For Doreen

With love & best wishes

from

General Davidson

26/4/24

PRINCESS SCHEHERAZADE, THE HEROINE OF
THE THOUSAND-AND-ONE NIGHTS, RANKS AMONG THE
GREAT STORYTELLERS OF THE WORLD

Stories from
The Arabian Nights

Retold by Laurence Housman
.. with drawings by ..
Edmond Dulac

Hodder and Stoughton
Limited   London

Made and Printed in Great Britain. Butler & Tanner Ltd., *Frome and London*

CONTENTS

ILLUSTRATIONS

ALI BABA

STORY OF THE WICKED HALF-BROTHERS

THE PRINCESS OF DERYABAR

SINDBAD THE SAILOR

ALADDIN

THEIR CHIEF IN A LOW BUT DISTINCT VOICE UTTERED THE TWO WORDS, "OPEN SESAME"

(Page 14)

ALI BABA AND THE FORTY THIEVES

IN a town in Persia lived two brothers named Cassim and Ali Baba, between whom their father at his death had left what little property he possessed equally divided. Cassim, however, having married the heiress of a rich merchant, became soon after his marriage the owner of a fine shop, together with several pieces of land, and was in consequence, through no effort of his own, the most considerable merchant in the town. Ali Baba, on the other hand, was married to one as poor as himself, and having no other means of gaining a livelihood he used to go every day into the forest to cut wood, and lading therewith the three asses which were his sole stock-in-trade, would then hawk it about the streets for sale.

One day while he was at work within the skirts of the forest, Ali Baba saw advancing towards him across the open a large company of horsemen, and fearing from their appearance that they might be robbers, he left his asses to their own devices and sought safety for himself in the lower branches of a large tree which grew in the close overshadowing of a precipitous rock.

Almost immediately it became evident that this very rock was the goal toward which the troop was bound, for having arrived they alighted instantly from their horses, and took down each man of them a sack which seemed by its weight and form to be filled with gold. There could no longer be any doubt that they were robbers. Ali Baba counted forty of them.

Just as he had done so, the one nearest to him, who seemed to be their chief, advanced toward the rock, and in a low but distinct voice uttered the two words, " Open Sesamé ! " Immediately the rock opened like a door, the captain and his men passed in, and the rock closed behind them.

For a long while Ali Baba waited, not daring to descend from his hiding-place lest they should come out and catch him in the act ; but at last, when the waiting had grown almost unbearable, his patience was rewarded, the door in the rock opened, and out came the forty men, their captain leading them.   When the last of them was through, " Shut, Sesamé ! " said the captain, and immediately the face of the rock closed together as before.   Then they all mounted their horses and rode away.

As soon as he felt sure that they were not returning Ali Baba came down from the tree and made his way at once to that part of the rock where he had seen the captain and his men enter.   And there at the word " Open, Sesamé ! " a door suddenly revealed itself and opened.

Ali Baba had expected to find a dark and gloomy cavern.   Great was his astonishment therefore when he perceived a spacious and vaulted chamber lighted from above through a fissure in the rock ; and there spread out before him lay treasures in profusion, bales of merchandise, silks, carpets, brocades, and above all gold and silver lying in loose heaps or in sacks piled one upon another.   He did not take long to consider what he should do.   Disregarding the silver and the gold that lay loose, he brought to the mouth of the cave as many sacks of gold as he thought his three asses might carry ; and having loaded them on and covered them with wood so that they

might not be seen, he closed the rock by the utterance of
the magic words which he had learned, and departed for
the town, a well-satisfied man.

When he got home he drove his asses into a small
court, and shutting the gates carefully he took off the
wood that covered the bags and carried them in to his
wife.   She, discovering them to be full of gold, feared that
her husband had stolen them, and began sorrowfully to
reproach him ; but Ali Baba soon put her mind at rest
on that score, and having poured all the gold into a great
heap upon the floor he sat down at her side to consider
how well it looked.

Soon his wife, poor careful body, must needs begin
counting it over piece by piece.   Ali Baba let her go on
for awhile, but before long the sight set him laughing.
" Wife," said he, " you will never make an end of it that
way.   The best thing to do is to dig a hole and bury it,
then we shall be sure that it is not slipping through our
fingers."   " That will do well enough," said his wife,
" but it would be better first to have the measure of it.
So while you dig the hole I will go round to Cassim's and
borrow a measure small enough to give us an exact reckoning.   " Do as you will," answered her husband, " but see
that you keep the thing secret."

Off went Ali Baba's wife to her brother-in-law's house.
Cassim was from home, so she begged of his wife the loan
of a small measure, naming for choice the smallest.   This
set the sister-in-law wondering.   Knowing Ali Baba's
poverty she was all the more curious to find out for what
kind of grain so small a measure could be needed.   So
before bringing it she covered all the bottom with lard,
and giving it to Ali Baba's wife told her to be sure and
be quick in returning it.   The other, promising to restore
it punctually, made haste to get home ; and there finding

the hole dug for its reception she started to measure the money into it. First she set the measure upon the heap, then she filled it, then she carried it to the hole; and so she continued till the last measure was counted. Then, leaving Ali Baba to finish the burying, she carried back the measure with all haste to her sister-in-law, returning thanks for the loan.

No sooner was her back turned than Cassim's wife looked at the bottom of the measure, and there to her astonishment she saw sticking to the lard a gold coin. "What?" she cried, her heart filled with envy, "is Ali Baba so rich that he needs a measure for his gold? Where, then, I would know, has the miserable wretch obtained it?"

She waited with impatience for her husband's return, and as soon as he came in she began to jeer at him. "You think yourself rich," said she, "but Ali Baba is richer. You count your gold by the piece, but Ali Baba does not count, he measures it! In comparison to Ali Baba we are but grubs and groundlings!"

Having thus riddled him to the top of her bent in order to provoke his curiosity, she told him the story of the borrowed measure, of her own stratagem, and of its result.

Cassim, instead of being pleased at Ali Baba's sudden prosperity, grew furiously jealous; not a wink could he sleep all night for thinking of it. The next morning before sunrise he went to his brother's house. "Ali Baba," said he, "what do you mean by pretending to be poor when all the time you are scooping up gold by the quart?" "Brother," said Ali Baba, "explain your meaning." "My meaning shall be plain!" cried Cassim, displaying the tell-tale coin. "How many more pieces have you like this that my wife found sticking to the bottom of the measure yesterday?"

Ali Baba, perceiving that the intervention of wives had

made further concealment useless, told his brother the true facts of the case, and offered him, as an inducement for keeping the secret, an equal share of the treasure.

" That is the least that I have the right to expect," answered Cassim haughtily. " It is further necessary that you should tell me exactly where the treasure lies, that I may, if need be, test the truth of your story, otherwise I shall find it my duty to denounce you to the authorities."

Ali Baba, having a clear conscience, had little fear of Cassim's threats ; but out of pure good nature he gave him all the information he desired, not forgetting to instruct him in the words which would give him free passage into the cave and out again.

Cassim, who had thus secured all he had come for, lost no time in putting his project into execution. Intent on possessing himself of all the treasures which yet remained, he set off the next morning before daybreak, taking with him ten mules laden with empty crates. Arrived before the cave, he recalled the words which his brother had taught him ; no sooner was " Open, Sesamé ! " said than the door in the rock lay wide for him to pass through, and when he had entered it shut again.

If the simple soul of Ali Baba had found delight in the riches of the cavern, greater still was the exultation of a greedy nature like Cassim's. Intoxicated with the wealth that lay before his eyes, he had no thought but to gather together with all speed as much treasure as the ten mules could carry ; and so, having exhausted himself with heavy labour and avaricious excitement, he suddenly found on returning to the door that he had forgotten the key which opened it. Up and down, and in and out through the mazes of his brain he chased the missing word. Barley, and maize, and rice, he thought of them all : but of sesamé never once, because his mind had become dark

3

to the revealing light of heaven.　And so the door stayed fast, holding him prisoner in the cave, where to his fate, undeserving of pity, we leave him.

Toward noon the robbers returned, and saw, standing about the rock, the ten mules laden with crates.　At this they were greatly surprised, and began to search with suspicion amongst the surrounding crannies and undergrowth.　Finding no one there, they drew their swords and advanced cautiously toward the cave, where, upon the captain's pronouncement of the magic word, the door immediately fell open.　Cassim, who from within had heard the trampling of horses, had now no doubt that the robbers were arrived and that his hour was come.　Resolved however to make one last effort at escape, he stood ready by the door; and no sooner had the opening word been uttered than he sprang forth with such violence that he threw the captain to the ground.　But his attempt was vain; before he could break through he was mercilessly hacked down by the swords of the robber band.

With their fears thus verified, the robbers anxiously entered the cave to view the traces of its late visitant. There they saw piled by the door the treasure which Cassim had sought to carry away; but while restoring this to its place they failed altogether to detect the earlier loss which Ali Baba had caused them.　Reckoning, however, that as one had discovered the secret of entry others also might know of it, they determined to leave an example for any who might venture thither on a similar errand; and having quartered the body of Cassim they disposed it at the entrance in a manner most calculated to strike horror into the heart of the beholder.　Then, closing the door of the cave, they rode away in the search of fresh exploits and plunder.

Meanwhile Cassim's wife had grown very uneasy at

her husband's prolonged absence ; and at nightfall, unable
to endure further suspense, she ran to Ali Baba, and telling
him of his brother's secret expedition, entreated him to
go out instantly in search of him.

Ali Baba had too kind a heart to refuse or delay comfort
to her affliction. Taking with him his three asses he set
out immediately for the forest, and as the road was familiar
to him he had soon found his way to the door of the cave.
When he saw there the traces of blood he became filled
with misgiving, but no sooner had he entered than his
worst fears were realized. Nevertheless brotherly piety
gave him courage. Gathering together the severed remains
and wrapping them about with all possible decency, he
laid them upon one of the asses ; then bethinking him
that he deserved some payment for his pains, he loaded
the two remaining asses with sacks of gold, and covering
them with wood as on the first occasion, made his way
back to the town while it was yet early. Leaving his
wife to dispose of the treasure borne by the two asses,
he led the third to his sister-in-law's house, and knocking
quietly so that none of the neighbours might hear, was
presently admitted by Morgiana, a female slave whose
intelligence and discretion had long been known to him.
" Morgiana," said he, " there's trouble on the back of
that ass. Can you keep a secret ? " And Morgiana's
nod satisfied him better than any oath. " Well," said
he, " your master's body lies there waiting to be pieced,
and our business now is to bury him honourably as though
he had died a natural death. Go and tell your mistress
that I want to speak to her."

Morgiana went in to her mistress, and returning presently
bade Ali Baba enter. Then leaving him to break to his
sister-in-law the news and the sad circumstances of his
brother's death, she, with her plan already formed,

hastened forth and knocked at the door of the nearest apothecary. As soon as he opened to her she required of him in trembling agitation certain pillules efficacious against grave disorders, declaring in answer to his questions that her master had been taken suddenly ill. With these she returned home, and her plan of concealment having been explained and agreed upon, much to the satisfaction of Ali Baba, she went forth the next morning to the same apothecary, and with tears in her eyes besought him to supply her in haste with a certain drug that is given to sick people only in the last extremity. Meanwhile the rumour of Cassim's sickness had got abroad; Ali Baba and his wife had been seen coming and going, while Morgiana by her ceaseless activity had made the two days' pretended illness seem like a fortnight: so when a sound of wailing arose within the house all the neighbours concluded without further question that Cassim had died a natural and honourable death.

But Morgiana had now a still more difficult task to perform, it being necessary for the obsequies that the body should be made in some way presentable. So at a very early hour the next morning she went to the shop of a certain merry old cobbler, Baba Mustapha by name, who lived on the other side of the town. Showing him a piece of gold she inquired whether he were ready to earn it by exercising his craft in implicit obedience to her instructions. And when Baba Mustapha sought to know the terms, " First," said she, " you must come with your eyes bandaged; secondly, you must sew what I put before you without asking questions; and thirdly, when you return you must tell nobody."

Mustapha, who had a lively curiosity into other folk's affairs, boggled for a time at the bandaging, and doubted much of his ability to refrain from question; but having on these considerations secured the doubling of his fee, he promised secrecy readily enough, and taking his cobbler's tackle in hand submitted himself to Morgiana's guidance and set forth. This way and that she led him blindfold, till she had brought him to the house of her deceased master. Then uncovering his eyes in the presence of the dismembered corpse, she bade him get out thread and wax and join the pieces together.

Baba Mustapha plied his task according to the compact, asking no question. When he had done, Morgiana again bandaged his eyes and led him home, and giving him a third piece of gold the more to satisfy him, she bade him good-day and departed.

So in seemliness and without scandal of any kind were the obsequies of the murdered Cassim performed. And when all was ended, seeing that his widow was desolate and his house in need of a protector, Ali Baba with brotherly piety took both the one and the other into his care, marrying his sister-in-law according to Moslem rule, and removing with all his goods and newly acquired treasure to the house which had been his brother's. And having also acquired the shop where Cassim had done business, he put into it his own son, who had already served an apprenticeship to the trade. So, with his fortune well established, let us now leave Ali Baba, and return to the robbers' cave.

Thither, at the appointed time, came the forty robbers, bearing in hand fresh booty; and great was their consternation to discover that not only had the body of Cassim been removed, but a good many sacks of gold as well. It was no wonder that this should trouble them, for so long as anyone could command secret access, the cave was useless as a depository for their wealth. The question was, What could they do to put an end to their present insecurity? After long debate it was agreed that

one of their number should go into the town disguised as
a traveller, and there, mixing with the common people,
learn from their report whether there had been recently
any case in their midst of sudden prosperity or sudden
death. If such a thing could be discovered, then they
made sure of tracking the evil to its source and imposing
a remedy.

Although the penalty for failure was death, one of the
robbers at once boldly offered himself for the venture,
and having transformed himself by disguise and received
the wise counsels and commendations of his fellows, he
set out for the town.

Arriving at dawn he began to walk up and down the
streets and watch the early stirring of the inhabitants.
So, before long, he drew up at the door of Baba Mustapha,
who, though old, was already seated at work upon his
cobbler's bench. The robber accosted him. " I wonder,"
said he, " to see a man of your age at work so early. Does
not so dull a light strain your eyes ? " " Not so much
as you might think," answered Baba Mustapha. " Why,
it was but the other day that at this same hour I saw well
enough to stitch up a dead body in a place where it was
certainly no lighter." " Stitch up a dead body ! " cried
the robber in pretended amazement, concealing his joy
at this sudden intelligence. " Surely you mean in its
winding sheet, for how else can a dead body be stitched ? "
" No, no," said Mustapha ; " what I say I mean ; but
as it is a secret, I can tell you no more." The robber
drew out a piece of gold. " Come," said he, " tell me
nothing you do not care to ; only show me the house
where lay the body that you stitched." Baba Mustapha
eyed the gold longingly. " Would that I could," he
replied ; " but alas ! I went to it blindfold." " Well,"
said the robber, " I have heard that a blind man remembers

ALI BABA DEPARTED FOR THE TOWN, A WELL-SATISFIED MAN

(Page 15)

his road ; perhaps, though seeing you might lose it, blind-fold you might find it again." Tempted by the offer of a second piece of gold, Baba Mustapha was soon persuaded to make the attempt. " It was here that I started," said he, showing the spot, " and I turned as you see me now." The robber then put a bandage over his eyes, and walked beside him through the streets, partly guiding and partly being led, till of his own accord Baba Mustapha stopped. " It was here," said he. " The door by which I went in should now lie to the right. And he had in fact come exactly opposite to the house which had once been Cassim's, where Ali Baba now dwelt.

The robber, having marked the door with a piece of chalk which he had provided for the purpose, removed the bandage from Mustapha's eyes, and leaving him to his own devices returned with all possible speed to the cave where his comrades were awaiting him.

Soon after the robber and cobbler had parted, Mor-giana happened to go out upon an errand, and as she returned she noticed the mark upon the door. " This," she thought, " is not as it should be ; either some trick is intended, or there is evil brewing for my master's house." Taking a piece of chalk she put a similar mark upon the five or six doors lying to right and left ; and having done this she went home with her mind satisfied, saying nothing.

In the meantime the robbers had learned from their companion the success of his venture. Greatly elated at the thought of the vengeance so soon to be theirs, they formed a plan for entering the city in a manner that should arouse no suspicion among the inhabitants. Passing in by twos and threes, and by different routes, they came together to the market-place at an appointed time, while the captain and the robber who had acted as spy made their way alone to the street in which the marked door

4

was to be found. Presently, just as they had expected, they perceived a door with the mark on it. "That is it!" said the robber; but as they continued walking so as to avoid suspicion, they came upon another and another, till, before they were done, they had passed six in succession. So alike were the marks that the spy, though he swore he had made but one, could not tell which it was. Seeing that the design had failed, the captain returned to the market-place, and having passed the word for his troop to go back in the same way as they had come, he himself set the example of retreat.

When they were all reassembled in the forest, the captain explained how the matter had fallen, and the spy, acquiescing in his own condemnation, kneeled down and received the stroke of the executioner.

But as it was still necessary for the safety of all that so great a trespass and theft should not pass unavenged, another of the band, undeterred by the fate of his comrade, volunteered upon the same conditions to prosecute the quest wherein the other had failed. Coming by the same means to the house of Ali Baba, he set upon the door, at a spot not likely to be noticed, a mark in red chalk to distinguish it clearly from those which were already marked in white. But even this precaution failed of its end. Morgiana, whose eye nothing could escape, noticed the red mark at the first time of passing, and dealt with it just as she had done with the previous one. So when the robbers came, hoping this time to light upon the door without fail, they found not one but six all similarly marked with red.

When the second spy had received the due reward of his blunder, the captain considered how by trusting to others he had come to lose two of his bravest followers, so the third attempt he determined to conduct in person.

Having found his way to Ali Baba's door, as the two others had done by the aid of Baba Mustapha, he did not set any mark upon it, but examined it so carefully that he could not in future mistake it. He then returned to the forest and communicated to his band the plan which he had formed. This was to go into the town in the disguise of an oil-merchant, bearing with him upon nineteen mules thirty-eight large leather jars, one of which, as a sample, was to be full of oil, but all the others empty. In these he purposed to conceal the thirty-seven robbers to which his band was now reduced, and so to convey his full force to the scene of action in such a manner as to arouse no suspicion till the signal for vengeance should be given.

Within a couple of days he had secured all the mules and jars that were requisite, and having disposed of his troop according to the pre-arranged plan, he drove his train of well-laden mules to the gates of the city, through which he passed just before sunset. Proceeding thence to Ali Baba's house, and arriving as it fell dark, he was about to knock and crave a lodging for the night, when he perceived Ali Baba at the door enjoying the fresh air after supper. Addressing him in tones of respect, " Sir," said he, " I have brought my oil a great distance to sell to-morrow in the market ; and at this late hour, being a stranger, I know not where to seek for a shelter. If it is not troubling you too much, allow me to stable my beasts here for the night."

The captain's voice was now so changed from its accustomed tone of command, that Ali Baba, though he had heard it before, did not recognize it. Not only did he grant the stranger's request for bare accommodation, but as soon as the unlading and stabling of the mules had been accomplished, he invited him to stay no longer in the outer court but enter the house as his guest. The captain, whose plans this proposal somewhat disarranged, endeavoured to excuse himself from a pretended reluctance to give trouble ; but since Ali Baba would take no refusal he was forced at last to yield, and to submit with apparent complaisance to an entertainment which the hospitality of his host extended to a late hour.

When they were about to retire for the night, Ali Baba went into the kitchen to speak to Morgiana ; and the captain of the robbers, on the pretext of going to look after his mules, slipped out into the yard where the oil-jars were standing in line. Passing from jar to jar he whispered into each, " When you hear a handful of pebbles fall from the window of the chamber where I am lodged, then cut your way out of the jar and make ready, for the time will have come." He then returned to the house, where Morgiana came with a light and conducted him to his chamber.

Now Ali Baba, before going to bed, had said to Morgiana, " To-morrow at dawn I am going to the baths ; let my bathing-linen be put ready, and see that the cook has some good broth prepared for me against my return." Having therefore led the guest up to his chamber, Morgiana returned to the kitchen and ordered Abdallah the cook to put on the pot for the broth. Suddenly while she was skimming it, the lamp went out, and, on searching, she found there was no more oil in the house. At so late an hour no shop would be open, yet somehow the broth had to be made, and that could not be done without a light. " As for that," said Abdallah, seeing her perplexity, " why trouble yourself ? There is plenty of oil out in the yard." " Why, to be sure ! " said Morgiana, and sending Abdallah to bed so that he might be up in time to wake his master on the morrow, she took the oil-can herself

GREATER STILL WAS THE EXULTATION OF A GREEDY NATURE LIKE CASSIM'S

(*Page* 17)

and went out into the court. As she approached the jar which stood nearest, she heard a voice within say, " Is it time ? "

To one of Morgiana's intelligence an oil-jar that spoke was an object of even more suspicion than a chalk-mark on a door, and in an instant she apprehended what danger for her master and his family might lie concealed around her. Understanding well enough that an oil-jar which asked a question required an answer, she replied quick as thought and without the least sign of perturbation, " Not yet, but presently." And thus she passed from jar to jar, thirty-seven in all, giving the same answer, till she came to the one which contained the oil.

The situation was now clear to her. Aware of the source from which her master had acquired his wealth, she guessed at once that, in extending shelter to the oil-merchant, Ali Baba had in fact admitted to his house the robber captain and his band. On the instant her resolution was formed. Having filled the oil-can she returned to the kitchen ; there she lighted the lamp and then, taking a large kettle, went back once more to the jar which contained the oil. Filling the kettle she carried it back to the kitchen, and putting under it a great fire of wood had soon brought it to the boil. Then taking it in hand once more, she went out into the yard and poured into each jar in turn a sufficient quantity of the boiling oil to scald its occupant to death.

She then returned to the kitchen, and having made Ali Baba's broth, put out the fire, blew out the lamp, and sat down by the window to watch.

Before long the captain of the robbers awoke from the short sleep which he had allowed himself, and finding that all was silent in the house, he rose softly and opened the window. Below stood the oil-jars ; gently into their midst he threw the handful of pebbles agreed on as a signal; but from the oil-jars came no answer. He threw a second and a third time; yet though he could hear the pebbles falling among the jars, there followed only the silence of the dead. Wondering whether his band had fled leaving him in the lurch, or whether they were all asleep, he grew uneasy, and descending in haste, made his way into the court. As he approached the first jar a smell of burning and hot oil assailed his nostrils, and looking within he beheld in rigid contortion the dead body of his comrade. In every jar the same sight presented itself, till he came to the one which had contained the oil. There, in what was missing, the means and manner of his companions' death were made clear to him. Aghast at the discovery and awake to the danger that now threatened him, he did not delay an instant, but forcing the garden-gate, and thence climbing from wall to wall, he made his escape out of the city.

When Morgiana, who had remained all this time on the watch, was assured of his final departure, she put her master's bath-linen ready and went to bed well satisfied with her day's work.

The next morning Ali Baba, awakened by his slave, went to the baths before daybreak. On his return he was greatly surprised to find that the merchant was gone, leaving his mules and oil-jars behind him. He inquired of Morgiana the reason. " You will find the reason," said she, " if you look into the first jar you come to." Ali Baba did so, and, seeing a man, started back with a cry. " Do not be afraid," said Morgiana, " he is dead and harmless; and so are all the others whom you will find if you look further."

As Ali Baba went from one jar to another, finding always the same sight of horror within, his knees trembled under him ; and when he came at last to the one empty oil-jar, he stood for a time motionless, turning upon Morgiana eyes of wonder and inquiry. " And what," he said then, " has become of the merchant ? " " To tell you that," said Morgiana, " will be to tell you the whole story ; you will be better able to hear it if you have your broth first."

But the curiosity of Ali Baba was far too great : he would not be kept waiting. So without further delay she gave him the whole history, so far as she knew it, from beginning to end ; and by her intelligent putting of one thing against another, she left him at last in no possible doubt as to the source and nature of the conspiracy which her quick wits had so happily defeated. " And now, dear master," she said in conclusion, " continue to be on your guard, for though all these are dead, one remains alive ; and he, if I mistake not, is the captain of the band, and for that reason the more formidable and the more likely to cherish the hope of vengeance."

When Morgiana had done speaking Ali Baba clearly perceived that he owed to her not merely the protection of his property but life itself. His heart was full of gratitude. " Do not doubt," he said, " that before I die I will reward you as you deserve ; and as an immediate proof from this moment I give you your liberty."

This token of his approval filled Morgiana's heart with delight, but she had no intention of leaving so kind a master, even had she been sure that all danger was now over. The immediate question which next presented itself was how to dispose of the bodies. Luckily at the far end of the garden stood a thick grove of trees, and under these Ali Baba was able to dig a large trench without attracting the notice of his neighbours. Here the remains of the thirty-seven robbers were laid side by side, the

trench was filled again, and the ground made level. As
for the mules, since Ali Baba had no use for them, he
sent them, one or two at a time, to the market to be sold.

Meanwhile the robber captain had fled back to the
forest. Entering the cave he was overcome by its gloom
and loneliness. " Alas ! " he cried, " my comrades, partners in my adventures, sharers of my fortune, how shall
I endure to live without you ? Why did I lead you to a
fate where valour was of no avail, and where death turned
you into objects of ridicule ? Surely had you died sword
in hand my sorrow had been less bitter ! And now what
remains for me but to take vengeance for your death and
to prove, by achieving it without aid, that I was worthy
to be the captain of such a band ! "

Thus resolved, at an early hour the next day, he
assumed a disguise suitable to his purpose, and going to
the town took lodging in a khan. Entering into conversation with his host he inquired whether anything of interest
had happened recently in the town ; but the other, though
full of gossip, had nothing to tell him concerning the
matter in which he was most interested, for Ali Baba,
having to conceal from all the source of his wealth, had
also to be silent as to the dangers in which it involved
him.

The captain then inquired where there was a shop for
hire ; and hearing of one that suited him, he came to
terms with the owner, and before long had furnished it
with all kinds of rich stuffs and carpets and jewellery
which he brought by degrees with great secrecy from the
cave.

Now this shop happened to be opposite to that which
had belonged to Cassim and was now occupied by the son
of Ali Baba ; so before long the son and the new-comer,
who had assumed the name of Cogia Houssain, became

THIS WAY AND THAT SHE LED HIM BLINDFOLD

(Page 21)

acquainted; and as the youth had good looks, kind manners, and a sociable disposition, it was not long before the acquaintance became intimate.

Cogia Houssain did all he could to seal the pretended friendship, the more so as it had not taken him long to discover how the young man and Ali Baba were related; so, plying him constantly with small presents and acts of hospitality, he forced on him the obligation of making some return.

Ali Baba's son, however, had not at his lodging sufficient accommodation for entertainment; he therefore told his father of the difficulty in which Cogia Houssain's favours had placed him, and Ali Baba with great willingness at once offered to arrange matters. "My son," said he, "to-morrow being a holiday, all shops will be closed; then do you after dinner invite Cogia Houssain to walk with you; and as you return bring him this way and beg him to come in. That will be better than a formal invitation, and Morgiana shall have a supper prepared for you."

This proposal was exactly what Ali Baba's son could have wished, so on the morrow he brought Cogia Houssain to the door as if by accident, and stopping, invited him to enter.

Cogia Houssain, who saw his object thus suddenly attained, began by showing pretended reluctance, but Ali Baba himself coming to the door, pressed him in the most kindly manner to enter, and before long had conducted him to the table, where food stood prepared.

But there an unlooked-for difficulty arose. Wicked though he might be, the robber captain was not so impious as to eat the salt of the man he intended to kill. He therefore began with many apologies to excuse himself; and when Ali Baba sought to know the reason, "Sir," said he, "I am sure that if you knew the cause of my

resolution you would approve of it.   Suffice it to say that
I have made it a rule to eat of no dish that has salt in it.
How then can I sit down at your table if I must reject
everything that is set before me ? ''

"If that is your scruple," said Ali Baba, "it shall
soon be satisfied," and he sent orders to the kitchen that
no salt was to be put into any of the dishes presently to
be served to the newly arrived guest. "Thus," said he
to Cogia Houssain, "I shall still have the honour, to which
I have looked forward, of returning to you under my own
roof the hospitality you have shown to my son."

Morgiana, who was just about to serve supper, received
the order with some discontent. "Who," she said, "is
this difficult person that refuses to eat salt ?   He must
be a curiosity worth looking at."   So when the saltless
courses were ready to be set upon the table, she herself
helped to carry in the dishes.   No sooner had she set eyes
on Cogia Houssain than she recognized him in spite of
his disguise ; and observing his movements with great
attention she saw that he had a dagger concealed beneath
his robe.   "Ah ! " she said to herself, "here is reason
enough ! For who will eat salt with the man he means
to murder ?   But he shall not murder my master if I
can prevent it."

Now Morgiana knew that the most favourable opportunity for the robber captain to carry out his design would
be after the courses had been withdrawn, and when Ali
Baba and his son and guest were alone together over their
wine, which indeed was the very project that Cogia Houssain had formed. Going forth, therefore, in haste, she
dressed herself as a dancer, assuming the head-dress and
mask suitable for the character.   Then she fastened a silver
girdle about her waist, and hung upon it a dagger of the
same material.   Thus equipped, she said to Abdallah the

cook, "Take your tabor and let us go in and give an
entertainment in honour of our master's guest."

So Abdallah took his tabor, and played Morgiana into
the hall. As soon as she had entered she made a low
curtsy, and stood awaiting orders. Then Ali Baba, seeing
that she wished to perform in his guest's honour, said
kindly, "Come in, Morgiana, and show Cogia Houssain
what you can do."

Immediately Abdallah began to beat upon his tabor
and sing an air for Morgiana to dance to ; and she, advancing with much grace and propriety of deportment, began
to move through several figures, performing them with the
ease and facility which none but the most highly practised
can attain to. Then, for the last figure of all, she drew
out the dagger and, holding it in her hand, danced a dance
which excelled all that had preceded it in the surprise
and change and quickness and dexterity of its movements.
Now she presented the dagger at her own breast, now at
one of the onlookers ; but always in the act of striking
she drew back. At length, as though out of breath, she
snatched his instrument from Abdallah with her left hand,
and, still holding the dagger in her right, advanced the
hollow of the tabor toward her master, as is the custom
of dancers when claiming their fee. Ali Baba threw in a
piece of gold ; his son did likewise. Then advancing it
in the same manner toward Cogia Houssain, who was
feeling for his purse, she struck under it, and before he
knew had plunged her dagger deep into his heart.

Ali Baba and his son, seeing their guest fall dead, cried
out in horror at the deed. "Wretch!" exclaimed Ali
Baba, " what ruin and shame hast thou brought on us ? "
" Nay," answered Morgiana, " it is not your ruin but your
life that I have thus secured ; look and convince yourself
what man was this which refused to eat salt with you ! "

So saying, she tore off the dead robber's disguise, showing the dagger concealed below, and the face which her master now for the first time recognized.

Ali Baba's gratitude to Morgiana for thus preserving his life a second time, knew no bounds. He took her in his arms and embraced her as a daughter. "Now," said he, "the time is come when I must fulfil my debt; and how better can I do it than by marrying you to my son?" This proposition, far from proving unwelcome to the young man, did but confirm an inclination already formed. A few days later the nuptials were celebrated with great joy and solemnity, and the union thus auspiciously commenced was productive of as much happiness as lies within the power of mortals to secure.

As for the robbers' cave, it remained the secret possession of Ali Baba and his posterity; and using their good fortune with equity and moderation, they rose to high office in the city and were held in great honour by all who knew them.

PIROUZE, THE FAIREST AND MOST HONOURABLY BORN

(*Page* 43)

THE STORY OF THE WICKED HALF-BROTHERS

In the city of Harran there once lived a King who had every happiness which life and fortune could bestow save that he lacked an heir. Although, according to royal custom, he had in his household fifty wives, fair to look upon and affectionate in disposition, and though he continually invoked on these unions the blessing of Heaven, still he remained childless; for which cause all his joy was turned to affliction, and his wealth and power and magnificence became as of no account.

Now one night as he slept there appeared before him an old man of venerable appearance who, addressing him in mild accents, spoke thus : "The prayer of the faithful among fifty has been heard. Arise, therefore, and go into the gardens of your palace and cause the gardener to bring you a pomegranate fully ripe. Eat as many of the seeds as you desire children, and your wish shall be fulfilled."

Immediately upon awaking the King remembered the dream, and going down into the gardens of the palace he took fifty pomegranate seeds, and counting them one by one ate them all. So in due course, according to the promise of his dream, each of his wives gave birth to a son, all about the same time. To this, however, there was an exception, for one of the fifty whose name was Pirouzè, the fairest and the most honourably born, she alone, as time went on, showed no sign of that which was

43

expected of her. Then was the King's anger kindled against her because in her alone the promise of his dream was not fulfilled; and deeming such a one hateful in the eyes of Heaven he was minded to put her to death. His vizier, however, dissuaded him. "Time alone can show," said he, "whether her demerits are so great as you now suppose. Let her go back to her own people, and remain in banishment until the will of Heaven shall declare itself, and if within due time she give birth to a son then can she return to you with all honour." So the King did as his vizier advised, and sent Pirouzè back to her own country to the court of the Prince of Samaria; and there before long she who had seemed barren had the joy of becoming a mother and gave birth to a son whom she named Codadad, that is to say, "the Gift of God." Nevertheless, because the King of Harran had put upon her so public a disgrace, the Prince of Samaria would send no word to him of the event; so the young Prince was brought up at his uncle's court, and there he learned to ride and to shoot and to perform such warlike feats as become a prince, and in all that country he had no equal for accomplishment or courage.

Now one day, when Codadad had reached the age of eighteen, word came to him that his father the King of Harran was engaged in war and surrounded by enemies; so the Prince said to his mother, "Now is it time that I should go and prove myself worthy of my birth and the equal of my brethren; for here in Samaria all is peace and indolence, but in Harran are hardship and dangers, and great deeds waiting to be done." And his mother said to him, "O my son, since it seems good to thee, go; but how wilt thou declare thyself to thy father, or cause him to believe thy word, seeing that he is ignorant of thy birth?" Codadad answered, "I will so declare myself by my deeds that before my father knows the truth he shall wish that it were true."

So he departed and came in princely arms to the city of Harran, and there offered his service to the King against all his enemies. Now, no sooner had the King looked upon the youth than his heart was drawn toward him because of his beauty and the secret ties of blood, but when he asked from what country he came, Codadad answered, " I am the son of an emir of Cairo, and wherever there is war I go to win fame, nor do I care in what cause I fight so long as I be proved worthy."

The Prince was not slow in making his valour known ; before long he had risen to the command of the whole army, not only over the heads of his brethren but also of the more experienced officers. And thereafter, when peace was re-established, the King, finding Codadad as prudent as he was valiant, appointed him governor to the young Princes.

Now this act, though justified by merit, could not fail to increase the hatred and jealousy which Codadad's brethren had long felt towards him. " What ? " they cried, " shall this stranger not only steal from us the first place in the King's favour, but must we also be in obedience to his ruling and judgment ? Surely if we do so we are no sons of a King."

So they conspired together how best to be rid of him. One said, " Let us fall upon him with our swords." " No, no," said another, " for so doing we shall but bring punishment upon ourselves. But let us so arrange matters as to draw on him the weight of the King's anger ; thus shall our vengeance be made both safe and complete."

To this the other Princes agreed ; so forming a design which seemed favourable to their end they approached Codadad, and besought his permission to go forth together on a hunting expedition, promising to return the same day. Codadad, deeming the request reasonable, immediately granted it : the brothers departed, but they did not return.

On the third day the King made inquiry as to the reason of their absence. Codadad replied that they were gone on a hunting expedition but had promised to return much sooner. Another day passed and the King grew anxious ; yet another, and he became furious ; and all his wrath was directed against Codadad. " O traitor," he cried, " why hast thou neglected thy trust and allowed my sons to go anywhere unaccompanied by thee ? Now go instantly and search for them, and if thou find them not, be assured that on thy head shall fall the penalty."

At these words the Prince was filled with sudden foreboding, for he knew that the brothers had no love for him, and well could he see now the danger into which he had fallen. All he could do, however, was to obey ; so furnishing himself with arms and a horse good for travelling, he set out in search of his brethren.

After some days employed in a fruitless quest he came to a desolate tract in the midst of which stood a castle of black marble. As he approached he beheld at an upper window a damsel of marvellous beauty, with torn garments, dishevelled hair, and a countenance expressive of the most lively affliction, who immediately that she set eyes on him wrung her hands and waived him away crying, " Oh, fly, fly from this place of death and the monster which inhabits it ! For here lives a black giant which feeds on human flesh, seizing all he can find. Even now in his dungeons you may hear the cries of those whom for his next meal he will devour."

" Madam," replied the Prince, " for my safety you need have no care. Only be good enough to inform me

THE LADY ADVANCED TO MEET HIM

(*Page* 50)

who you are and how you came to be in your present
plight." " I come from Cairo," she replied, " where my
birth gives me rank.   And as I was travelling from thence
on my road to Bagdad this monstrous negro suddenly fell
upon us, and having slain my escort brought me hither
a captive, to endure, if Heaven refuses me succour,
things far worse than death.   But though I know my
own peril I will not see others perish in a vain attempt
to rescue me, therefore once more I entreat you to fly
ere it be too late."

But even as she spoke, the negro, a horrible and
gigantic monster of loathsome appearance, came in sight
moving rapidly toward the palace.   No sooner had he
caught sight of the Prince than he rushed upon him with
growls of fury, and drawing his scimitar aimed at him a
blow which, had it found him, must there and then have
ended the fight.   The Prince, however, swerved nimbly
under the stroke, and reaching his farthest, wounded the
giant in the knee ; then wheeling his charger about before
the negro could turn on his maimed limb he attacked him
from the rear, and with one fortunate blow brought him
to earth.   Instantly, before the giant could gather up his
huge length and regain his vantage, Codadad spurred
forward and with a single sweep of his sword smote off
his head.

Meanwhile, all breathless above, the lady had leaned
watching the contest.   Now, seeing that victory was
secured, she gave free vent to her joy and gratitude.   " O
prince of men ! " she cried, " now is revealed to me the
high rank to which thou wast born.   Finish, then, thy
work ; take from the girdle of yonder wretch the keys of
the castle and come quickly to the release of me and my
fellow-prisoners."

The Prince did according to her directions ; as he

7

opened the gates and entered the forecourt the lady advanced to meet him, ready, had he permitted it, to throw herself in gratitude at his feet. And now, as he beheld near at hand the beauty which had charmed him from a distance, Codadad realized how great had been his fortune, and with his whole heart rejoiced at the deliverance of one in whose nature so much virtue and grace seemed blended.

But while he was thus lost in the contemplation of her loveliness there arose from the basement of the castle a dreadful sound of crying and lamentation. " What is that ? " inquired the Prince. " It is the cry of the prisoners," replied the lady, " to whom, I doubt not, the opening of the gates has betokened the monster's return. Come, therefore, quickly and relieve them of their misery." And so saying she pointed to the door which led to the place of confinement.

Thither, accompanied by the lady, went Codadad with all speed. Descending by a dark stair he came upon a vast cavern dimly lighted, around the walls of which a hundred prisoners lay chained. Instantly he set to work to loose their bonds, informing them at the same time of the death of their captor and of their freedom from all further danger. At these unexpected tidings the captives raised a cry of joy and thanksgiving; but great as was their surprise at such unlooked-for deliverance, greater still was that of the Prince when, on bringing them to the light, he discovered that forty-nine of the hundred whom he had released were his own brethren.

The Princes received the cordial embraces of their deliverer with little embarrassment, for the disaster into which they had fallen had caused them almost entirely to forget their original intent. Satisfied with expressing in

proper terms their obligation and gratitude toward Codadad, they now joined eagerly in his survey of the castle ;
there upon examination they found an extraordinary
variety and wealth of booty, consisting for the most part
of merchandise which the negro had pillaged from passing
caravans, some of it actually belonging to those whom
Codadad had so recently rescued.

The Prince accordingly ordered the merchants each to
take what he recognized as his own ; and this being done
he divided the rest equally between them. The question
then arose how they should remove their plunder from a
place so desolately situated, where it would seem impossible
to procure means of conveyance ; but on a further search
they found not only the camels of the merchants, but also
the horses on which the Princes of Harran had ridden ;
and as, at their approach, the black slaves who were in
charge of the stables fell into headlong flight, Codadad
and his companions found themselves left in undis-
puted possession. The merchants therefore loaded their
camels, and with renewed protestations of gratitude
departed on the several roads by which their avocations
called them.

When they were gone Codadad's next care was to
inquire of the lady in what direction she wished to travel,
promising that he and the Princes would conduct her
in safety to any place she might name. The lady
replied, thanking him for his generous offer. " But
wherever I go," said she, " it cannot be to my own
country, for not only is it too far distant, but cruel misfortune has separated me from it for ever. And since you
have put me under so great an obligation, let me now
confess the truth which before I thought it prudent to
conceal. My dignity of rank is far higher than that to
which I recently laid claim ; in me you behold a King's

daughter, and if it will interest you to hear the story of my misfortunes, I shall be happy to recount it." Assured of the lively sympathy of her auditors she began as follows :

A CITY AMONG THE ISLES NAMED DERYABAR
(*Page* 55)

THE STORY OF THE PRINCESS OF DERYABAR

My father was the King of a city among the isles named Deryabar, and I was his only child; for, in spite of his many prayers directed to that end, Heaven had not granted him a son. And for this cause, though he bestowed upon my education all imaginable care, the sight of me remained displeasing to him. In order the better to forget his sorrow he spent his days in hunting, and so he chanced on the event which led to all our misfortunes. For one day, as he was riding unattended in the forest, night overtook him and he knew not which way to turn. Presently in the distance he perceived a light, and advancing towards it he came upon a hut within which a monstrous negro stood basting an ox that roasted before the fire. In the farther corner of the hut lay a beautiful woman with hands bound, and a face betokening the deepest affliction, while at her feet a young child, between two and three years of age, stretched up its arms and wailed without ceasing.

At this sight my father was filled with compassion, but his desire to effect her rescue was restrained for a while by fear that a failure might only make matters worse. In the meantime the giant, having drained a pitcher of wine, sat down to eat. Presently he turned himself about and addressed the lady. " Charming Princess," said he, " why will you not accept the good things which are within your reach ? Only yield to me the love that I demand and you will find in me the gentlest and most considerate of lords." To these advances, however, the lady replied with resolution and courage. " Vile monster," she cried, " every time I look at you does but increase my hatred and loathing toward you. Unchangeable as the foulness of your appearance is the disgust with which you inspire me ! "

These words of violent provocation were no sooner uttered than the negro, beside himself with rage, drew his sword, and seizing the lady by the hair, lifted her from the ground in preparation for the blow that would have ended all. Whereupon, seeing that not a moment was to be lost, my father drew his bow and let fly an arrow with so good an aim that, pierced to the heart, the giant fell dead. Immediately entering the hut my father raised the lady from the swoon into which she had fallen, and severing her bonds gave her the needed reassurance that all danger was now over. Before long he learned in answer to his inquiries that she had been wife to a chief of the Saracens, in whose service the slain giant had, on account of his great strength, occupied a position of trust. This, however, he had shamelessly betrayed; for having conceived a violent passion for his master's wife, he first persuaded the chief into an expedition which terminated in his death, and then returning in haste carried away by force not only the lady but her child also. From this degrading bondage my father's act had now saved her ; but though thus relieved of immediate danger, the wife of the Saracen chief was both solitary and friendless, for not only was she too far removed from her own land to return to it unaided, but she had small hope, should she ever arrive there, of securing for her son his rightful inheritance. This being the case my father, moved with compassion, determined to adopt the child as his own; and as the lady gratefully accepted his proposal, the next day, as soon as it was light, he returned to Deryabar bringing with him mother and son.

Thus it came about that the son of a Saracen chief was brought up in my father's palace like a Prince of the blood royal; and so, on attaining to manhood, having both grace and good looks to recommend him, he came to forget the comparative lowliness of his origin, and aspiring to become my father's heir, had the presumption to demand my hand in marriage.

A claim so audacious merited the severest punishment, yet my father merely remarked that he had other views concerning me, and with so lenient a rebuke would have passed the matter by. His refusal, however, excited in the proud youth the liveliest resentment; seeing that he could not obtain his ambition by fair means he immediately entered into conspiracy, and having treacherously slain my father, caused himself to be made King in his place. Fresh from this monstrous crime he renewed his suit for my hand, and was preparing to enforce it by violence, when the vizier, who alone of all my father's court had remained faithful to his memory, found means to convey me from the palace to a sailing vessel which was leaving harbour the same night.

Here for a time I seemed to have reached safety, but when we had been only three days at sea a violent storm arose, and the ship, driving helplessly before it, struck upon a rock and went down leaving as sole survivor the one who least wished to be spared. How I was saved I know not, nor how long I lay unfriended by the desolate shore upon which I had been cast; but scarcely had the consciousness of life returned to me when I heard a multitudinous sound of swift galloping; and presently, feeling myself lifted by men's hands, I turned and saw halting

8

near me a troop of Arab horsemen, and at their head a youth royally arrayed and beautiful as the morning. Thus when my fortunes were at their lowest I beheld him whom Heaven had sent not only to afford me that deliverance of which I stood so much in need, but also to restore me to the rank due to my birth. For let me confess that after this young Prince had succoured me with the most tender solicitude, conducting me in all honour to his own palace and there lodging me under his mother's protection, I experienced towards him a feeling of duty and gratitude such as would have made his lightest wish my law. When therefore with an ardent and ever-increasing devotion he desired me to become his bride, I could not, upon the completion of my recovery, refuse him the happiness he sought.

But the festivities of our marriage were scarcely ended, when suddenly by night the city in which we dwelt was attacked by a band of travelling marauders. The attack was so unexpected and so well planned that the town was stormed and the garrison cut to pieces before any news of the event had reached the palace. Under cover of darkness we managed to escape, and fleeing to the sea-shore took refuge on a small fishing boat, in which we immediately put out to sea, hoping to find in the rude winds and waves a safer shelter than our own walls had afforded us.

For two days we drifted with wind and tide, not knowing any better direction in which to turn; upon the third we perceived with relief a ship bearing down upon us, but as we watched its approach our satisfaction was soon changed to apprehension and dread, for we saw clearly that those on board were neither fishermen nor traders, but pirates. With rude shouts they boarded our small barque, and seizing my husband and myself carried

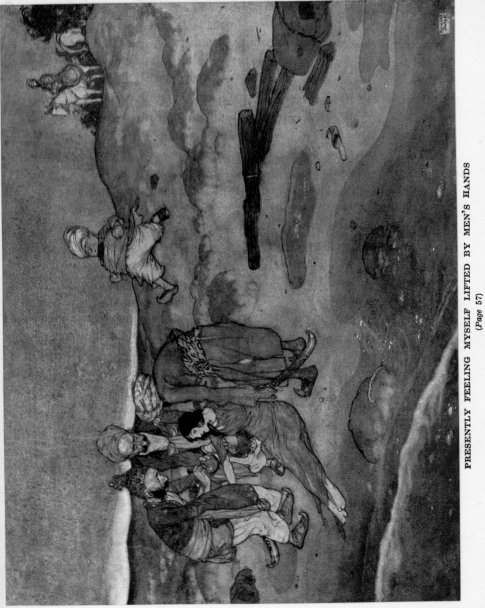

PRESENTLY FEELING MYSELF LIFTED BY MEN'S HANDS

(Page 57)

us captive to their own vessel. Here the one who was
their leader advanced towards me and pulled aside my
veil; whereupon a great clamour instantly arose among
the crew, each contending for the possession of me. The
dispute upon this point grew so warm that presently they
fell to fighting; and a bitter and deadly conflict was
maintained till at last only a single pirate was left. This
one, who now regarded himself as my owner, proceeded
to inform me of what was to be my fate. " I have," he
said, " a friend in Cairo who has promised me a rich
reward if I can supply him with a slave, more beautiful
than any of those that his harem now contains. The
distinction of earning me this reward shall be yours.
But tell me," he went on, turning towards the place
where my husband stood bound, " who is this youth that
accompanies you ? Is he a lover or a brother, or only a
servant ? " " Sir," said I, " he is my husband." " In
that case," he replied, " out of pity we must get rid of
him, for I would not afflict him needlessly with the sight
of another's happiness." And so saying, he took my
husband, all bound as he was, and threw him into the sea.

So great was my grief at the sight of this cruel deed,
that had I not been bound myself I should undoubtedly
have sought the same end to my sufferings. But for the
sake of future profit the pirate took the most watchful
care of me, not only so long as we were on board the ship
but also when, a few days later, we came to port and
there joined ourselves to a large caravan which was about
to start on the road to Cairo. While thus travelling in
apparent safety, we were suddenly attacked by the terrible
negro who lately owned this castle. After a long and
dubious conflict the pirate, and all who stood by him,
were slain, while I and those of the merchants who had
remained timorously looking on were seized, and brought

hither as prisoners destined as it seemed for a fate far more lingering and terrible. The rest of my story, brave Prince, I need not here recount, since the shaping of it was so largely in your own hands, and since to you alone is owed the happiness of its conclusion.

When the Princess of Deryabar had thus finished the tale of her wanderings, Codadad hastened to assure her how deep was his sympathy in all her misfortunes. " But if you will allow yourself," he continued, " to be guided by me, your future life shall be one of safety and tranquillity. You have but to come as my bride, and the King of Harran will offer you an honourable welcome to his court ; while, as regards myself, my whole life shall be devoted to securing for you that happiness which your grace and noble qualities prove that you deserve. And that you may not regard this proposal as too presumptuous, I have now to inform you, and also these Princes, concerning my birth and rank. For I, too, am a son of the King of Harran, born to him at the court of Samaria by his wife the Princess Pirouzè, whom he had sent unjustly into banishment."

This declaration on the part of Codadad so accorded with the inclinations of the Princess that she at once yielded her consent, and as the castle was full of provisions suitable for the occasion, preparations were made first to solemnize the marriage, and then for all together to set forth on the return journey to Harran. As for the Princes, though they received Codadad's news with every outward protestation of joy, they were in fact more filled with apprehension and jealousy than before, for they could not but fear that his favour with the King would be greatly increased and become far more dangerous to their interests when the true facts of his birth were revealed. No sooner,

therefore, had Codadad and the Princess passed to their
nuptials, than his brethren entered into a conspiracy to
slay him ; and at the first halt upon the homeward journey,
taking advantage of the lack of protection which a tent
affords, they came upon their brother by night, and
stabbing him in a hundred places as he lay asleep, left
him for dead in the arms of his bride. They then broke
up the camp and returned with all haste to the city of
Harran, where, with a falsely invented tale, they excused
themselves to the King for their long absence.

In the meantime Codadad lay so spent by loss of blood
that there remained in him no sign of life. The Princess
his wife, distraught with grief, had already given him up
for dead. " O Heaven," she cried, bathing his body with
her tears, " why am I thus ever condemned to bring on
others disaster and death, and why for a second time have
I been deprived of the one I was about to love ? "

As thus she continued to cry in piteous lamentation,
and to gaze on the senseless form lying before her, she
thought that she perceived on the lips a faint motion of
breath. At once her hope revived, and springing to her
feet she ran instantly in the direction of the nearest
village, hoping to find there a surgeon or one that had skill
in the binding of wounds. Returning after a time with
the aid that she had summoned she found to her grief
the place where Codadad had lain left vacant, nor was
there any trace or indication of the fate which had over-
taken him.

Overwhelmed by this final catastrophe, and believing
that some wild beast must have devoured him, she suffered
herself to be led away by the surgeon, who, in pity for
one so greatly afflicted, placed her under the shelter of
his own roof, and lavished upon her every mark of con-
sideration and respect. So, when she had sufficiently

recovered from her griefs to find utterance, he gathered from her own lips all the circumstances of her story, her name and rank, the high and valiant deeds of the Prince her husband, and the base ingratitude of his brethren. And perceiving that her grief and sufferings had so robbed her of the desire of life that without some end on which to direct her will she would presently pass into a decline, the surgeon endeavoured to arouse her to the pursuit of that just vengeance which the murder of her husband had earned. " Do not," he said, " let the death of so noble a Prince become a benefit to his enemies. Let us go together to the King of Harran, and make known to him the guilt of these wicked brethren. For surely the name of Coda-dad should live in story; but if you, whose honour he saved, now sink under your affliction his name perishes with you, and you have not retrieved your debt."

These words roused the Princess from her deep des-pondency; forming her resolution on the surgeon's advice, she arose instantly and prepared herself for the journey, and with such haste and diligence did she pursue her project that within two days she and her companion arrived at the city of Harran.

Here strange news awaited them; for at all the cara-vanseri it was told how lately there had come to the city an exiled wife of the King, Princess Pirouzè by name, in-quiring for news of her lost son; and how, as now appeared, this son had already been under a feigned designation at his father's court, and after performing many exploits and deeds of heroism had disappeared none knew whither. Forty-nine sons had the King by different wives, but all these, it was declared, he would willingly put to death so only that Codadad might be restored to him.

Now when the Princess of Deryabar heard this, she said, " I will go to the Queen Pirouzè and make known to her the fate of her son, and when we have wept together and drawn comfort from each other in our grief then we will go before the King, and demand vengeance on the murderers." But the surgeon said, "Have a care what you do; for if the Princes of Harran learn of your arrival, they will not rest till they have done to you as they did to your husband. Let us therefore proceed with secrecy, so as to ensure safety, and do you on no account let your presence here be known till the King has been thoroughly informed of the whole matter." Then leaving the Princess in a place discreetly chosen, he went forth into the streets and began to direct his steps towards the palace. Presently he was met by a lady mounted upon a mule richly caparisoned, and behind her followed a great troop of guards and attendants. As she approached the populace ran out of their houses and stood in rows to see her go by, and when she passed all bowed down with their faces to the earth. The surgeon inquired of a beggar standing near whether this was one of the King's wives. "Yes, brother," replied the beggar, "and the best of them all; for she is the mother of Prince Codadad, whom, now that he is lost, all hold in love and reverence. And thus each day she goes to the mosque to hear the prayers which the King has ordered for her son's safe return."

Seeing his course now clear the surgeon went and stood at the door of the mosque, waiting the Queen's departure, and when she came forth with all her attendants he plucked one of them by the sleeve and said to him, "If the Queen would have news of her son, Prince Codadad, let her send for the stranger who will be found waiting at the door of her palace." So, as soon as Pirouzè had returned to her apartments, the slave went in and gave his mistress the message. Then she sent in all haste and caused the surgeon to be brought before her. And the surgeon pros-

trated himself and said, " O Queen, let not the grief of
the tidings which I bear be visited upon me but on them
that were the cause of it." And she answered him, " Have
peace, and say on ! " So he told her, as has been here
set forth, the full story of all the courage and prowess of
Codadad, and of his generosity towards his brethren, also
of his marriage to the Princess of Deryabar and of what
followed after. But when he came to speak of the slaying
of her son, the tender mother, as though receiving in her
own body the strokes of the murderers, fell forward upon
the ground, and there for a while lay motionless without
sign of life. When however the surgeon, aided by her
women, had restored her to consciousness, then Pirouzè,
putting aside all personal grief, set her mind upon the
accomplishment of the duty which now lay before her.
" Go instantly," she said, " and tell the Princess of Deryabar that the King will shortly receive her with all the
honour due to her rank. As for yourself, be assured that
your services will be remembered."

Hardly had the surgeon departed, when the King
himself entered, and the sight of his Queen's deep affliction
at once informed him that something dreadful must have
occurred. " Alas," she cried, " our son no longer exists,
nor is it even possible to pay to his body those last rites
which were due to his rank and virtue, for stricken by
treacherous hands and left to perish unprotected he has
fallen a prey to wild beasts so that not a trace of him
remains." She then proceeded to inform her husband
of all the horrible circumstances which the surgeon had
narrated.

But before she had ended the King became so transported with rage and grief that he could no longer delay
the setting in motion of his just vengeance. Repairing in
haste to the hall of audience, where courtiers and suitors

THE PRINCESS DERYABAR

(*Page* 66)

stood waiting, he summoned to him his grand vizier with so much fury of countenance that all trembled for their lives. " Go instantly," he cried, " arrest all the Princes, and convey them under a strong guard to the prison assigned for murderers ! " The vizier, not daring to question an order so terribly uttered, went forth and fulfilled the King's command with all speed. On his return to the palace for the presentation of his report, a further order almost equally surprising awaited him. The King described to him a certain inn lying in a poor quarter of the city. " Go thither," said he, " take with you slaves and high attendants, a white mule from the royal stables, and a guard of honour, and bring hither with all the respect due to her rank the young Princess whom you shall find there."

The vizier, with revived spirits, went forth to fulfil this second mission, so much more agreeable to him than the first ; and presently there arose from the streets leading to the palace the acclamations of the populace because of the magnificence and splendour which announced the arrival of the unknown Princess. The King, as a token of respect, stood waiting at the palace gates to receive her, and taking her hand he led her to the apartments of the Queen Pirouzè. Here at the meeting of mother and wife a scene of the most tender and heart-rending affliction took place. The King himself was so moved by it that he had not the heart to refuse to them any request. So when they came and besought for the absent those funeral honours which under other circumstances would have been his due, he gave orders for a dome of marble to be erected on the plain by which the city of Harran lies surrounded. And with such speed was the work put in hand, and so large was the number of men employed upon it, that within three days the entire building was completed.

On the day following the obsequies began. All was done with the greatest solemnity and splendour. First came the King attended by his vizier and all the officers and lords of his palace ; and entering the tomb, in which lay an effigy of Codadad, they seated themselves on carpets of mourning bordered with gold. Then followed the chiefs of the army mounted upon horses and bewailing the loss of him who had led them to victory ; behind these came old men upon black mules, with long robes and flowing beards ; and after these maidens on white horses, with heads unveiled, bearing in their hands baskets of precious stones. Now when these had approached and compassed the dome three times about, then the King rose up to speak the dismissal of the dead. Touching with his brow the tomb whereon the effigy lay, he cried in a loud voice, " O my dear son, O light of mine eyes, O joy that is lost to me for ever." After him all the lords and the chiefs and the elders came and prostrated themselves in like manner ; and when the ceremony was ended the doors of the tomb were shut and all the people returned to the city.

Now after this there was prayer and fasting in the mosque for eight days, and on the ninth the King gave orders that the Princes were to be beheaded. But meanwhile the neighbouring powers, whose arms the King of Harran had defeated, as soon as they heard that Codadad was dead, banded themselves together in strong alliance, and with a great host began to advance upon the city. Then the King caused the execution to be postponed, and making a hasty levy of his forces went forth to meet the enemy in the open plain. And there battle was joined with such valour and determination on both sides that for a time the issue remained doubtful. Nevertheless, because the men of Harran were fewer in number, they began to be surrounded by their enemies ; but at the very moment when all seemed lost they saw in the distance a large body of horsemen advancing at the charge ; and while both combatants were yet uncertain of their purpose, these fell furiously and without warning upon the ranks of the allies, and throwing them into sudden disorder, drove them in rout from the field.

With the success of their arms thus established the two leaders of the victorious forces advanced to meet each other in the presence of the whole army, and great was the joy and astonishment of the King when he discovered in the leader of the lately arrived troop his lost son Codadad. The Prince, for his part, was equally delighted to find in his father's welcome the recognition for which he had yearned.

When the long transport of their meeting embrace was over, the Prince, as they began to converse, perceived with surprise how much was already known to the King of past events. "What ? " he inquired, " has one of my brothers awakened to his guilt, and confessed that which I had meant should ever remain a secret ? " " Not so," replied the King, " from the Princess of Deryabar alone have I learned the truth. For she it was who came to demand vengeance for the crime which your brothers would still have concealed."

At this unlooked-for news of the safety of the Princess and of her arrival at his father's court, Codadad's joy was beyond words, and greatly was it increased when he heard of his mother's reinstatement in the King's favour with the honour and dignity due to her rank. He now began to perceive how events had shaped themselves in his absence, and how the King had already become informed of the bond that existed between them. As for the rest of his adventures, together with the circumstance which

had led to his disappearance and supposed death, they
were soon explained.   For when the Princess had left
Codadad in her desperate search for aid, there chanced
that way a travelling pedlar ; and he, finding the youth
apparently deserted and dying of his wounds, took pity
on him, and placing him upon his mule bore him to his
own house.   There with medicinal herbs and simple arts
unknown in the palaces of kings he had accomplished a
cure which others would have thought impossible, so that
in a short time Codadad's strength was completely restored.
Thereupon the Prince, impatient for reunion with those
whom he loved, bestowed on the pedlar all the wealth
that he possessed, and immediately set forth toward the
city of Harran.

On the road news reached him of the fresh outbreak
of hostilities, followed by the invasion of his father's territory.   Passing from village to village he roused and armed
the inhabitants, and by the excellence of his example made
such soldiers of them that they were able in the fortunate
moment of their arrival to decide the issue of the conflict
and give victory to the King's arms.

" And now, sire," said the Prince in conclusion, " I
have only one request to make : since in the event all
things have turned out so happily, I beg you to pardon
my brothers in order that I may prove to them in the
future how groundless were the resentment and jealousy
that they felt toward me."

These generous sentiments drew tears from the King's
eyes and removed from his mind all doubt as to the wisdom
of the resolution he had been forming.   Immediately
before the assembled army he declared Codadad his heir,
and, as an act of grace to celebrate his son's return, gave
orders for the Princes to be released.   He then led
Codadad with all speed to the palace, where Pirouzè

and her daughter-in-law were anxiously awaiting them.

In the joy of that meeting the Prince and his wife were repaid a thousandfold for all the griefs and hardships they had undergone : and their delight in each other's society remained so great that in all the world no happiness has been known to equal it. The Princes half died of shame when the means by which their pardon had been procured was revealed to them ; but before long the natural insensibility of their characters reasserted itself and they recovered.

AT SO ARROGANT A CLAIM ALL THE COURTIERS BURST INTO LOUD LAUGHTER

(*Page* 76)

THE STORY OF THE MAGIC HORSE

In the land of the Persians there lived in ancient times a King who had three daughters and an only son of such beauty that they drew the eyes of all beholders like moon-rise in a clear heaven. Now it was the custom in that country for a great festival to be held at the new year, during which people of all grades, from the highest to the lowest, presented themselves before the King with offerings and salutations. So it happened that on one of these days there came to the King as he sat in state three sages, masters of their craft, bringing gifts for approval. The first had with him a peacock of gold which was so constructed that at the passing of each hour it beat its wings and uttered a cry. And the King, having proved it, found the gift acceptable and caused the inventor thereof to be suitably rewarded. The second had made a trumpet so that if placed over the gates of a city it blew a blast against any that sought to enter; and thus was the city held safe from surprise by an enemy. And when the King had found that it possessed that property, he accepted it, bestowing on its maker a rich reward.

But the gift of the third sage, who was an Indian, appeared more prodigious than all, for he had brought with him a horse of ivory and ebony, for which he claimed that, at the will of its owner, or of anyone instructed in the secret, it would rise above the earth and fly, arriving at distant places in a marvellously short space of time.

75

The King, full of wonder at such a statement, and eager to test it, was in some doubt as to how he might do so, for the Indian was unwilling to part with the secret until secure of the reward which in his own mind he had fixed on. Now it happened that at a distance of some three leagues from the city there stood a mountain the top of which was clearly discernible to all eyes; so, in order that the Indian's word might be proved, the King, pointing to it, said, " Go yonder, and bring back to me while I wait the branch of a palm-tree which grows at the foot of that mountain; then I shall know that what you tell me is true."

Instantly the Indian set foot in the stirrup and vaulted upon his charger, and scarcely had he turned a small peg which was set in the pommel of the saddle, when the horse rose lightly into the air and bore him away at wondrous speed amid the shouts of the beholders; and while all were still gazing, amazed at so sudden a vanishing, he reappeared high overhead, bearing the palm branch, and descending into their midst alighted upon the very spot from which he had started, where, prostrating himself, he laid the branch at the King's feet.

The King was so delighted when the wonderful properties of the horse had been thus revealed to him, that, eager to possess it, he bade the Indian name his own reward, declaring that no price could be too great. Then said the sage, " Since your Majesty so truly appreciates the value of my invention, I do not fear that the reward I ask for will seem too high. Give me in marriage the hand of the fairest of your three daughters, and the horse shall be yours."

At so arrogant a claim all the courtiers burst into loud laughter; the King alone, consumed with the desire of possessing the wonderful treasure, hesitated as to what

answer he should give. Then the King's son, Prince
Firouz Schah, seeing his father lend ear to so shameful a
proposal, became moved with indignation. Determined
to defend his sister's honour and his own, he addressed
the King. "Pardon me, sire," said he, "if I take the
liberty of speaking. But how shall it be possible for one
of the greatest and most powerful monarchs to ally himself to a mere nobody? I entreat you to consider what
is due not to yourself alone but to the high blood of your
ancestors and of your children."

"My son," replied the King of Persia, "what you say
is very true, so far as it goes; but you do not sufficiently
consider the value of so incomparable a marvel as this
horse has proved itself to be, or how great would be my
chagrin if any other monarch came to possess it. And
though I have not yet agreed to the Indian's proposal,
I cannot incontinently reject it. But first I must be
satisfied that the horse will obey other hands besides
those of its inventor, else, though I become its possessor,
I may find it useless."

The Indian, who had stood aside during this discussion,
was now full of hope, for he perceived that the King had
not altogether rejected his terms, and nothing seemed
likelier than that the more he became familiar with the
properties of the magic horse the more would he wish to
possess it. When, therefore, the King proposed that the
horse should be put to a more independent trial under
another rider, the Indian readily agreed; the more so
when the Prince himself, relinquishing his apparent opposition, came forward and volunteered for the essay.

The King having consented, the Prince mounted, and
eager in his design to give his father opportunity for cooler
reflection, he did not wait to hear all the Indian's instructions, but turning the peg, as he had seen the other do

when first mounting, caused the horse to rise suddenly in the air, and was carried away out of sight in an easterly direction more swiftly than an arrow shot from a bow.

No sooner had the horse and its rider disappeared than the King became greatly concerned for his son's safety; and though the sage could justly excuse himself on the ground that the young Prince's impatience had caused him to cut short the instructions which would have ensured his safe return, the King chose to vent upon the Indian the full weight of his displeasure; and cursing the day wherein he had first set eyes on the magic horse, he caused its maker to be thrown into prison, declaring that if the Prince did not return within a stated time the life of the other should be forfeit.

The Indian had now good cause to repent of the ambition which had brought him to this extremity, for the Prince, of whose opposition to his project he had been thoroughly informed, had only to prolong his absence to involve him in irretrievable ruin. But on the failure of arrogant pretensions the sympathy of the judicious is wasted; let us return therefore to Prince Firouz Schah, whom we left flying through the air with incredible swiftness on the back of the magic steed.

For a time, confident of his skill as a rider and undismayed either by the speed or altitude of his flight, the Prince had no wish to return to the palace; but presently the thought of his father's anxiety occurred to him, and being of a tender and considerate disposition he immediately endeavoured to divert his steed from its forward course. This he sought to do by turning in the contrary direction the peg which he had handled when mounting, but to his astonishment the horse responded by rising still higher in the air and flying forward with redoubled swiftness. Had courage then deserted him, his situation might have become perilous; but preserving his accustomed coolness he began carefully to search for the means by which the speed of the machine might be abated, and before long he perceived under the horse's mane a smaller peg, which he had no sooner touched than he felt himself descending rapidly toward the earth, with a speed that lessened the nearer he came to ground.

As he descended, the daylight in which hitherto he had been travelling faded from view, and he passed within a few minutes from sunset into an obscurity so dense that he could no longer distinguish the nature of his environment, till, as the horse alighted, he perceived beneath him a smooth expanse ending abruptly on all sides at an apparent elevation among the objects surrounding it.

Dismounting he found himself on the roof of a large palace, with marble balustrades dividing it in terraces, and at one side a staircase which led down to the interior. With a spirit ever ready for adventure Prince Firouz Schah immediately descended, groping his way through the darkness till he came to a landing on the farther side of which an open door led into a room where a dim light was burning.

The Prince paused at the doorway to listen, but all he could hear was the sound of men breathing heavily in their sleep. He pushed the door and entered; and there across an inner threshold he saw black slaves lying asleep, each with a drawn sword in his hand. Immediately he guessed that something far more fair must lie beyond; so, undeterred by the danger, he advanced, and stepping lightly across their swords passed through silken hangings into the inner chamber. Here he perceived, amid surroundings of regal magnificence, a number of couches, one of which stood higher than the rest. Upon each of these a fair damsel lay asleep; but upon that which was raised above its fellows lay a form of such perfect and enchanting beauty that the Prince had no will or power to turn away after once beholding it. Approaching the sleeper softly, he kneeled down and plucked her gently by the sleeve ; and immediately the Princess—for such if rank and beauty accorded she needs must be—opened to him the depths of her lustrous eyes and gazed in quiet amazement at the princely youth whose handsome looks and reverent demeanour banished at once all thought of alarm.

Now it so happened that a son of the King of India was at that time seeking the hand of the Princess in marriage ; but her father, the King of Bengal, had rejected him owing to his ferocious and disagreeable aspect. When therefore the Princess saw one of royal appearance kneeling before her she supposed he could be no other than the suitor whom she knew only by report, and shedding upon him the light of her regard, " By Allah," she said, smiling, " my father lied in saying that good looks were lacking to thee ! "

Prince Firouz Schah, perceiving from these words and the glance which accompanied them, that her disposition towards him was favourable, no longer feared to acquaint her with the plight in which he found himself ; while the Princess, for her part, listened to the story of his adventures with lively interest, and learned, not without secret satisfaction, that her visitor possessed a rank and dignity equal to her own.

Meanwhile the maidens who were in attendance on the Princess had awakened in dismay to the unaccountable apparition of a fair youth kneeling at the feet of their mistress, and, dreading discovery by the attendants, were all at a loss what to do. The Princess, however, seeing that they were awake, called them to her with perfect composure and bade them go instantly and prepare an inner chamber where the Prince might sleep and recover from the fatigues of his journey; at the same time she gave orders for a rich banquet to be prepared against the time when he should be ready to partake of it. Then when her visitor had retired, she arose and began to adorn herself in jewels and rich robes and to anoint her body with fragrance, giving her women no rest till the tale of her mirror contented her; and when all had been done many times over, and the last touch of art added to her loveliness, she sent to inquire whether the Prince had yet awaked and were ready to receive her.

Upon the receipt of that message the Prince rose eagerly, and dressing in haste, although it was scarcely yet day, heard everywhere within the palace sounds of preparation for the feast that was being got ready in his honour.

Before long the Princess herself entered to inquire how he had slept, and being fully assured on that score, she gave orders for the banquet to be served. Everything was done in the greatest magnificence, but the Princess was full of apologies, declaring the entertainment unworthy of so distinguished a guest. "You must pardon me, Prince," she said, "for receiving you with so little state, and after so hasty a preparation; but the chief of the eunuchs does not enter here without my express permission, and I feared that elsewhere our conversation might be interrupted."

Prince Firouz Schah was now convinced that the inclinations of the Princess corresponded with his own; but though her every word and movement increased the tenderness of his passion, he did not forget the respect due to her rank and virtue. One of her women attendants, however, seeing clearly in what direction matters were tending, and fearing for herself the results of a sudden

11

discovery, withdrew secretly, saying nothing to the rest, and running quickly to the chief of the guards she cried, "O miserable man, what sorry watch is this that thou hast kept, guarding the King's honour; and who is this man or genie that thou hast admitted to the presence of our mistress? Nay, if the matter be not already past remedy the fault is not thine!"

At these words he quickly leapt up in alarm, and going secretly he lifted the curtain of the inner chamber, and there beheld at the Princess's side a youth of such fair and majestical appearance that he durst not intrude unbidden. He ran shrieking to the King, and as he went he rent his garments and threw dust upon his head. "O sire and master," he cried, "come quickly and save thy daughter, for there is with her a genie in mortal form and like a king's son to look upon, and if he have not already carried her away, make haste and give orders that he be seized, lest thou become childless."

The King at once arose and went in great haste and fear to his daughter's palace. There he was met by certain of her women, who, seeing his alarm, said, "O sire, have no fear for the safety of thy daughter; for this young man is as handsome of heart as of person, and as his conduct is chaste, so also are his intentions honourable."

Then the King's wrath was cooled somewhat; but since much remained which demanded explanation he drew his sword and advanced with a threatening aspect into the room where his daughter and the Prince still sat conversing. Prince Firouz Schah, observing the new-comer advance upon him in a warlike attitude, drew his own sword and stood ready for defence; whereupon the King, seeing that the other was the stronger, sheathed his weapon, and with a gesture of salutation addressed him courteously. "Tell me, fair youth," he said, "whether you are man or

AS HE DESCENDED THE DAYLIGHT FADED
(Page 79)

devil, for though in appearance you are human, how else than by devilry have you come here ? "

" Sire," replied the youth, " but for the respect that is owing to the father of so fair a daughter, I, who am a son of kings, might resent such an imputation. Be assured, however, that by whatever means I have chosen to arrive, my intentions now are altogether human and honourable ; for I have no other or dearer wish than to become your son-in-law through my marriage with this Princess in whose eyes it is my happiness to have found favour."

" What you tell me," answered the King, " may be all very true ; but it is not the custom for the sons of kings to enter into palaces without the permission of their owners, coming, moreover, unannounced and with no retinue or mark of royalty about them. How, then, shall I convince my people that you are a fit suitor for the hand of my daughter ? "

" The proof of honour and kingship," answered the other, " does not rest in splendour and retinue alone, though these also would be at my call had I the patience to await their arrival from that too distant country where my father is King. Let it suffice if I shall be able to prove my worth alone and unaided, in such a manner as to satisfy all." " Alone and unaided ? " said the King ; " how may that be ? " " I will prove it thus," answered the Prince. " Call out your troops and let them surround this palace ; tell them that you have here a stranger, of whom nothing is known, who declares that if you will not yield him the hand of your daughter in marriage he will carry her away from you by force. Bid them use all means to capture and slay me, and if I survive so unequal a contest, judge then whether or no I am fit to become your son-in-law."

The King immediately accepted the proposal, agreeing

to abide by the result; yet was he grieved that a youth of such fair looks and promise should throw away his life in so foolhardy an adventure. As soon as day dawned he sent for his vizier and bade him cause all the chiefs of his army to assemble with their troops and companies, till presently there were gathered about the palace forty thousand horsemen and the same number of foot; and the King gave them instructions, saying, " When the young man of whom I have warned you comes forth and challenges you to battle, then fall upon and slay him, for in no wise must he escape." He then led the Prince to an open space whence he could see the whole army drawn up in array against him. " Yonder," said the King, pointing, " are those with whom you have to contend; go forth and deal with them as seems best to you."

" Nay," answered the Prince, " these are not fair conditions, for yonder I see horsemen as well as foot; how shall I contend against these unless I be mounted ? " The King at once offered him the best horse in his stables, but the Prince would not hear of it. " Is it fair," he said, " that I should trust my life under such conditions to a horse that I have never ridden ? I will ride no horse but that upon which I came hither."

" Where is that ? " inquired the King. " If it be where I left it," answered the Prince, " it is upon the roof of the palace."

All who heard this answer were filled with laughter and astonishment, for it seemed impossible that a horse could have climbed to so high a roof. Nevertheless the King commanded that search should be made, and there, sure enough, those that were sent found the horse of ebony and ivory standing stiff and motionless. So though it still seemed to them but a thing for jest and mockery obeying the King's orders they raised it upon their shoulders, and bearing it to earth carried it forth into the open space before the palace where the King's troops were assembled.

Then Prince Firouz Schah advanced, and leaping upon the horse he cried defiance to the eighty thousand men that stood in battle array against him. And they, on their part, seeing the youth so hardily set on his own destruction, drew sword and couched spear, and came all together to the charge. The Prince waited till they were almost upon him, then turning the peg which stood in the pommel of his saddle he caused the horse to rise suddenly in the air, and all the foremost ranks of the enemy came clashing together beneath him. At that sight the King and all his court drew a breath of astonishment, and the army staggered and swung about this way and that, striking vainly up at the hoofs of the magic horse as it flew over them. Then the King, full of dread lest this should indeed be some evil genie that sought to carry his daughter away from him, called to his archers to shoot, but before they could make ready their bows Prince Firouz Schah had given another turn to the peg, and immediately the horse sprang upward and rose higher than the roof of the palace, so that all the arrows fell short and rained destruction on those that were below.

Then the Prince called to the King, " O King of Bengal, have I not now proved myself worthy to be thy son-in-law, and wilt thou not give me the hand of thy daughter in marriage ? " But the King's wrath was very great, for he had been made foolish in the eyes of his people, and panic had broken the ranks of his army and many of them were slain ; and by no means would he have for his son-in-law one that possessed such power to throw down the order and establishment of his kingdom. So he cried back to the Prince, saying, " O vile enchanter, get hence as thou valuest thy life, for if ever thou darest to return and set foot within my dominions thy death and not my daughter shall be thy reward!" Thus he spoke in his anger, forgetting altogether the promise he had made.

Now it should be known that all this time the Princess had been watching the combat from the roof of the palace; and as her fear and anxiety for the Prince had in the first instance been great, so now was she overjoyed when she saw him rise superior to the dangers which had threatened him. But as soon as she heard her father's words she became filled with fresh fear lest she and her lover were now to be parted; so as the Prince came speeding by upon the magic horse she stretched up her arms to him, crying, " O master of the flying bird, leave me not desolate, for if thou goest from me now I shall die."

No sooner did Prince Firouz Schah hear those words than he checked his steed in its flight, and swooping low he bore down over the palace roof, and catching the Princess up in his arms placed her upon the saddle before him; and straightway at the pressure of its rider the horse rose under them and carried them away high in air, so that they disappeared forthwith from the eyes of the King and his people.

But as they travelled the day grew hot and the sun burned fiercely upon them; and the Prince looking down beheld a green meadow by the side of a lake: so he said, " O desire of my heart, let us go down into yonder meadow and seek rest and refreshment, and there let us wait till it is evening, so that we may come unperceived to my father's palace, and when I have brought thee thither safely and secretly, then will I make preparation so that thou mayest appear at my father's court in such a manner as befits thy rank."

TILL THE TALE OF HER MIRROR CONTENTED HER

(Page 81)

12

So the Princess consenting, they went down and sat by the lake and solaced themselves sweetly with love till it was evening. Then they rose up and mounted once more upon the magic horse and came by night to the outskirts of the city where dwelt the King of Persia. Now in the garden of the summer palace which stood without the walls all was silence and solitude, and coming thither unperceived the King's son led the Princess to a pavilion, the door of which lay open, and placing before it the magic horse he bade her stay within and keep watch till his messenger should come to take her to the palace which he would cause to be prepared for her.

Leaving her thus safely sheltered, the Prince went into the city to present himself before the King his father; and there he found him in deep mourning and affliction because of his son's absence; and his father seeing him, rose up and embraced him tenderly, rejoicing because of his safe return, and eager to know in what way he had fared. And the Prince said, "O my father, if it be thy good will and pleasure, I have come back to thee far richer than I went. For I have brought with me the fairest Princess that the eyes of love have ever looked upon, and she is the daughter of the King of Bengal; and because of my love for her and the great service which she rendered me when I was a stranger in the midst of enemies, therefore have I no heart or mind or will but to win your consent that I may marry her." And when the King heard that, and of all that the Princess had done, and of how they had escaped together, he gave his consent willingly, and ordered that a palace should be immediately got ready for her reception that she might on the next day appear before the people in a manner befitting her rank.

Then while preparation was going forward, the Prince sought news concerning the sage, for he feared that the

King might have slain him. " Do not speak of him," cried the King. " Would to Heaven that I had never set eyes on him or his invention, for out of this has arisen all my grief and lamentation. Therefore he now lies in prison awaiting death."

" Nay," said the Prince, " now surely should he be released and suitably rewarded, seeing that unwittingly he hath been the cause of my fortune ; but do not give him my sister in marriage."

So the King sent and caused the Indian to be brought before him clad in a robe of rank. And the King said to him, " Because my son, whom thy vile invention carried away from me, hath returned safe and sound, therefore will I spare thy life. And for the reward of thine ingenuity I give thee this robe of honour ; but now take thy horse, whatever it may be, and go, nor ever appear in my sight again. And if thou wilt marry, seek one of thine own rank, but do not aspire to the daughters of kings."

When the Indian heard that, he dissembled his rage, and bowing himself to the earth departed from the King's presence. And, as he went everywhere in the palace ran the tale how the King's son had returned upon the magic horse bringing with him a Princess of most marvellous beauty, and how they had alighted in the gardens of the summer palace that lay outside the walls.

Now when this was told him the Indian at once saw his opportunity, and going forth from the city in haste he arrived at the summer palace before the messenger with the appointed retinue which the Prince and the King were sending. So coming to the pavilion in the garden he found the Princess waiting within, and before the door the horse of ivory and ebony. Then was his heart uplifted for joy, the more so when he perceived how far the damsel exceeded in loveliness all that had been told of her. Entering the chamber where she sat he kissed the ground at her feet; and she, seeing one that wore a robe of office making obeisance before her, spake to him without fear, saying, "Who art thou?"

The sage answered, "O moon of beauty, I am but the dust which lies upon the road by which thou art to travel. Yet I come as a messenger from the King's son who hath sent me to bring thee with all speed to a chamber in the royal palace where he now awaits thee."

Now the Indian was of a form altogether hideous and abominable. The Princess looked at him, therefore, in surprise, saying, "Could not the King's son find anyone to send to me but thee?" The sage laughed, for he read the meaning of her words. "O searcher of hearts," he said, "do not wonder that the Prince hath sent to thee a man whose looks are unattractive, for because of his love toward thee he is grown exceeding jealous. Were it otherwise, I doubt not that he would have chosen the highest and most honourable in the land; but, being what I am, he has preferred to make me his messenger."

When the Princess heard that, she believed him, and because her impatience to be with her lover was great, she yielded herself willingly into his hands. Then the sage mounted upon the horse and took up the damsel behind him; and having bound her to his girdle for safety, he turned the pin so swiftly that immediately they rose up into the air far above the roof of the palace and in full view of the royal retinue which was even then approaching.

Now because his desire to be with his beloved was so strong, the Prince himself had come forth before all others to meet her; and when he saw her thus carried away captive, he uttered a loud cry of lamentation, and stretched out his hands toward her. The cry of her lover reached the ears of the Princess, and looking down she saw with wonder his gestures of grief and despair. So she said to the Indian, " O slave, why art thou bearing me away from thy lord, disobeying his command ? " The sage answered, " He is not my lord, nor do I owe him any duty or obedience. May Heaven repay on him all the grief he has brought on me, for I was the maker of this horse on which he won thee, and because he stole it from me I was cast into prison. But now for all my wrongs I will take full payment, and will torture his heart as he hath tortured mine. Be of good cheer, therefore, for doubt not that presently I shall seem a more desirable lover in thine eyes than ever he was."

On hearing these words the Princess was so filled with terror and loathing that she endeavoured to cast herself from the saddle ; but the Indian having bound her to his girdle, no present escape from him was possible.

The horse had meanwhile carried them far from the city of the King of Persia, and it was yet an early hour after dawn when they arrived over the land of Cashmire. Assured that he was now safe from pursuit, and perceiving an uninhabited country below him, the Indian caused the horse to descend on the edge of a wood bordered by a stream. Here he made the Princess dismount, and was proceeding to force upon her his base and familiar attentions, when the cries raised by the Princess drew to that spot a party of horsemen who had been hunting in the neighbourhood. The leader of the party, who chanced to be no other than the Sultan of that country, seeing a fair damsel undergoing ill-treatment from one of brutish and malevolent aspect, rode forward and demanded of the Indian by what right he so used her. The sage boldly declared that she was his wife and that how he used her was no man's business but his own. The damsel, how-

ever, contradicted his assertion with indignation and scorn,
and so great were her beauty and the dignity of her bearing that her statement of the case had only to be heard
to be believed. The Sultan therefore ordered the Indian
to be bound and beaten, and afterwards to be led away
to the adjacent city and there cast into the deepest dungeon. As for the Princess and magic horse, he caused
them to be brought to the palace, and there for the damsel
he provided a magnificent apartment with slaves and
attendants such as befitted her rank; but the horse,
whose properties remained secret, since no other use
for it could be discovered, was placed in the royal
treasury.

Now though the Princess was full of joy over her
escape from the Indian, and of gratitude to her deliverer,
she could not fail to read in the Sultan's manner towards
her the spell cast by her beauty. And, in fact, no later
than the next day, awakened by sounds throughout the
whole city of tumult and rejoicing, and inquiring as to
the reason, she was informed that these festivities were
the prelude to her own nuptials with the Sultan which
were to be celebrated that very day before sundown.

At this news her consternation was so great that she
immediately swooned away, and remained for a long while
speechless. But no sooner had she recovered possession
of her faculties than her resolution was formed, and when
the Sultan entered, as is customary on such occasions, to
present his compliments and make inquiries as to her
health, she fell into an extravagance of attitude and speech,
so artfully contrived that all who beheld her became convinced of her insanity. And the more surely to effect her
purpose, and at the same time to relieve her feelings, she
made a violent attack upon the Sultan's person; nor did
she desist until she had brought him to recognize that all

hopes for the present consummation of the nuptials were useless.

On the following day also, and upon every succeeding one, the Princess showed the same violent symptoms whenever the Sultan approached her. It was in vain that all the wisest physicians in the country were summoned into consultation. While some declared that her malady was curable, others, to whose word the Princess by her actions lent every possible weight, declared that it was incurable; and in no case was any remedy applied that did not seem immediately to aggravate the disorder.

And here for a while we must leave the Princess and return to Prince Firouz Schah, whose affliction no words can describe. Unable to endure the burden of his beloved one's absence in the splendours of his father's palace, or to leave her the victim of fate without an attempt at rescue, he put on the disguise of a travelling dervish, and departing secretly from the Persian court set out into the world to seek for her.

For many months he travelled without clue or tidings to guide him; but as Heaven ever bestows favour on constancy in love, so it led him at last to the land of Cashmire, and to the city of its Sultan. Now as he drew near to it by the main road, he fell into conversation with a certain merchant, and inquired of him as to the city and the life and conditions of its inhabitants. And the merchant looked at him in surprise, saying, " Surely you have come from a far country not to have heard of the strange things which have happened here, for everywhere in these regions and among all the caravans goes the story of the strange maiden, and the ebony horse, and the waiting nuptials."

Now when the Prince heard that, he knew that the end of his wanderings was in sight : so looking upon the

city with eyes of gladness, " Tell me," he said, " for I
know none of these things." So the merchant told him
truly all that has here been narrated; and having ended
he said, " O dervish, though you are young, you have in
your eyes the light of wisdom ; and if you have also in
your hands the power of healing, then I tell you that in
this city fortune awaits you, for the Sultan will give even
the half of his kingdom to any man that shall restore
health of mind to this damsel."

Then the King's son felt his heart uplifted within him,
howbeit he knew well that the fortune he sought would
not be of the Sultan's choosing ; so parting from the
merchant, he put on the robe of a physician, and went
and presented himself at the palace.

The Sultan was glad at his coming, for though many
physicians had promised healing and had all failed, still
each new arrival gave him fresh hopes. Now as the sight
of a physician seemed ever greatly to increase the Princess's
malady, the Sultan led him to a small closet or balcony,
that thence he might look upon her unperceived. So
Prince Firouz Schah, having travelled so many miles in
search of her, saw his beloved seated in deep despondency
by the side of a fountain ; and ever with the tears falling
down from her eyes she sighed and sang. Now when he
heard her voice and the words, and beheld the soft grief
of her countenance, then the Prince knew that her disorder
was only feigned ; and he went forth and said to the Sultan,
" This malady is curable ; but for the cure something is
yet lacking. Let me go in and speak with the damsel
alone, and on my life I promise that if all be done according to my requirements, before this time to-morrow the
cure shall be accomplished."

At these words the Sultan rejoiced greatly, and he
ordered the doors of the Princess's chamber to be opened

13

to the physician. So Firouz Schah passed in, and he and his beloved were alone together. Now because of his grief and wanderings and the growth of his beard, the face of the Prince was so changed that the Princess did not know him; but seeing one before her in the dress of a physician she rose up in pretended frenzy and began to throw herself about with violence, until from utter exhaustion she fell prostrate. Thereupon the Prince drew near, and called her gently by name; and immediately when she heard his voice she knew him, and uttered a loud cry. Then the King's son put his mouth to her ear and said, " O temptation of all hearts, now spare my life and have patience, for surely I am come to save thee; but if the Sultan learn who I am we are dead, thou and I, because his jealousy is great." So she replied, saying, " O thou that bringest me life, tell me what I shall do ? " The Prince said, " When I depart hence let it appear that I have restored to thee the possession of thy faculties; howbeit the full cure is to come after. Therefore when the Sultan comes to thee, be sad and meek and do not repulse him as thou hast done aforetime. Yet have no fear but that I will keep thee safe from him to the last." And so saying he left the Princess and returned to the Sultan, and said to him, " Go in and see whether the cure be not already at work; but approach not near to her, for though the genie that possessed her is bound he is not yet cast forth: nevertheless to-morrow before noon the remedy shall be complete."

So the Sultan went and found her even as he had been told; and with joy and gratitude he returned to Firouz Schah, saying, " Truly thou art a healer and the rest are but bunglers and fools. Now, therefore, give orders and all shall be done according to thy will. Doubt not that thy reward shall be great."

THE BANQUET SERVED

(*Page* 81)

Then the Prince said, " Let the horse of ivory and ebony which was with her at the first be brought forth and set again in the place where it was found, and let the damsel also be brought and put into my hand ; and it shall be that when I have set her upon the horse, then the evil genie that held her shall be suddenly loosed, passing from her into that which was aforetime his place of bondage. So shall the remedy be complete, and the Princess find joy in her lord before the eyes of all."

Now when the Sultan heard that, the mystery of the ebony horse seemed plain to him, and its use manifest. Therefore he gave orders that with all speed the thing should be done as the physician of the Princess required it.

So early on the morrow they brought the horse from the royal treasury, and the Princess from her chamber, and carried them to the place where they were first found ; and all about, a great crowd of the populace was gathered to behold the sight. Then Prince Firouz Schah took the Princess and set her upon the horse, and leaping into the saddle before her he turned the pin of ascent, and immediately the horse rose with a great sound into the air, and hung above the heads of the affrighted populace. And the King's son leaned down from the saddle and cried in a loud voice, " O Sultan of Cashmire, when you wish to espouse Princesses which seek your protection, learn first to obtain their consent." And so saying he put the horse to its topmost speed, and like an arrow on the wind he and the Princess were borne away, and passed and vanished, and were no more seen in that land.

But in the city of the King of Persia great joy and welcome and thanksgiving awaited them; and there without delay the nuptials were solemnized, and through all the country the people rejoiced and feasted for a full month.　But because of the grief and affliction that it had caused him the King broke the ebony horse and destroyed its motions.　As for the maker thereof, the Sultan of Cashmire caused him to be put to a cruel death : and thus is the story of the sage and his invention brought to a full ending.

SO STRANGE OF FORM AND SO BRILLIANT AND DIVERSE IN HUE

(*Page* 110)

THE FISHERMAN AND THE GENIE

THERE was once an old fisherman who lived in great poverty with a wife and three children. But though poorer than others he ever toiled in humble submission to the decrees of Providence, and so, at the same hour each day, he would cast his net four times into the sea, and whatever it brought up to him therewith he rested content.

One day, having cast for the first time, he found his net so heavy that he could scarcely draw it in; yet when at last he got it to shore all that it contained was the carcass of an ass.

He cast a second time, and found the draught of the net even heavier than before. But again he was doomed to disappointment, for this time it contained nothing but a large earthenware jar full of mud and sand. His third attempt brought him only a heap of broken old bottles and potsherds : fortune seemed to be against him. Then, committing his hope to Providence, he cast for the fourth and last time; and once more the weight of the net was so great that he was unable to haul it. When at last he got it to land, he found that it contained a brazen vessel, its mouth closed with a leaden stopper, bearing upon it the seal of King Solomon.

The sight cheered him. " This," thought he, " I can sell in the market, where I may get for it enough to buy a measure of corn ; and, if one is to judge by weight, what lies within may prove yet more valuable."

Thus reckoning, he prised out the stopper with his knife, and turning the vessel upside down looked for the contents to follow. Great was his astonishment when nothing but smoke came out of it. The smoke rose in a thick black column and spread like a mist between earth and sky, till presently, drawing together, it took form ; and there in its midst stood a mighty Genie, whose brows touched heaven while his feet rested upon ground. His head was like a dome, his hands were like flails, and his legs like pine-trees ; his mouth was black as a cavern, his nostrils were like trumpets, his eyes blazed like torches, and his wings whirled round and over him like the simoom of the desert.

At so fearful a sight all the fisherman's courage oozed out of him ; but the Genie, perceiving him, cried with a loud voice, " O Solomon, Prophet of God, slay me not, for never again will I withstand thee in word or deed."

" Alas ! " said the fisherman, " I am no prophet ; and as for Solomon, he has been dead for nearly two thousand years. I am but a poor fisherman whom chance has knocked by accident against thy door."

" In that case," answered the Genie, " know that presently thou wilt have to die."

" Heaven forbid ! " cried the fisherman ; " or, at least, tell me why ! Surely it might seem that I had done thee some service in releasing thee."

" Hear first my story," said the Genie, " then shalt thou understand."

" Well, if I must ! " said the fisherman, resigning himself to the inevitable ; " but make it short, for truly I have small stomach left in me now for the hearing of tales."

" Know, then," said the Genie, " that I am one of those spirits which resisted the power and dominion of

Solomon; and when, having brought into submission all the rest of my race, he could not make me yield to him either reverence or service, he caused me to be shut up in this bottle, and sealing it with his own seal cast it down into the depths of the sea.

" Now when I had lain there prisoner for a hundred years, I swore in my heart that I would give to the man that should release me all the treasures attainable in heaven or earth.   But when none came to earn so great a reward in all the hundred years that followed, then I swore that I would give to my liberator earthly riches only ; and when this gift also had lain despised for yet another hundred years, then would I promise no more than the fulfilment of three wishes.   But thereafter finding that all promises and vows were vain, my heart became consumed with rage, and I swore by Allah that I would only grant to the fool that should release me his own choice of the most cruel form of death by which he should die. Now therefore accept that mercy which I still offer and choose thy penalty ! "

When the fisherman heard this he gave himself up for lost, yet he did not the less continue by prayer and supplication to entreat the Genie from his purpose.   But when he found that there was no heart left in him to be moved, then for the first time he bestirred his wits, and remembering how that which is evil contains far less wisdom than that which is good, and so falls ever the more readily into the trap prepared for it, he spoke thus : " O Genie, since thou art determined on my death, there is yet a certain thing touching thine honour that I would first know.   So, by the Ineffable Name, which is the seal of Solomon, I will ask thee one question, and do thou swear to answer it truly."

The Genie was ready enough to give the oath as desired.

Then said the fisherman, "How is it that one so great as thou art, whose feet o'er-step the hills and whose head out-tops the heaven—how can such an one enter into so small a vessel to dwell in it ? Truly, though mine eyes tell me I have seen it, I cannot any longer believe so great a marvel."

"What ? " cried the Genie, "dost thou not believe what I have already told thee ? "

"Not till I have seen it done can I believe it," said the fisherman.

Thereupon, without more waste of words, the Genie, drawing his limbs together and folding himself once more in a thick veil of smoke, descended from his vast altitude into the narrow neck of the brazen vessel till not one shred or film of him remained to view. Then the fisherman with a quick hand replaced the leaden stopper, and laughing, cried to the Genie, "Choose now, thou in thy turn, by what manner of death thou wilt die."

The Genie, hearing himself thus mocked, made violent efforts to escape ; but the power of the seal of Solomon held him fast, and the fisherman, ceasing not all the while to revile him for the treachery and baseness which were now to receive their due reward, began to carry the vessel back to the sea's brink. "Now," said he, "thou shalt return to the place whence I drew thee. And here on the shore I will build myself a hut, and to every fisherman that comes near I will say, ' Look that you fish not in these waters, for herein lies bound a wicked genie that has sworn to put to a cruel death whoever dares to release him.' "

"Nay, nay," cried the Genie, "I did not mean what I said. Ask of me now, and I will give you all the treasures that the world contains, or that your heart can find in it to desire, if only you will set me free ! "

The fisherman, being of a mild spirit and with no heart for revenge, sat down to consider what he should do, and all the while the imprisoned Genie continued to appeal to him for compassion with loud promise and lamentation. So, at last, the fisherman, having the fear of God before his eyes, after he had extracted from the Genie a most solemn vow to leave him unharmed, drew out the stopper of lead and released him.

No sooner was he out and restored to his true form than the Genie, turning himself about, lifted his foot and with his full strength smote the brazen vessel far out to sea; and the fisherman, beholding that act, began to repent him of his mercy and to tremble again for dear life.

But the Genie, seeing his fear, broke into huge laughter, and striding on ahead of him cried, " Come, fisherman, and follow me, for now I will lead you to fortune ! "

Meekly at his heels went the old fisherman, and leaving behind them the habitations of men they ascended a mountain and entered upon a desert tract guarded by four hills, in the centre of which lay a broad lake. Here the Genie stopped, and pointing to a place where fish were swimming in abundance bade the fisherman cast in his net. The fisherman did as he was told, and when he drew in his net he found that it contained four fish each of a different colour, a red, a white, a blue, and a yellow : never in his life had he seen the like of them. The Genie bade him take and offer them to the Sultan, assuring him that if he did so they should bring him both fortune and honours. Then he struck the ground with his foot, and immediately the earth opened its mouth and swallowed him as the dry desert swallows the rain.

The fisherman, wondering no less at his safe deliverance than at the marvel of these occurrences, made his way in haste to the city; and there presenting himself at the palace he begged that the four fish might be laid at the Sultan's feet, as a humble offering from the poorest of his subjects.

No sooner had the monarch seen them, so strange of form and so brilliant and diverse in hue, than his longing to taste of them became strongly awakened; so by the hand of his vizier, he sent them to the cook to be prepared forthwith for the royal table. As for the poor fisherman, he received no fewer than four hundred pieces of gold from the Sultan's bounty, and returned to his family rejoicing in an affluence which surpassed his utmost expectations.

The cook meanwhile, proud of an opportunity to exhibit her culinary skill on dainties so rare, scaled and cleaned the fish and laid them in a frying-pan over the fire. But scarcely had she done so when the wall of the kitchen divided, and there issued forth from it a damsel of moon-like beauty richly apparelled, holding a rod of myrtle in her hand. With this she struck the fish that lay in the frying-pan, and cried:

> "O fish of my pond,
> Are ye true to your bond?"

And immediately the four fishes lifted their heads from the frying fat and answered:

> "Even so, the bond holds yet;
> Paid by thee, we pay the debt.
> With give and take is the reckoning met."

Thereupon the damsel upset the pan into the fire and retired through the wall in the same way that she had come, leaving the four fish all charred to a cinder.

The cook, beholding her labour thus brought to naught, began to weep and bewail herself, expecting no less than instant dismissal, and was still loud in her lamentations when the vizier arrived to see if the fish were ready.

On hearing her account of what had occurred, the vizier was greatly astonished, but feared to bring so strange a report to the Sultan's ears while the cravings of the royal appetite were still unsatisfied; so recalling the fisherman by a swift messenger, he bade him procure in all haste four more fish of the same kind, promising to reward him according to the speed with which he accomplished the task. So spurred, and by the additional favour of fortune, the fisherman fulfilled his mission in an astonishingly short space of time; but no sooner was the second lot of fish placed upon the fire in the vizier's presence than once again the wall opened, and the damsel appearing as before, struck the frying-pan with her rod, and cried :

"O fish of my pond,
Are ye true to your bond ? "

And immediately the fish stood up on their tails in the frying fat and replied :

"Even so, the bond holds yet ;
Paid by thee, we pay the debt.
With give and take is the reckoning met."

Whereupon she upset the pan into the fire and departed as she had come.

The vizier, perceiving that so strange an event might no longer be kept from the royal knowledge, went and informed the Sultan of all that had occurred ; and the monarch as soon as he had heard the tale, now rendered more eager for the satisfaction of his eyes than he had previously been for the indulgence of his appetite, sent for the fisherman, and promised him yet another four hundred pieces of gold if he could within a given time procure four more fishes similar to those he had already brought on the previous occasions.

If the fisherman had been prompt at the vizier's bidding, he made even greater speed to fulfil the royal command, and before the day was over—this time in the presence of the Sultan himself—four fish, of four diverse colours like to the first, were cleaned and laid into the pan ready for frying. But scarcely had they touched the fat when the wall opened in a clap like thunder, and there came forth with a face of rage a monstrous negro the size of a bull, holding in his hand the rod of myrtle. With this he struck the frying-pan, and cried in a terrible voice :

> " O fish from the pond,
> Are ye true to your bond ? "

And when the fish had returned the same answer that the others had made before them, without more ado the negro overturned the pan upon the fire and departed as he had come.

When the Sultan's eyes had seen that marvel he said to his vizier, " Here is mystery set before us ! Surely these fish that talk have a past and a history. Never shall I rest satisfied until I have learned it." So causing the fisherman to be brought before him, he inquired whence the fish came. The fisherman answered, " From a lake between four hills upon the mountain overlooking the city." The Sultan inquired how many days' journey it might be, and the fisherman replied that it was but a matter of a few hours going and returning. Then to the Sultan and his court it seemed that the old man was mocking them, for none had heard tell of any lake lying among the hills so near to that city ; and the fisherman, seeing his word doubted, began to fear that the Genie was playing him a trick ; for if the lake were now suddenly

THE DAMSEL UPSET THE PAN

(*Page* 110)

to vanish away, he might find his fortunes more undone at the end than at the beginning.

Yet the Sultan, though his vizier and all his court sought to dissuade him, was firmly resolved on putting the matter to the proof; so he gave orders that an escort and camping tents should be immediately got ready, and, with the fisherman to guide, set forth to find the place that was told of.

And, sure enough, when they had ascended the mountain which all knew, they came upon a desert tract on which no man had previously set eyes; and there in its midst lay the lake filled with four kinds of fish, and beyond it stretched a vast and unknown country.

At this sight, so mysterious and unaccountable, of a strange region lying unbeknownst at the gates of his own capital, the monarch was seized with an overwhelming desire to press forward in solitary adventure to the discovery of its secret. To the cautious counsels of his vizier he turned a deaf ear; but since it would not be safe for his subjects to know of his departure on an errand so perilous, it was given out that he had been stricken by sudden sickness. The door of the royal tent was closed, and at the dead of night the Sultan, admitting none but the vizier into his confidence, set out secretly on his adventure.

Journeying by night and resting by day, he arrived on the third morning within sight of a palace of shining marble which, with its crowd of domes and minarets, stood solitary among the hills. No sign of life was about it, and when he drew near and knocked at the gates none came to answer him. Then, finding the doors unfastened, he took courage and entered; and advancing through chambers where gold lay as dust, and by fountains wherein pearls lay poured out like water, he found only solitude to greet him.

Wandering without aim among innumerable treasures unguarded and left to waste, the Sultan grew weary, and sat down in an embrasure to rest. Then it seemed to him that not far off he could hear a sorrowful voice chant verses of lamentation. Following the sounds with wonder he came to a curtained doorway, and passing through found himself in the presence of a fair youth richly dressed, seated upon a couch and bearing upon his countenance tokens of extreme grief and despondency. To the Sultan's proffered greeting the youth returned salutation, but did not stir from his seat. " Pardon me," he said, " for not rising ; but my miserable condition makes it impossible." Having said this he again broke into doleful lamentation ; and when the Sultan inquired as to the cause of so many tears, " See for yourself," he cried, " what I am now made into ! " And lifting the skirt of his robe he revealed himself all stone from his waist to the soles of his feet, while from the waist upwards he was as other men. Then as he observed upon his visitor's countenance the expression of a lively curiosity and astonishment, " Doubtless," he went on, " as you now know the secret of my miserable condition you will wish also to hear my story." And he related it as follows :

THE CUP OF WINE CONTAINS A SLEEPING-DRAUGHT
(*Page* 119)

THE STORY OF THE KING OF THE EBONY ISLES

"My father was King of the city which once stood about this palace. He was lord also of the Ebony Isles that are now the four hills which you passed on your way hither. When I succeeded to the throne upon his death, I took to wife my own cousin, the daughter of my uncle with whom I lived for five years in the utmost confidence and felicity, continually entertained by the charm of her conversation and the beauty of her person, and happy in the persuasion that she found in me an equal satisfaction.

"One day, however, it chanced, in the hour before dinner when the Queen was gone to bathe and adorn herself, that I lay upon a couch beside which two female slaves sat fanning me; and they, supposing me to be asleep, began to talk concerning me and their mistress. 'Ah!' said one, 'how little our lord knows where our mistress goes to amuse herself every night while he lies dreaming!' 'How should he know?' returned the other, 'seeing that the cup of wine which she gives him each night contains a sleeping-draught, that causes him to sleep sound however long she is absent. Then at daybreak when she returns she burns perfumes under his nostrils, and he waking and finding her there guesses nothing. Pity it is that he cannot know of her treacherous ways, for surely it is a shame that a king's wife should go abroad and mix with base people.'

"Now when I heard this the light of day grew dark

119

before my eyes; but I lay on and made no sign, awaiting my wife's return. And she coming in presently, we sat down and ate and drank together according to custom; and afterwards, when I had retired and lain down, she brought me with her own hands the cup of spiced wine, inviting me to drink. Then I, averting myself, raised it to my lips, but instead of drinking, poured it by stealth into my bosom, and immediately sank down as though overcome by its potency, feigning slumber. Straightway the Queen rose up from my side, and having clothed herself in gorgeous apparel and anointed herself with perfumes, she made her way secretly from the palace, and I with equal secrecy followed her.

" Soon passing by way of the narrower streets, we arrived before the city gates; and immediately at a word from her the chains fell and the gates opened of their own accord, closing again behind us as soon as we had passed. At last she came to a ruined hut, and there entering I saw her presently with her veil laid aside, seated in familiar converse with a monstrous negro, the meanest and most vile of slaves, offering to him in abject servility dainties which she had carried from the royal table, and bestowing upon him every imaginable token of affection and regard.

" At this discovery I fell into a blind rage, and drawing my sword I rushed in and struck the slave from behind a blow upon the neck that should have killed him. Then believing that I had verily slain him, and before the Queen found eyes to realize what had befallen, I departed under cover of night as quickly as I had come, and returned to the palace and my own chamber.

" On awaking the next morning I found the Queen lying beside me as though nothing had happened, and at first I was ready to believe it had all been an evil dream; but presently I perceived her eyes red with weeping, her hair dishevelled, and her face torn by the passion of a grief which she strove to conceal. Having thus every reason to believe that my act of vengeance had not fallen short of its purpose, I held my tongue and made no sign.

"But the same day at noon, while I sat in council, the Queen appeared before me clad in deep mourning, and with many tears informed me how she had received sudden news of the death of her father and mother and two brothers, giving full and harrowing details of each event. Without any show of incredulity I heard her tale; and when she besought my permission to go into retirement and mourn in a manner befitting so great a calamity, I bade her do as she desired.

"So for a whole year she continued to mourn in a privacy which I left undisturbed; and during that time she caused to be built a mausoleum or Temple of Lamentation—the same whose dome you see yonder—into which she withdrew herself from all society; while I, believing the cause of my anger removed and willing to humour the grief which my act had caused her, waited patiently for her return to a sane and reasonable state of mind.

"But, as I learned too late, matters had not so fallen: for though in truth the negro was grievously wounded, being cut through the gullet and speechless, it was not the will of Heaven that he should die; and the Queen having by her enchantments kept him in a sort of life, no sooner was the mausoleum finished than she caused him to be secretly conveyed thither, and there night and day tended him, awaiting his full recovery.

"At length, when two years were over and her mourning in no wise abated, my curiosity became aroused; so going one day to the Temple of Lamentation I entered unannounced, and placing myself where I might see and not be seen, there I discovered her in an abandonment of

16

fond weeping over her miserable treasure whose very life was a dishonour to us both. But no sooner in my just resentment had I started to upbraid her, than she—as now for the first time realizing the cause of her companion's misfortune—began to heap upon me terms of the most violent and shameful abuse; and when, carried beyond myself, I threatened her with my sword, she stood up before me, and having first uttered words of unknown meaning, she cried:

> 'Be thou changed in a moment's span;
> Half be marble, and half be man!'

And at the word I became even as you see me now—dead to the waist, and above living yet bound. Yet even so her vengeance was not satisfied. Having reduced me to this state, she went on to vent her malice upon the city and islands over which I ruled, and the unfortunate people who were my subjects. Thus by her wicked machinations the city became a lake and the islands about it the four hills which you have seen; as for the inhabitants, who were of four classes and creeds, Moslems, Christians, Jews and Persians, she turned them into fish of four different colours: the white are the Moslems, the red are Persian fire-worshippers, the yellow are Jews, and the blue Christians. And now having done all this she fails not every day to inflict upon me a hundred lashes with a whip which draws blood at every stroke: and when these are accomplished she covers my torn flesh with hair-cloth and lays over it these rich robes in mockery. Of a surety it is the will of Heaven that I should be the most miserable and despised of mortals!"

Thus the youth finished his story, nor when he had ended could he refrain from tears. The Sultan also was greatly moved when he heard it, and his heart became full of a desire to avenge such injuries upon the doer of them. " Tell me," he said, " where is now the monster of iniquity ? " " Sir," answered the youth, " I doubt not she is yonder in the mausoleum with her companion, for thither she goes daily so soon as she has measured out to me my full meed of chastisement : and as for this day my portion has been served to me, I am quit of her till to-morrow brings the hour of fresh scourgings."

Now when this was told him the Sultan saw his way plain. " Be of good cheer," he said to the youth, " and endure with a quiet spirit yet once more the affliction she causes thee ; for at the price of that single scourging I trust, by the will of Heaven, to set thee free."

So on the morrow the Sultan lay in close hiding until sounds reached him which told that the whippings had begun ; then he arose and went in haste to the mausoleum, where amid rich hangings and perfumes and the illumination of a thousand candles, he found the black slave stretched mute upon a bed, awaiting in great feebleness the recovered use of his sawn gullet. Quickly, with a single sword-stroke, the avenger took from him that poor remnant of life which enchantment alone had made possible : then having thrown the body into a well in the courtyard below, he lay down in the dead man's place, drawing the coverlet well over him. Soon after, fresh from her accustomed task of cruelty, the enchantress entered, and falling upon her knees beside the bed she cried, " Has my lord still no voice wherewith to speak to his servant ? Surely, for lack of that sound, hearing lies withered within me ! " Then the Sultan, taking to himself the thick speech of a negro, said, " There is no strength or power but in God alone ! "

On hearing those words, believing that her companion's speech was at last restored to him, the Queen uttered a

cry of joy. But scarcely had she begun to lavish upon
him the tokens of her affection when the pretended negro
broke out against her in violent abuse. "What!" he
cried, "dost thou expect favour at my hands, when it is
because of thee that for two years I have lain dumb and
prostrate? How darest thou speak to me or look for any
recompense save death! Nay!" he went on in answer
to her astonished protests, "have not the cries and tears
and groans of thy husband kept me continually from rest :
and has not Heaven smitten me for no other reason than
because thou wouldst not cease from smiting him? So
has the curse which thou didst seek to lay upon him fallen
doubly upon me."

"Alas!" cried the enchantress, "have I unknowingly
caused thee so great an ill? If it be so, then let my lord
give command, and whatever be his desire it shall be
satisfied."

Then said the Sultan, "Go instantly and release thy
husband from spell and torment : and when it is done,
return hither with all speed."

Thus compelled, in great fear and bewilderment and
sorely against her will, the Queen sped to the chamber
in the palace where her husband lay spell-bound. Taking
a vessel of water she pronounced over it certain words
which caused it instantly to boil as though it had been
set on a fire : then throwing the water over him, she
cried :

> "Spell be loosed, and stone grow warm,
> Yield back flesh to the human form."

And immediately on the word his nature came to him
again, and he leaped and stood upon his feet. But the
Queen's hatred towards him was by no means abated.
"Go hence quickly," she cried, "since a better will than
mine releases thee! But if thou tarry or if thou return

GREAT WAS THE ASTONISHMENT OF THE VIZIER
(Page 127)

thou shalt surely die!"   Thankful for his deliverance the
youth stayed not to question, but departing went and hid
himself without, while the Queen returned in haste to the
mausoleum where her supposed lover awaited her.   There,
eager for restoration to favour, she informed him of what
she had done, supposing that to be all.

"Nay," said the other, still speaking with the thick
voice of a negro; "though thou hast lopped the branch
of the evil thou hast not destroyed the root.   For every
night I hear a jumping of fishes in the lake that is between
the four hills, and the sound of their curses on thee and
me comes to disturb my rest.   Go instantly and restore
all things to their former state, then come back and give
me thy hand and I shall rise up a sound man once more."

Rejoicing in that promise and the expectations it held
out to her of future happiness, the Queen went with all
speed to the border of the lake.   There taking a little
water into her hand, and uttering strange words over it,
she sprinkled it this way and that upon the surface of the
lake and the roots of the four hills, and immediately where
had been the lake a city appeared, and instead of fishes
inhabitants, and in place of the four hills four islands.
As for the palace, it stood no longer removed far away
into the desert but upon a hill overlooking the city.

Great was the astonishment of the vizier and the Sultan's escort which had lain encamped beside the lake to
find themselves suddenly transported to the heart of a
populous city, with streets and walls and the hum of
reawakened life around them; but a greater and more
terrible shock than this awaited the Queen upon her return
to the mausoleum to enjoy the reward of her labours.
"Now," she cried, "let my lord arise, since all that he
willed is accomplished!"

"Give me thy hand!" said the Sultan, still in a voice

of disguise; "come nearer that I may lean on thee!" And as she approached he drew forth his sword which had lain concealed beside him in the bed, and with a single blow cleft her wicked body in twain.

Then he rose and went quickly to where in hiding lay the young King her husband, who learned with joy of the death of his cruel enemy. He thanked the Sultan with tears of gratitude for his deliverance, and invoked the blessings of Heaven upon him and his kingdom. "On yours too," said the Sultan, "let peace and prosperity now reign! And since your city is so near to mine, come with me and be my guest that we may rejoice together in the bonds of friendship."

"Nay," answered the young King, "that would I do willingly, but your country lies many a day's journey from my own. I fear the breaking of the spell which held me and my subjects has brought you farther than you wished."

It was in fact true that the Ebony Isles had now returned to the place from which they had originally come. The Sultan put a smiling face upon the matter: "I can well put up with the tedium of my journey," said he, "if only you will be my companion. Nay, let me speak frankly to one whose demeanour in affliction has won my heart; I am childless and have no heir. Come with me and be my son, and when I am dead unite our two kingdoms under a single ruler." The young King, who had conceived for his deliverer an equal affection, could not withstand so noble and generous an offer; and so with a free exchange of hearts on both sides the matter was arranged.

After a journey of some months the Sultan arrived again at his own capital, where he was welcomed with great rejoicings by the people, who had long mourned over his strange and unexplained absence.

As for the old fisherman who had been the immediate cause of the young King's deliverance, the Sultan loaded him with honours and gave his daughters in marriage to sons of the blood royal, so that they all continued in perfect happiness and contentment to the end of their days.

PRINCESS BADOURA

(*Page* 131)

THE HISTORY OF
BADOURA, PRINCESS OF CHINA,
AND OF CAMARALZAMAN, THE ISLAND PRINCE

THE story of Aboulhassan, the Prince of Persia, had
come to an end and the light of morning was full.
Then said Dinarzade, "Another story, O sister, another
story!" Scheherazade made answer, "If my Lord will
suffer me to live for another day, there is yet one more tale
that I could tell. The history of Prince Camaralzaman
and of his bride Badoura is far more entrancing than that
which I have just given; but it is too long to be told now."

Then she was silent; and Shahriar could not bring
himself to order her death till he had heard that story
also. So once more he let his oath stay unfulfilled and de-
ferred sentence; and the next night, wakened in the
small hours towards dawn, Scheherazade, opening a
mouth of loveliness and filling it with wise and sweet
words, took up the thread of her tale and began:

O King, live for ever! About twenty days' sail from
the coast of Persia there lies in the open sea an island
which is called Khaledan, a country wealthy and pros-
perous and containing many large and well-inhabited
towns. Its ruler in ancient times was a king named
Shahzaman. As a reward for his many virtues, he had
gathered about him a large and well-proportioned household, four wives, the daughters of kings, and sixty concu-
bines; but, in spite of so generous a provision for that
which only Heaven can bestow, he had no son; and as

131

time went on, and he grew old, his bones wasted, and his heart became filled with affliction ; and he said to his Vizier, " Now in a little while I shall die ; then will my name perish, and my Kingdom pass to others, for I have not a son to come after me. Tell me, is there anything I can do to avert so great a calamity ? "

His Vizier answered, " When human means fail, it is then that we must rely on Heaven, for often these evils are sent to remind us of our dependence on Him who alone holds power. Fast, therefore, and pray, and perform ablutions, and when that is done make a great banquet, and call to it the poor and needy ; it may be that among them will be found one pure and righteous soul whose blessing will thus descend on thee, for the fulfilment of thy desire."

The King did as his Vizier advised : he made a great feast, and called to it all whose poverty might give virtue to their petition : and bidding them pray that he might have a son, caused meat to be set before them ; so they did eat and were filled.

This holy act had the desired effect ; one of the King's four Queens immediately conceived, and in course of time presented him with a son as fair as a full moon on a cloudless night. When the midwives and nurses carried him to his father, the King seeing his beauty and transported with joy at the event, named him Camaralzaman, that is to say Moon of the Age ; and he sent out orders, on pain of death to any who disobeyed, that for seven days the drums were to beat and every house in the city to be decorated in sign of thanksgiving. Never were such rejoicings heard.

The Prince was reared and educated with all care and magnificence until he attained the age of fifteen. For the polish of his manners and the enlightenment

of his brain the wisest and most accomplished men in
the Kingdom were chosen; and since from the first
he displayed a modest and docile disposition, combined
with a fine understanding, he became, as he approached
the years of manhood, the most virtuous and eligible heir
to a throne that monarch or people could find it in their
hearts to desire.

He was of surpassing comeliness and grace, perfect
in form and stature; and his father loved him so tenderly
that he could scarcely bear to be away from him either
by night or day. This devotion to his son was, indeed,
so excessive, that the King himself was perturbed by it,
for always accompanying it was a terror lest the Prince
might die.

One day he said to his Grand Vizier, " How came it
that my happiness in the possession of such a son gives
me anxiety rather than rest? When I was childless I
was miserable, and now that the desire of my heart
has been satisfied, I am full of dread lest he also should
die childless and my hope of posterity fail? Calamities
and accidents come when we least expect them, and
so it seems to me now that the Prince being vigorous and
strong is in greater danger of death than I who am near
the grave. For him a thousand perils are waiting, while
I have nothing to fear but old age. If, therefore, I may
not see my son married in my own lifetime I shall die in
a state more miserable than that which I endured before
he was born."

His Vizier said, " The Prince is still full young, but
nothing forbids that he should marry if, by the will of
Allah, we can find one worthy of him."

" As for that," said the King, " Heaven cannot have
willed to send into the world a form of beauty and of
virtue so pre-eminent without also providing a fitting

match for it. Doubt not, if the Prince himself is willing, that some maiden not too far beneath him will be found capable of sustaining the honour."

So Shahzaman sent for his son, and Camaralzaman came and stood before him, and when he saw the King seated in state upon his throne, though not having his lords round him, the Prince bade reverence take the place of love, and with his head bowed down toward the ground waited in submission for the royal word to be spoken.

Thus he stood before his father humbly as a stranger; for never before had the King so received him, and he wondered why he had been summoned, and in his heart there was a fear.

The King perceiving his reserve said to him, "My son, can you now guess for what reason I have sent for you?" But the Prince answered, "My lord, I would not so presume; for it is not in the power of one so young as I am to fathom the thoughts of the hearts of Kings. Only when I hear the true reason from your Majesty's lips will my brain become enlightened."

So he spoke, with all the decorum, and deference, and virtue, and prudent modesty which had been instilled in him by the preceptors of his youth; and Shahzaman, his father, loved him for it, and said in his heart, "Never was King blessed with such a son as I."

Then he said to the Prince, "What thou lackest in years of man's estate thou hast already gained in wisdom and understanding; therefore as a man I speak to thee. Know, then, it is my wish that thou shouldst marry, so that before my days are ended I may rejoice in the assurance of my posterity."

When Camaralzaman heard these words he no longer hung his head, but stood up straight; and as he made answer to the King his face flushed and his eyes grew bright ; and said he, " O my father, is it into bondage you would deliver me ere I become a man ?   Lo, here am I, the son of Kings, and all my life till now have I been free, and my soul has been free within me, because I have not gone in the way of women nor inclined my heart toward them ; but if I marry, then by their cunning and guile will my soul and my freedom be taken from me.   Far rather would I drink the cup of death."

When King Shahzaman heard that, the light of day darkened before him, for never until now had his son gone against his wish or disobeyed his word.   But, because he loved the youth very tenderly, he forgave him and thought not at this time to punish him ; for he said to himself, " At present he is full young, and excess of virtue hath caused his manhood to slumber."   So he forbore, and waited till another year should have passed, and withdrew not from his son the light and favour of his countenance.

So Camaralzaman continued in undisturbed life to receive the instructions of his preceptors, and every day he increased in beauty and comeliness of form, in modesty of mind, and in grace of manner and in elegance of deportment.   Added to which, he became accomplished in verse, and eloquence, and rhetoric and the divine sciences, so that the flower of his form and the honey of his understanding made together a thing of inconceivable loveliness and attraction.   Even as a magical willow-branch bearing peach-blossom and fruit at one season, so was he.

Now when another year was completed, his father having once more consulted with the Grand Vizier, sent for him again, and said, " This time, O my son, listen to my word, and obey ; for now have thy years touched manhood, and unless thou beget children thy virtue and wisdom are wasted.   Therefore if thou wilt marry her whom I shall now choose for thee, I will also make thee ruler over all my dominions; so with mine eyes shall I see my kingdom and my posterity established, and rejoice in thee before I die."

But the Prince had listened so well to the preceptors set over him to guard his virtue, and had pondered so deeply the books which wise men had written in their old age, when delight had fled from them and when all that they had done in the past seemed only to be vanity, that his mind, even though his heart softened to his father's request, remained as aforetime. Therefore, abasing himself in fear and reverence at the King's feet, he said, "O my father, not so can I find happiness, or strength, or wisdom wherewith to rule others, seeing that if I marry I cease to be ruler of myself. In all things outward it is Allah's will that I should obey you; but in this which comes from within and concerns myself alone, I can obey the voice of no man, however wise he may be. Yet, by all the seers and poets and soothsayers is the same thing told, that woman is a calamity, and that from her spring all the weaknesses and afflictions of men." And so saying with sweetness, and modulation of tone, and grace of gesture, Camaralzaman began to recite to his father all the words of the poets; and there was not a poet who had written poetry in his old age whose verses did not bear out the contention.

So when the King had heard the verses of the poets and the words of the ancients arrayed against him, he returned no answer; for he said to himself: "I doubt not but that before another year shall have run that voice within will have spoken differently to my son than it speaks now, and the words of the sages will have far less weight with him then than the glance of some woman's eye." Once more, therefore, letting his tenderness extinguish his resentment, he forgave the Prince's disobedience and received him back into his favour.

But to his Grand Vizier Shahzaman said, " Now twice, O Vizier, have I come to thee for advice, and what profit has it been ?   When I consulted thee first as to marrying my son thy word was for it ; yet no sooner did I mention it to him than his mind rebelled.   This time also, it was on thy advice that I sought to bribe him by the offer of power ; but when I offered him the Crown, so little did he care that he seemed almost not to have heard me.   What better advice, then, wilt thou give me now so that my patience may be rewarded and my heart obtain its desire ? "

The Vizier answered, " O King, thy son hath presumed on thy forbearance, knowing well thy tenderness, and when thou hast spoken with him it hath been privately and as a father.   But when a year hence the time comes to speak with him again on this matter, then speak not to him privately any more, but before all the people, with the emirs and the viziers and the troops standing by. Then he will no longer dare to oppose thee, since to do so before all those witnesses would be an offence treasonable and worthy of death."

So the King accepted the advice of his Vizier, and when another year had gone by he summoned the Prince to his presence on a day of festival, when all about him were the dignitaries and chamberlains of his court, the viziers of the provinces, and the emirs of neighbouring states who paid tribute to Shahzaman as their Sultan. Thus he sat in all his power and splendour, and Camaralzaman came in and drew near, and stood before him, being then in his eighteenth year, with the early bloom of manhood beginning to show upon his cheek.   Allah, who loves to give beauty to virtue, had clothed him in comeliness and crowned his features with joy ; his eyes were like pools of deep water and their glances flashed like

18

a fountain in the sun ; and from head to foot whether he moved or stood he was perfect in dignity and grace.

As he approached, thrice he bent and kissed the ground in sign of obedience and reverence, and thereafter stood upright, with hands folded behind his back, waiting to hear the King's pleasure.

Shahzaman spoke. " Once more, O my son, I have sent for thee to declare my will. Twice ere this have I been tender and patient, not forcing an inclination that was not ripe. But now thou art come to man's estate, and the season of waiting is ended. Therefore my command is that thou marry a daughter of kings, whom presently I shall choose for thee ; so shall I have joy in thee before I die, seeing the establishment of my posterity."

When Camaralzaman heard these words he shut fast his lips and stood speechless for a while. But as his eye fell on all those lords assembled as witnesses as to what he should say, wrath kindled in his blood and the fire of youth mounted to his brain and he spoke swiftly and unadvisedly.

" Surely," he said, " thou art a man of great age and little sense thus to talk, having already been answered ! Twice before hast thou asked me, and twice have I refused. Thinkest thou with all these cooks to make a better broth of me, having thyself failed ? I swear now that rather than marry I will drink the cup of perdition and die : for no man shall possess himself of my body to give it to another while my will is contrary ! " And so saying Camaralzaman unclasped his hands from behind his back, and rolling up his sleeves stood before his father all quivering with anger.

Greatly was Shahzaman, the King, disturbed at receiving so public an affront from the son whom he loved so tenderly. For a moment he sat speechless, seeing in the eyes of those around him the reflection of his humiliation and shame; then his energy returned to him, and rising from his throne he uttered so terrible a cry of wrath that at once Camaralzaman became conscious of the enormity of his offence, and his hasty anger departed leaving only contrition and fear.

Then, at the King's command, the memlooks came and seized him, and having first bound his hands, dragged him before the throne.

The extremity of Shahzaman's wrath now broke into words, and while the Prince stood speechless before him, his head bowed down and with drops of anguish upon his brow, he loaded him with a volume of abuse which did not spare even the Queen's unblemished reputation. " Woe to thee," he cried, " baseborn child of iniquity and deceit! Is it thus that a King is to be answered in the presence of his people ? Is it thus that a son nurtured in the tenderest affection casts insult on the head of his father ? Had such language been uttered by one of the common people, it had been less disgraceful and more pardonable than coming from thee."

Then he commanded the memlooks to take him away and imprison him in the deepest dungeon of the castle, which had long stood neglected and empty.

Servants of the Prince hearing of that order went in haste and prepared the chamber for his reception; they swept the walls of its cobwebs, and wiped the damp from the floors; they placed in it a bedstead, and on it laid a mattress and a leather covering and cushions; they also provided a large lantern and a candle, for even in the daytime the place was dark. To this dungeon came Camaralzaman escorted by his guard, and when all had been made secure and a eunuch set outside to keep watch, there they left him.

Camaralzaman threw himself upon the couch weeping, for bitterly now did he repent of his injurious conduct to his father; yet even in his affliction he ceased not to inveigh against marriage. " Malediction upon women ! " he cried, " alas, why were they invented to give sting to the affections and divide father and son ! Had Allah refrained from creating women, certainly I should not have been here ! "

Thus in his misfortune did Camaralzaman find truths to comfort him. Meanwhile the King, his father, was suffering an equal affliction, and lacking the philosophy of youth he sought to find comfort in laying the blame for all that had happened upon the Grand Vizier. " See, O Vizier ! " he cried, " what comes of taking counsel with thee ! Thou alone hast been the cause of my son's undoing; for had I spoken to him privately on this matter as aforetime, he would not have answered me otherwise than as a son should and in such manner as would have made forgiveness possible. Now, therefore, since we are brought to this pass by the foolishness of thy wisdom, it is for thee to devise means by which we may find a remedy."

The Vizier replied: " O King, let the Prince stay where he is for another fifteen days, so shall he have time to cool himself. I doubt not that thereafter his mind toward marriage will be all that your heart can desire. Better to him then will seem the bride's chamber than the stone walls of his prison."

Shahzaman took the Vizier's advice and slept on it, or rather slept not at all, for the loss of his son so troubled him that he lay awake all night tossing restlessly from side to side and longing for the light of day.

Far better did Camaralzaman fare; for when night came the eunuch brought lantern and candle, and having prepared a table set food before him. The Prince ate

THE KING OF CHINA AND BADOURA
(*Page* 159)

little and thought much, sorrow for his ill-conduct having severed his appetite in half, and when he had finished he called for water and washed his hands from all taint of food; then he performed the ablution preparatory to prayer, and recited with his accustomed regularity the prayers of sunset and nightfall. After that he sat upon the couch reciting extracts from the Koran: he recited the chapters from " The Cow " and " The Family of Emran " and " The Two Preventives "; and having done all these things he commended his soul to Allah and laid himself down upon the couch, whereon was a mattress of figured satin showing its pattern on both sides and stuffed abundantly with ostrich plumes. And when sleep drew near he took off his outer raiment and clothed himself in a fine shirt of waxed linen, and wrapped about his head a kerchief of blue muslin so that he seemed like the moon on its fourteenth night. Then with the lantern at his feet and the candle at his head, he covered himself with the sheet and fell into the sleep of the just from which he awakened not till after the third hour, knowing naught of the hidden event which then awaited him, or what Allah, who knoweth all secrets, had decreed should befall.

Now in the floor of this dungeon was an old well malodorous and foul through long disuse; and in this well dwelt a female Genie or Efreet, named Meymooneh, a monster of bad ancestry and of tremendous power to set evil above good. Toward midnight, when the hour for her nightly wanderings had come, Meymooneh rose up like a bubble from the bottom of the well and lifting her head over the brim saw a light which had not been there formerly and under it a couch whereon lay someone asleep.

Full of wonder, she drew up her feet to earth, and advancing, cautiously turned back the coverlet from

the sleeper's face. Thereafter she stood for a whole
hour lost in wonder and astonishment at the beauty
which she found there : perfect in all its lines and colour
and texture was the loveliness of the sleeping youth, and
there arose from his body an odour like fragrant musk.
Meymooneh snuffed at it, and her heart became enlarged,
lifting her thoughts toward Heaven. " Blessed be Allah ! "
she cried, " surely He must be good to have created this
thing." And as she continued to gaze, her mind acquired
a benevolence which had long since been strange to it.
" By Allah," she said, " in no way will I injure him ;
rather will I watch over and protect him from any that
may seek to do him harm." And so saying she stooped
over the youth and kissed him between the eyes.

Then elated of heart she spread her wings and smiting
the earth with her heel sprang upward and floated away
into space, till the heavens about her were clear. As
she rose up through clouds she heard above her head a
flapping of wings, and there passed one she knew by
his tail to be Dahnash, an Efreet greatly inferior in power
to herself. After him she went like a hawk, pounced
and caught him by the scruff.

Dahnash, perceiving into whose clutches he had
fallen, quivered through all his members, and imploring
pardon for his existence cried, " I conjure thee by
the Most High Name and the sign on the Seal of Solomon
that this time and for the present thou shouldst release
me. So will I go upon my errand and return presently."

Then said Meymooneh, " By the high oath which
thou hast sworn, what errand art thou after ? "

Dahnash answered, " I have seen once with mine
eyes that which should make the wicked virtuous, and
the foul-minded clean ; therefore I am in haste to make
known the story of it to others less virtuous than

thou art; so that they too may see it and find reward."

"Though I am more virtuous than thou art," replied Meymooneh, "yet shalt thou tell me thy story, else I will pluck off every scale from thy body and every feather from thy wings and throw thee to the bottomless pit. And if what thou tellest be not true then also shalt thou fare as I have said."

Then said Dahnash, "O Meymooneh, if my word be not true, invent for me what tortures thou wilt and I will accept them. I am come to-night from the farthest isles of China, which are the dominions of King Gaiour, who is lord also of the Seas and of the Seven Palaces. There have I seen the Princess, his daughter, for whom also these palaces were built; surely there is none like her in all the world! Her hair is as dark as the night of separation and exile, and her face is like the dawn when lovers meet to embrace; her nose hath both point and edge, and her cheeks are like petals of anemone filled with wine. When she speaks, wisdom flows from her tongue; and when she moves, her feet faint with delight under the burden of the loveliness laid on them. The King's love for her is so great that there is no limit to what he will bestow on her if only it may add to her happiness; therefore in her honour hath he built the seven palaces: the first is of crystal, the second of marble, the third of steel, the fourth of onyx, the fifth silver, the sixth is of inlaid gold, and the seventh of all manner of jewels. Also these palaces are most sumptuously furnished, and around them lie gardens embellished with everything that can soothe the senses and delight the eye. Yet all this is but as a shade when the beauty of the Princess shines in the midst of it. Because the fame of her incomparable loveliness has gone far and wide, many kings and powerful princes come to demand

19

her hand in marriage. But so tender is the King's love for her, that in all these years without her free consent he has married her to none. Many a time has he sought to persuade her, but it is all in vain. 'For where,' says the Princess, 'shall I have honour and freedom such as I enjoy now? Here I sit at thy side in council and am a ruler over men; but if I marry then will my husband rule me.' And now there has come to the court of King Gaiour, another monarch, so dreaded and so powerful that his suit cannot be refused. Nevertheless the Princess, whose name is Badoura, will not consent; and having threatened to kill herself rather than submit, the King now treats her as insane in order to excuse himself, and hath shut her up in one of her palaces with ten old women to look after her. There she has been confined for a whole year, but the imprisonment has done nothing either to change her will or diminish the enchantment of her beauty. So to-night when I saw her lying asleep every evil thought and passion died within me, for so holy is her beauty that I respected her even as I respect myself. Come, Meymooneh, and you shall see what is indeed a miracle and a wonder!"

So far had Dahnash proceeded, when Meymooneh impatiently interrupted him. First, she cuffed him over the head, and then spitting in his face cried with laughter, "O fool, what eyes have you to behold beauty, or what tongue to tell of it? This Princess that you speak of is, I doubt not, a poor insignificant creature not worth looking at. What would you say, then, if I showed you my own beloved? Little talk would there be then of this fine Princess of yours; you would have but to look at him once and you would go crazy with jealousy."

Dahnash replied humbly, "O Mistress of language and of facts, far be it from me to deny beauty that you

yourself have verified ; but neither can I deny that which
I, in turn, have beheld and think to be incomparable.
All I can ask, therefore, is that you should accompany me
to the bedchamber of this adorable Princess, where
she now lies sleeping, and judge for yourself."

" Not so," answered Meymooneh, " wherefore should
I travel to the far ends of China merely to prove thy
folly and thy falsehood ? Here close at hand is the
tower wherein my beloved lies prisoner ; come, then, and
see for yourself the face of him whose loveliness even
in sleep puts all other beauty to scorn."

So they descended, and passing through the roof
and floors of the tower came to the dungeon below,
where Camaralzaman lay sleeping. There by the bedside
Meymooneh put forth her hand and drew back the sheet ;
and Dahnash gazed with awe and remained silent, for
doubt swayed him. Nevertheless after a while he said,
" O Meymooneh, though my word may seem hard to
believe, yet do I still say that she whom I saw is fairer
than this youth ; and needs must it be so, since the
fairest woman is by her sex made fairer than the fairest
man. But for that, these two whom we contend over
might be twin flowers from the same stem, so like are
they."

When Meymooneh heard that she struck him a hard
blow over the head with her wing, crying, " Go, accursed
one, fly back to China, lift up thy beloved and bring
her quickly to this place ; so when we see them side by
side shall it be manifest which one is the more beautiful.
Then if I am right thou shalt pay forfeit to me, and if
thou art right I will pay."

Then with inconceivable swiftness Dahnash departed ;
and within an hour returned bearing the Princess in his
arms. She was clad in a gown of finest silk with two

borders of gold, and when the Efreet laid her upon the bed beside Camaralzaman, the two proved to be so alike that they might have been twin brother and sister. Nevertheless Meymooneh and Dahnash continued to say each to each, " My beloved is more beautiful than thine." Nor was agreement possible between them.

Therefore after much strife, wherein Dahnash, though physically worsted, stuck to his opinion, they determined to refer the matter to an arbitrator, and by his sentence to abide.

Then Meymooneh struck the ground with her foot and cried " Kashkash ! " Instantly the earth opened and there arose from it an Efreet hideous to look upon ; he was blind of an eye, and lame of a leg, and upon his back he carried a hump bigger than the rest of his body ; and when he saw Meymooneh he prostrated himself before her, saying, " O Mistress and daughter of Kings, what dost thou require of me ? "

Meymooneh told him of the contention that had arisen between them, and showing him the Prince and Princess lying side by side called on him to say which was the more beautiful of the two.

But Kashkash, having considered them for a while with great attention, replied, " When mortals are endowed with such beauty as these, then only themselves can decide. Let us, then, awake them each in turn, and the one that draws from the other the most violent protestations of love and admiration shall be esteemed the more beautiful."

This proposal was approved both by Meymooneh and Dahnash.

Thereupon Meymooneh transformed herself into a flea, and leaping upon Camaralzaman's neck bit him in a soft place. The youth put up his hand and rubbed to allay the smarting ; then moving sideways he touched something that stirred, and starting up saw by his side a maiden of most marvellous beauty.

No sooner had he beheld her than all his reasons against marriage were confounded and put to flight ; and he said within his heart, " What God desireth will come to pass, and what He desireth not will not happen." Then taking the Princess by the hand, he endeavoured gently to rouse her, and ceasing not to invoke her with words and kisses of tenderness, he would infallibly have awakened her had not Dahnash bound her by a spell.

Then, seeing how fast she slept, " What ! " cried the Prince, " must the love of Camaralzaman admit an impediment such as this ? Awake, O beloved ! " Carried away by his words he was tempted for a moment to assail her rudely, but then the nobility of his nature reasserted itself and respect for her beauty and innocence constrained him. Then he bethought himself, and said, " Doubtless this is the honourable maiden to whom the King, my father, intended to marry me. Oh, why, instead of argument, did he not show me her face ? So would none of this trouble have come about ! "

Then perceiving upon the Princess's finger a ring, he drew it off and exchanged it for his own, saying, " Since I may not yet possess myself of the owner I will take this." And having so done, he turned his back to her and slept.

Then Meymooneh, jealous of the testimony which Camaralzaman had given to the Princess's beauty, transformed herself again into a flea, and entering beneath the clothes of Badoura, the beloved of Dahnash, bit her sharply ; whereupon she opened her eyes and sat up ; and there at her side beheld a youth snoring in his sleep, with eyelashes shading roseate cheeks and a mouth like the seal of Solomon. No sooner had she seen him than her heart was filled with contending emotions. " Oh me ! " she cried, " what disgrace is this that has come upon me to be lying in the same bed with a stranger ? But, by Allah, he is so beautiful that I have much ado not to love him to distraction. Nay, if this be the Prince who came demanding my hand in marriage of my father, I would have been willing to marry him ten times over had I but known beforehand."

So saying she seized Camaralzaman by the arm and shook him so violently that, saving for the enchantment, he must surely have awakened.

Thereat she lost patience. " Self-satisfied youth," she cried, " is this the way to behave to a Princess upon the night of her bridal ? What ? has so much beauty made thee proud ? " Then as love began to devour her heart, " O my lord," she cried, " light of mine eyes, and moon of my existence, arise, awake out of sleep ! " And forthwith seizing his hand she began kissing it. While she was doing so she saw her ring upon his little finger, and uttered a cry of astonishment ; while even greater became her amaze when she found upon her own hand a strange ring. This, she thought, must surely mean that she had become wedded to him in her sleep, so putting away all false modesty and fear she lay down again by his side, and fell fast asleep.

Then Meymooneh and Dahnash, seeing how evenly between the pair the balance of love and admiration was divided, composed their difference ; and Dahnash, taking the sleeping Princess upon his shoulder, carried her back to China.

When Camaralzaman awoke the next morning to find no maiden at his side, he supposed that the King, his father, had caused her to be carried away secretly, in order that thereby his desire for her might be increased. So he called to the slave who guarded him and said, " Tell me of the lady who slept with me last night : how came she, and who brought her ? "

The slave replied, " O Prince, there was no lady ; how could any lady get in while I slept all night across the doorway, and had the key ? "

This answer so infuriated the Prince that he fetched the slave a buffet which knocked him over ; then tying him to the well rope he let him down into the well, though it was the middle of winter ; and this he continued to do, now up, now down, saying as he did so, " When thou hast told me the truth I will let thee go."

After a while the unfortunate slave, at the last gasp for wretchedness, cried, " O Prince, restore to me my life and I will tell thee all."

So Camaralzaman drew him up and laid him to drain upon the floor.

Then the eunuch, with shiverings and chattering of teeth, said, " Alas, Master, in my present plight I have not tongue nor wits to tell thee the whole story. Suffer me to go hence and get dry, then will I return." So Camaralzaman let him go.

Off ran the eunuch, and without stopping came even as he was into the presence of Shahzaman, the King. Shahzaman was complaining to the Grand Vizier of the misery he had endured and the restless night he had passed, when the slave entered all a-drench with wetness and forthwith uttered his tidings. " O King," he cried, " insanity hath seized on thy son, and thus hath he done to me ! He saith there hath been a lady in his bed, when there hath been no lady ; and because I cannot tell him how she came or how she went, or where now he can find her, see from what a drowning I have escaped ! "

When the King heard these words his sorrow for his son and his wrath against the Vizier knew no bounds. " Go, accursed," he cried, " this is thy doing. Go to the Prince and discover the true cause of his malady ; then come again and tell me."

So the Vizier hastened, treading upon his skirts as he went forth in fear of the King's anger, and coming to the tower found the Prince not mad at all, but seated upon the couch reciting verses from the Koran with the utmost composure.

" O Prince," cried the Vizier, " the mere sight of thee relieves me of affliction ; but so have I the more reason to complain of that vile slave who attends on thee, and hath said shameful things concerning thee to thy father, the King."

" I also," answered the Prince, " have great reason to complain of him ; but let that be for a while, and tell me now what has become of the lady who slept with me last night ? For I know my father must have sent her to me for a just purpose, and to cure me of my folly : which indeed she hath done. So let that sweet remedy return to me and you shall find me sane."

" Of a truth, Prince," replied the Vizier, " the King, thy father, sent no lady to thee, and all that thou sayest now is mystery. Bethink thee, shut in here a prisoner, how canst thou have seen any lady with thine eyes except in a dream ? "

" O ill-omened old man," cried the Prince, " thou wilt be saying next that I saw her only with my ears ! " And approaching the Vizier he seized him by the beard, which was long, and twisting it this way and that, cried, " Tell me the truth, or I will treat thee as I did the slave ! "

Then the Vizier, to save himself from further ill-treatment, replied even as the slave had done, and said,

" O Prince, I am not free to reveal the secrets of my master, but I will take to him any message wherewith you may be pleased to entrust me."

" Go, then," answered the Prince, " and tell my father that I repent of my former words and will marry the lady he sent to me last night, but no other, though he should put me to a thousand deaths ! "

So the Vizier, as soon as Camaralzaman had let go of his beard, returned in haste to the King and said to him, " O my lord, what the slave says is true ; the Prince hath been seized with insanity of the most violent kind ; yea, he heareth with his eyes, and seeth with his ears, and declareth a lady hath slept with him, whom he will marry and no other."

Then Shahzaman went himself to see the Prince and to learn the truth of this matter, for he doubted the Vizier's word. And when he came to the prison, his son received him with so much respect, and contrition and devotion, that he turned upon the Vizier with eyes of anger and reproach, crying, " O wretch, why hast thou afflicted me with lies ? " But the Vizier only shook his head sorrowfully, waiting for the truth to reveal itself.

Then said the King, " O my son, what day of the week is it ? " Camaralzaman answered, " To-day is Saturday, to-morrow is Sunday, the next day is Monday, then comes Tuesday, then Wednesday, then Thursday and then Friday."

" Praise be to Allah ! " cried the King, " my son is not mad, for he knows the days of the week." Then he said to Camaralzaman, " Tell me, my son, who is this lady who, you say, slept with you last night ; for truly I know nothing about her."

" O my lord," replied the Prince, " I pray that you cease to mock me, for though I have deserved it through my

20

folly, yet now am I ready and eager to marry this lady whom you have chosen for me, since her beauty delights me, and her manners, even in her sleep, fascinate me."

On hearing these words the King was as much astonished as the Vizier had been; but the countenance of his son was so full of ingenuousness and truth that he was not as incredulous as the others had been before him. "I swear to you, my son," said he, "that I know nothing of this matter. What my Vizier has told you, he invented to appease your anger. But now tell me everything, just as it happened, for whether it be true or no, this event has given me cause for rejoicing."

Then the Prince sat down by his father's side and told him everything, and when he had finished he showed him the ring for proof that his tale was true; and the King was so convinced by his son's manner and by all the incidents of the story, that he had not a word to say against it.

Therefore was his heart uplifted, and he said to Camaralzaman, "Though all these things be mysteries in the hands of Allah, so deep that we may not fathom them, yet now hast thou convinced me that thou art not as was said of thee. Keep, therefore, that precious mind to which Heaven hath given light, and possess thyself in patience till the mystery hath resolved itself."

But Camaralzaman replied, "Alas, O my father, to what term of imprisonment dost thou now condemn me? for if thou canst not find for me this maiden who hath ravished my heart, surely I shall die of anguish. So great is my love and my distraction that I cannot wait for her even an hour."

Upon this the King smote his palms together, and cried, "Now are we in the hands of Allah, where no mortal power can avail!" Then he took his son gently by the hand and led him back to the palace: and there

CAMARALZAMAN CURES BADOURA

(Page 171)

the Prince threw himself down upon a bed of sickness, too weak to rise or look up : and Shahzaman seated himself at his side, mourning and weeping for his grief, and leaving him neither by day nor night.

But after a while his Vizier came to him and said, " O King of the Age, how long shall thy people seek for thee, and not find thee ? Thy troops murmur that they have none to lead them to the field, and in the city corruption grows rife because the seat of judgment stays empty. This sickness into which the Prince has fallen comes only from grief ; and as his grief increases thine, so does thine give nourishment to his. Therefore I entreat your Majesty to provide some better relief for the complaint both of the Prince and of the people. Here in the city his spirits languish and his strength returns not ; but take him to the palace which is upon the shore looking toward the islands ; there shall his soul, on the days when thou art absent, find peace and refreshment. And do thou, O King, on two days in each week return to the affairs of state, which need thy presence, to give audiences and to hold councils, else out of these two evils which are upon us there may grow a greater."

So Shahzaman did as his Vizier advised him, and caused the Prince to be carried, all wasted as he was with grief, to a pavilion which was upon the shore, and there on the days when affairs of state caused the King to be absent Camaralzaman lay and looked out over the sea.

While these things were happening in the land of Khaledan, Dahnash had conveyed the Princess of China safely back to her own bed. There the next morning she awoke, unstained by travel and with her raiment undisturbed ; nor was she conscious that she had been anywhere but where she now was. No sooner, therefore, did she perceive on looking to left and right that the youth who had lain in her bosom was no longer near her than her heart became agitated and her reason confounded, and she uttered a loud cry.

All her women came running; and her nurse, who was the chief, inquired what misfortune had befallen her. The Princess, who continued to search among the bed-clothes, said, "Vexatious and contrary old woman, what have you done with the beautiful youth who slept last night in my bosom, or how comes it that I have mislaid him?"

At these words the nurse was shocked in her morals and confounded in her understanding, and she answered, "O mistress, what mean these disgraceful words! Surely thy bosom is guiltless of any such deed, and no youth, whether beautiful or otherwise, has been near thee."

Badoura answered, "He had black eyes and a lovely face, and a mouth like the seal of Solomon, and his eyebrows were joined where I kissed them; and he was here sleeping at my side from nightfall to nigh upon daybreak."

"Princess," answered her nurse, "thou hast had an unpermissible dream and art talking nonsense. No such young man hath been near thee, nor would I have permitted it."

Then the Princess lifting her hand in anger saw upon it the ring which Camaralzaman had given her in exchange for her own, and cried to her nurse, "Woe to thee, O deceitful! Have I also dreamed this ring which is not mine and lost that which belonged to me?" And so saying she started to belabour her nurse so unmercifully, that she would assuredly have killed her had not all the other women and the eunuchs lifted up their voices in lamentation; whereupon the Princess, who greatly disliked loud noises, desisted.

So the nurse, escaping from her vengeance, fled and

acquainted the King with all that had happened and with the story which the Princess had told her.

The King came in haste and found that which till now he had only pretended concerning his daughter apparently come true. For excess of reason had fled to her brain, and rushing this way and that she was searching for her beloved in every cupboard, and under every article of furniture, crying, "Where is the beautiful youth who slept in my bosom last night? He belongs to me; he is mine. If I do not find him I shall die."

When her father saw and heard this he inquired no further, but ordered the slaves and eunuchs to seize her, and bind her with chains lest she should do herself or others an injury.

So they put a chain about her neck and fastened her to a window of the palace looking toward the sea, that so by the will of Allah her thoughts might have rest and her reason be restored. And the King, loving her tenderly and greatly distressed at the condition she had fallen into, caused a proclamation to be issued to all sages, astrologers, and men skilled in such matters, saying, "Whosoever shall cure my daughter of her present malady, to him will I give her hand in marriage together with the half of my kingdom; and whoso fails to cure her, having offered, his head will I strike off and set it above the gates of my palace as a warning to others." This he continued to do till forty of the wisest physicians and astrologers had lost their heads. Then the supply failed; and the Princess, whom the offer of any husband other than the one she sighed for threw into paroxysms of wrath, was as far from a cure at the end as at the beginning. Thus she remained for the space of three years, sitting at a window with a chain about her neck and looking out over the sea.

Now the nurse of the Princess Badoura had a son named Marzavan, who was a great traveller. He was foster-brother to the Princess ; when they were children she had been to him as his own sister ; and the two loved each other tenderly. So on the day when he returned from his travels he went to the palace to get tidings of the Princess, and there over the gates were ranged the heads of the forty wise men. This surprised him greatly, and when on inquiring into the matter he learned the cause, he heard also of the unhappy state into which the Princess had fallen. The news troubled him far more deeply than the death of forty wise men who had been found foolish, but, unwilling to trust to the judgment of others in such a case, being himself also well skilled in medicine, he besought his mother to obtain for him an interview with the Princess.

This was a difficult matter, for the door of the chamber was strictly guarded, and no one had access to it except the nurse herself. So urgent, however, was her son's entreaty, that at last she consented and set about finding the means. To this end she said to the eunuch who was on guard at the door, " You know well my devotion to the Princess, and my desire to do anything that may alleviate her affliction, therefore I am come to ask you for a favour. I have a daughter whom my mistress from her earliest childhood, when I nursed them together, has ever regarded with the tenderest affection. She has lately married, and the Princess, hearing of this event, has expressed a wish to see her. Allow this to be ; and do not doubt that Heaven will reward you for your goodness."

The eunuch readily consented in spite of the strictness of his orders. " Let her come at night," he said, "or bring her yourself, after the King has retired :

then the door shall be open and no one need know of it."

Accordingly, the next night, the nurse disguised Marzavan in woman's attire, and taking his hand in hers led him to the palace. The eunuch let them pass without suspicion; but as soon as they were in the Princess's presence, and the door shut behind them, the nurse said, " O mistress, I have brought gladness to you to-night; for this is no woman but my son Marzavan, who, having returned from his travels, wished greatly to see you."

No sooner did the Princess hear the name of Marzavan than she sprang joyfully forward, the full length of her chain, and being held back by it, she stretched her hands toward him, crying, " O brother, come to me ! " When Marzavan beheld her in that unhappy plight, then for weeping he could not look at her, but turned away his head and covered his eyes. Then said Badoura, " Dost thou also think that I am mad like the rest of them ? Nay, hear my story and be undeceived, for it is true."

Then she told Marzavan everything; and he, perceiving that she was in love, doubted no longer, for he knew that such passion and such a desire for beauty could arise neither out of madness nor of a dream. So when she besought his aid he pondered deeply what he might do, and then said, " O sister, have patience yet a little while, and I will go search through the world for thy missing friend. Be assured that if he lives I will find him." Then they embraced as brother and sister in full affection ; and Marzavan departed.

The next day he set out once more upon his travels, and continued to journey from city to city, and island to island for the space of some months. At first, wherever he went, he heard men speaking of the beauty of the Princess Badoura and of the strange malady that afflicted

21

her; but presently, as he changed from country to country, her name ceased to be upon men's lips, and he heard instead of one by name Camaralzaman, a prince of the Islands of Khaledan, who for three years had suffered from a grievous affliction of body and a desolation of spirit to which there seemed no remedy.

Marzavan did not delay when he heard that story; but inquiring for the nearest route he took ship and sailed from the city of Torf, where these tidings had first reached him, to the islands of Khaledan, a whole month's voyage; and all the way he was glad so that his heart sang. But on the day when the ship approached the dominions of Shahzaman, there arose a great storm which broke the mast and carried away the sail and capsized the vessel.

Marzavan, thrown overboard with the rest, was caught by a strong current and carried shorewards; and as fate would have it, since the destiny of all are in the hands of the Most High, the current bore him toward that part of the coast where stood the palace of the King; and there at that time, in the pavilion looking toward the sea, sat Shahzaman attended by his Vizier; and the head of Camaralzaman lay upon his lap; and a eunuch was whisking the flies from him.

The Vizier, looking out from the terrace, saw in the water below him the shipwrecked Marzavan, tossed this way and that and unable to land; so his heart was moved with pity and he came running to the King and crying, " Permit me, O my lord, to open the gates of the court and put forth my hand to save yonder man who is now drowning. For since a just action is never without reward, it may be he shall bring us good."

Shahzaman replied, " Thou art the cause of all our trouble, and I doubt not that coming by thy hand this drowning man will bring us more. Yet I cannot forbid thee to save his life : only be sure that he comes not near us to spy upon my son in his affliction and report it to others. If he do, his head and thine shall be forfeit."

So the Vizier ran, and opening the gates of the court leaned down, and caught Marzavan by the hair and drew him up to dry land. And Marzavan came forth from the sea all lost to consciousness, his stomach filled with water and his eyes protruding. The Vizier waited till his spirit had returned to him ; then he took from him his clothes and clad him in others and put on his head the turban of an attendant and said to him, " Now, as I have saved thy life, do my bidding and save mine also. Cast down thine eyes, speak not, look not into any chamber as we go, but follow closely where I lead lest worse befall thee."

Then said Marzavan, " What is this peril that I am not to see ? "

The Vizier answered, " It is the King's son, who is sorely afflicted for the loss of a fair damsel that came to him but once and is gone again, none knows where. That is the story, and on pain of death all who hear it must believe it." And the Vizier sighed heavily, for at this time life was hard to him and belief difficult.

When the half-drowned Marzavan heard that, his heart went up like a singing bird, and he skipt at the Vizier's heels like a squirrel. And when they came by the chamber where Camaralzaman was lying, with the King seated beside him, then Marzavan turned swiftly and went in and stood before him ; and no sooner had he seen the Prince than, with an exclamation of joy, he cried : " Extolled be the perfection of him who hath given beauty its pair ! Lo, the eyes are hers, the complexion is hers, the lips and the cheeks are hers ! "

At these words the knees of the Vizier went from

under him, and he prayed succour of death : but on the heart of Camaralzaman there descended a coolness and a refreshment, and turning his tongue in his mouth, he signalled with his hand to Shahzaman to make the young man sit down.

The King, seeing the look of joy upon his son's face, easily forgave the intrusion which had earned death ; and having placed Marzavan in the seat at the Prince's side, he bade him recount his history and whence and why he came.

So Marzavan told of the country from which he had come and of its King and people, and of all the events of his journey, but of the real cause which had brought him he said nothing. And the Prince listened and waited, for he saw that something was concealed : and all the while, since hope had returned to him, his countenance grew bright and his strength of body increased. So presently he made a sign for his father to raise him to a sitting posture ; and the King, full of joy, lifted him, and placed cushions behind him and under him. Thus after three years of lying down did Camaralzaman sit up. So after a while Shahzaman, seeing how by the conversation of Marzavan the Prince was restored to health, went away and left them ; and the Vizier departed also.

Then, seeing that they were alone, Marzavan spoke low in the ear of Camaralzaman saying, " O Prince, thy sorrow is at an end ; for she whom thou lovest is the Princess Badoura, daughter of the King of China and my own foster-sister : and I am come through the world seeking thee because of my devotion to her, who, for love of thee, now lieth in chains. All that hath happened unto thee with thy father hath happened to her also with her father, yea, and worse things also." So he went on and told him all.

Now when Camaralzaman had heard the story of the Princess, and of her sufferings and constancy, and of all the useless cures for her malady that had been tried, his heart was divided in its joy by an overflowing of sorrow, even as a rich country is divided and broken by a stream when it floods its banks; and he said to Marzavan, "Alas! how may I bring her the true cure, seeing that we dwell in such different parts of the world, and my father will not suffer me to be out of his sight even for one day?"

Marzavan answered, "For thy health's sake he will allow thee that one, and it shall suffice. For to-morrow thou shalt say to him, 'Let me go out into the hills for a day and a night, that I may hunt and recover my strength,' and surely he shall not deny it to thee. And when thou hast found that for which thou art in search, I know that thou wilt return to him. But we will take with us two spare horses and saddlebags, with money sufficient for our journey, and when we have started upon our way I will provide, so that we may not be pursued and over-taken."

At these words the Prince rejoiced greatly, and it all came about even as Marzavan had planned. For on the morrow the King, rejoicing that his son's health was so quickly restored, granted him the permission he sought, saying only, "Be not absent, my son, longer than one night, for while thou art away from me I have no joy left." Camaralzaman answered, "The night of sorrow will end, then shall I return." So he took leave of his father and departed.

For the whole of that day until the evening Camaralzaman and Marzavan went in the direction they had chosen, setting their faces for the open country and the seaport lying beyond. And when it was night they ate and drank,

fed their beasts, and rested for a while; then they re-
mounted and journeyed on. At daybreak they came
to a spacious tract of forest; there Marzavan took one
of the led horses and killed it, stripping the flesh from its
bones; next he took the garments which Camaralzaman
had worn on the previous day, and after tearing them
this way and that daubed them with blood.

Camaralzaman inquired why he did this : and Marzavan
answered, " When we return not great search will be
made for thee, and I doubt not, if it went far enough,
we should be overtaken. But when the searchers come
upon this they will suppose that a wild beast has fallen
upon thee and devoured thee; and that I, fearing
the King's wrath, have fled away. Doubtless the news
will bring great sorrow to thy father's heart; but when
thou returnest with thine errand safely accomplished,
he shall be recompensed with joy."

The Prince sorrowfully commended the plan which
Marzavan had devised for the safety of their enterprise;
and so they continued upon their way unmolested, and
after much travelling by land and water, and many
adventures not to be told of here, they arrived at the
capital of the dominions of King Gaiour, where the
Princess Badoura lay in captivity.

Marzavan did not take Camaralzaman to his own
house, but to a public khan, where for three days they
remained recovering from the fatigues of their journey. Then, having clothed the Prince in the garb of a
merchant-doctor with all the signs and instruments of
his calling, he conducted him to the gates of the palace;
standing before which Camaralzaman began, on the
instructions of Marzavan, to cry in a loud voice, " Look
at me, for I am learned ! Marvel at me, for I am wise !
I am the healer, the calculator, the astrologer; I know

the cause of all maladies and their cure. If anyone, be he king or peasant, is in affliction, let him come to me!"

The people were greatly astonished to hear once more an astrologer so bold of tongue; and pitying him for his youth and wondering at the beauty of his form, they pointed to the heads which were over the palace gates, saying, "While there is time save thyself; for if the King hear thee thy head will be joined to those."

Nevertheless Camaralzaman continued to cry with a loud voice; till at last the King heard him, and said to his Vizier, "Go down, and bring this astrologer in."

So the Vizier went out and fetched him, and Camaralzaman came and bowed himself before the King. And when the King looked at him, his heart also was moved with pity toward the stranger, as the heart of the people had been, because of his youth and the beauty of his form. And he said to him, "My son, comply not with my conditions; for I have bound myself with an oath, and whoso goes in to visit my daughter but cannot cure her, his head must I strike off; and of a truth you have but to look over my palace gate to see that her malady is obstinate. Nevertheless if you can cure her she is yours, and the half of my kingdom is yours also."

Camaralzaman said, "To those conditions, O King, I am agreed!" Then the King, sighing heavily, sent for the eunuch and bade him conduct the astrologer to the apartment of the Princess.

The eunuch led the way; but when they were come to the corridor wherein Badoura's chamber was situated, so great was the joy of the Prince that he hastened and went before; and the eunuch called after him, "Tarry, good sir, and be not so hasty before the event, for I alone have the key that shall bring thee to thy death! Never was any other astrologer in such haste to depart from life as thou."

"Friend," answered Camaralzaman, "they had not such science as I have to make them glad: for they could not tell what the end would be, but I know it already, nay, even without entering that door of which thou hast the key I can cure the Princess of her malady."

The eunuch, astonished to be met with so much confidence, ceased from his taunts, and admitted the Prince to the antechamber. "If thou canst do that," he said, "thou art indeed the wonder of the world. Truly were I only permitted to see such a marvel accomplished, I should account myself rich."

Thereupon Camaralzaman seated himself against the curtain which divided the outer from the inner chamber and wrote the following prescription:

"He whom estrangement hath afflicted is cured when the vow of the beloved is accomplished; and the heart of exile findeth restoration in union with that which was lost. Love alone can heal those whom love hath persecuted."

Underneath this prescription he added the following words:

"From the distracted, the passionate, the perplexed, the famished with longing, the captive of transport and ardent desire, Camaralzaman, son of Shahzaman, King of Khaledan, to the peerless one of her age, the pre-eminent among Hooris, the Princess Badoura, daughter of Gaiour, King of the Isles of China and lord of the seven Palaces. Behold the slave of the ring who, sleepless and inflamed by love, now awaits the call of his Beloved."

Then, having enclosed the ring which at their first meeting he had exchanged for his own, he sealed the

CAMARALZAMAN FINDS THE TALISMAN
(*Page* 173)

22

missive, and putting it into the hands of the eunuch bade him carry it to his mistress.

No sooner had the Princess Badoura received the missive and the ring than she knew at once from whom it came. Whereupon joy overthrew her reason, and leaping up in a transport of exultation she pressed her feet against the wall, and breaking the chains which bound her ran forth and threw herself into the arms of Camaralzaman.

Speechless with joy she kissed him without ceasing; even as a pigeon when it feeds its young, so upon the lips of Camaralzaman fell the kisses of the Princess Badoura. Then came the nurse, crying aloud for gladness to behold the joy of her mistress and the healing of her malady accomplished; and presently after her came the King. For to him had run the eunuch in swift haste bringing tidings of the event—how that without entering her chamber the astrologer had cured her. " What ? " cried the King, " can such news be true ? " " O my lord," answered the eunuch, " let thine own eyes look upon her and be blest; for she hath broken her chains of iron, and coming forth to the astrologer she falleth upon him and kisseth him, and never will she let him go."

So Gaiour the King came and found it even as the eunuch had said. Full of joy to behold so sweet a sight, he embraced first the Princess and then the Prince, thanking him with tears of gratitude for the debt which he owed him. And when he inquired further and learned of Camaralzaman his name, and his true rank, and of the country from which he came, with all the strange story of his love and the grief of his separation, then his satisfaction and delight knew no bounds. And so on that very day the nuptials were celebrated, and word of rejoicing went forth through the whole of the King's dominions.

The hearts of Prince Camaralzaman and his bride were now so full of happiness that for many months they wist not the passing of time, and waking or sleeping it seemed to them as one day. But while their joy thus decked itself in the colours of immortality, the Prince one night had a dream, wherein he beheld his father Shahzaman, lying as at the point of death. And in his dream it seemed that he heard him say, " O my son, whom in thy grief I so tenderly cherished, wherefore hast thou acted thus, leaving me in my old age to die alone? "

So sharp was the sting of that dream upon his conscience that, sighing, the Prince woke; and his wife hearing him made inquiry as to his grief. " Alas! " answered Camaralzaman, " in my happiness with thee I had forgotten my father." And thereupon he recounted his dream. So the next day the Princess Badoura went to her father, and having told him all, besought leave for Camaralzaman to return for a while to his own land so that he might comfort his father in his old age.

The King readily granted his daughter's request. Then said Badoura, " If my husband goes I must go too." " Why so? " inquired her father. " Because," said she, " if you separate us there is no power in the world that shall keep me alive."

Now the King had learned during the years of his daughter's captivity, that anything which she said she meant. Therefore with much grief and reluctance at being so compelled, he granted her request; and having accorded them permission to be absent for a whole year, he made preparation for their departure. In order that they might appear at the court of Shahzaman in the splendour that became their rank, he presented them with many changes of costly apparel, and having provided a large train of horses, dromedaries, and attendants, he bade them an affectionate farewell, and with many tears watched them depart.

For a whole month Camaralzaman and his bride travelled in comfort and luxury by the route that they had chosen, and greatly was the Prince's heart rejoiced by the thought of seeing his father once more and presenting to his eyes the lovely and innocent cause of all their past affliction. Therefore, early and late they journeyed on, only stopping to rest at night and during the heat of each day.

And so it chanced that one day, about noon, they came to a spacious meadow shaded by trees, and there at the Prince's command the tents were pitched; and the Princess went into her pavilion and lay down to sleep.

Now when she lay down, the heat being very great, she took off her outer robe and her girdle. And the Prince, coming in later, saw the girdle lying, and knotted within its folds a large stone, red as blood, inscribed with strange characters which, in the darkness of the tent, he could not read. Being curious, therefore, to see what words were upon this talisman which the Princess carried so secretly in her apparel, he unfastened the knot, and taking the stone went forth from the tent to examine it.

Scarcely had he done so when, with a strange cry, a bird swooped down from the tree above his head, caught up the stone in its beak, and flew away with it. Camaralzaman, fearing to lose what, for all he knew, might be a precious talisman, ran after the bird, throwing up his arms, shouting and endeavouring in all possible ways to make it let go the stone. But the bird flew on from tree to tree, and from valley to valley, never so fast that Camaralzaman could not keep pace with it, but never coming within his reach, or letting go of the talisman. So the flight went on and so the chase continued, till several hours had passed and it began to grow dark. Then the bird, uttering once more its strange cry, went up to the topmost branch of a high tree and settled itself to roost.

The pursuit had now led Camaralzaman so far and in so many directions, that he no longer knew which way to turn. So, commending himself to Allah, he lay down at the foot of the tree and slept.

In the morning, with a loud rustling of feathers, the bird awakened him, and still carrying the stone in its beak, sprang out of the tree and continued its flight. And as Camaralzaman rose and followed, it presently became apparent that at whatever rate he went, the bird went too; so when he ran the bird flew fast, and when he could run no more it waited for him, flying from point to point and never disappearing from view.

" By Allah ! " cried Camaralzaman, " this is wonderful ! This chase will lead me either to great fortune or to death." So without giving up he went on; and thus he followed the bird for ten days, living upon roots and drinking of the streams that he crossed; and every night he slept at the foot of some tree while the bird perched in its topmost branches.

Thus on the tenth day he was brought to the outskirts of a large city. Then, like a flash, the bird flew over it and disappeared; and Camaralzaman following, footsore and weary, came to the city gates and passed through. Here for some time he wandered, solitary and without hope, not knowing what to do nor of whom to seek aid; and coming presently to the other side of the city, he found there a harbour with much shipping and merchandise, and people plying their trade and talking in

many languages.   And as he walked along the shore, still
uncertain what course to pursue, he came upon an old
man working in a garden of flowers ; and when he halted
the old man looked up.

The gardener, seeing a stranger at his gate, came
forward, and saluting him in the name of Allah, bade
him come in. " I see by your dress," said he, " that
you are a Mussulman as I also am ; and great is your
good fortune to have escaped until now the wrath of the
inhabitants, for they are unbelievers and idolaters, and
fierce is their hatred for those who are of the true faith.
Therefore come quickly into my house, and disguise
yourself ; else is your life not safe."

Camaralzaman was thankful to have found a friend
in such a moment of need ; and after his host had supplied
him with food and drink and made him rest for a while,
then without concealment he confided to him the whole
of his story. Greater than ever had now become his
longing to reach the island of Khaledan, for there not
only did he hope to find his father still alive, but to be
reunited with his wife, the Princess Badoura. Inquiring
therefore of the old gardener, he learned that there were
two routes ; the longer being for the greater part of the
way by land—a year's journey, and the shorter by sea.
" But if," said the gardener, " you would go by sea, then
you must wait for the merchant ship which sails every
year to the Island of Ebony, for through that country
lies your way. Had you but come a few days earlier,
you would have been in time ; but now the ship has left the
harbour and will not return for another year. If you
decide upon this course, then while you wait my house
is open to you, and if you are willing to share my work
and be my assistant, you shall also have a fair share of
the profits."

Camaralzaman gladly accepted the proposition, for better by far is work, however hard or humble it may be, than the idleness of unavailing regret. So for a whole year he lived with the old gardener as if he had been his son, wearing a blue smock down to his knees, working with a hoe, tending plants, tilling the soil, and carrying its produce for sale to the market. And every day he looked out over the sea for the merchant vessel which was to arrive and bear him back to his own country and to the arms of his beloved.

Now turn we to the Princess Badoura, whom we left lying asleep in her tent. When she awoke she inquired after her husband, the Prince, but he was not to be found; some had seen him go into the tent, but no one had seen him come out. Then, as she put on her dress, she noticed that the knot in her girdle had been untied and that the stone was missing. "Alas, O Beloved, what hast thou done?" she cried. "Ignorant of its virtues thou hast taken from me the talisman which unites us; now surely if thou hast lost it we shall be separated for ever." And as time went on her distress and her certainty of misfortune became greater; for she knew that had not the Prince already lost the talisman its infallible virtues would by now have brought him back to her. Knowing therefore that if the talisman were indeed lost, he also was lost to her, and that when found, he would return to her again, she made no useless delay in proceeding to her destination. Yet was there now great peril if the absence of the Prince were discovered, lest she and her women and all the wealth which her father had bestowed on her might fall a prey to the men who formed their escort. For this reason she concealed the matter from all but her women, and having dressed herself in some of her husband's clothes, and put into her litter a girl slave wearing the royal veil, she went forth from her tent and gave orders for the camp to be struck and their journey resumed. So, for many days she continued to travel by land and sea, till she came before a city set on a height with a great harbour lying below ; and when she inquired its name of the inhabitants they said to her, " This is the city of Ebony, wherein dwells King Amanos, and he has a beautiful daughter whose name is Hayatelne-foos."

Presently word went to the palace that a stranger prince of very noble appearance, accompanied by a large retinue, had arrived in the harbour and was seeking admission to the city. Whereupon the King sent in haste certain high dignitaries of his court to give welcome and to conduct the supposed Prince into his presence. And no sooner had he beheld the noble appearance of his guest and the graciousness of her bearing than he gave orders for a great banquet to be prepared, appointed that she should be lodged in the palace, and extended to her for three days an entertainment of the most royal magnificence.

During the whole of these festivities the Princess bore herself exactly as Camaralzaman would have done, doing honour to that rank and name which for her own protection she had assumed. Therefore the heart of King Amanos was drawn greatly towards her, and when she began to speak of departure, he said, " Wherefore, O Prince, shouldst thou seek to leave a country where happiness and power can be thine ? For behold, I am an old man and childless, save for one daughter, whose beauty and perfection resemble thine. But, for me, the cares of state have become too heavy a burden, and I sigh to be released from them. Remain with us, therefore,

23

and I will give to thee even now the hand of my daughter and the sceptre and rule of my kingdom."

At this proposal, so generously expressed, the face of Badoura became covered with bashfulness, for strange indeed to a woman was this offer of a kingdom and a bride. Yet at her father's court she had long since become learned in the affairs of state, and to rule a kingdom had ever been her desire; moreover, since by the loss of the talisman she and her husband seemed destined to eternal separation, there was no cause that she could see why her life should not thus be dedicated; there was also some peril in a refusal, which the King would be certain to take as an affront both to himself and his daughter. So after pondering the matter for a while she lifted her head and spoke to the King as follows :

" O King, if I delayed for one moment my acceptance of so splendid an offer, it was only a knowledge of unworthiness which held me back. Yet to delay longer might seem to throw a doubt on the discretion of your royal mind. Beset by these two dangers I place myself entirely in your Majesty's hands; and if I may have your promise of the guidance and counsel which I shall constantly need, then I will unreservedly accept your Majesty's proposal. To hear is to obey."

The marriage being thus agreed on, the nuptial ceremony was fixed for the following day. The pretended Prince, putting a bold face upon the matter, informed the officers of her escort of the coming event, saying also that the Princess Badoura had given it her approval. As for her women, their silence was already assured since, as partners to the deception, their very lives depended on it.

So on the morrow King Amanos gathered together his emirs, viziers, and captains, and having presented to them the Princess Badoura as his destined son-in-law and heir, he placed her upon the throne and gave orders for the nuptial ceremony to commence. And when the day of rejoicings was ended, the Princess Badoura was conducted to the bridal chamber.

But no sooner did Badoura find herself by the side of the beautiful Princess Hayatelnefoos than the thought of her beloved Camaralzaman overwhelmed her with grief, and committing herself to prayer and recitation, she continued at her devotions till the bride lay fast asleep. And thus she did the next night and on the night following.

Finding herself thus neglected by the husband of whom she had received such glowing reports, the Princess Hayatelnefoos was filled with a depression of spirit which immediately became visible in her looks; and when her father, King Amanos, discerning his daughter's grief, inquired what was amiss, she informed him that her husband, whom she already loved most tenderly, had conceived for her an aversion so intense that to avoid all intimacy of conversation he committed himself to prayer, and thus continued till weariness and sleep overcame her.

At this news the countenance of King Amanos was darkened, and he said to his daughter, " If the Prince does not treat thee with the respect due from a husband to a wife, he shall be divested of his royal dignity and banished from my kingdom."

This threat so afflicted the heart of Hayatelnefoos, to whom the thought of separation from her husband was already unbearable, that on their next meeting she confided to Badoura her grief, informing her also of the King's words and of the danger that threatened her.

Then said Badoura, " O amiable and charming Princess,

though thou canst not be my wife thou canst be my friend. Hear first my story, and then, if thou art unable to pardon me thou canst at least have the satisfaction of depriving me of life." And forthwith she proceeded to give the full story of her adventures.

When she had finished, Hayatelnefoos replied, " O Princess, I should indeed be unworthy of your confidence, if such a tale of misfortune had failed to win not only my pity, but my devotion. Henceforth we two are of one mind, and will have between us but one heart and one desire for the preservation of thy life and honour and the restoration of thy husband."

Thereupon the two Princesses embraced with the tenderest affection, and from that day on, concealing from all others the true facts, they lived together in the greatest amity and concord ; while the Princess Badoura continued in her husband's name to rule over the city of Ebony, giving law and justice to all.

Prince Camaralzaman, meanwhile, was living with the old gardener, tilling the soil, and carrying each day fruit and vegetables to the market. The time was now near for the merchant vessel which he was awaiting to return ; but having lost the talisman of which he had come in quest, he had little hope of a successful issue to the adventure. So one day, when the inhabitants of the city were making holiday and all the markets were closed, the Prince, released from labour, sat in deep dejection of spirit under the trees of the garden away from the sound of festival, when suddenly he heard a strange cry of birds and in the leaves overhead he saw one furiously attacking another with beak and claw. So desperate was the fight, that before many minutes were over one of the birds fell dead at his feet, and the conqueror, uttering a loud cry of triumph, flew swiftly away.

But hardly had it disappeared, when two other birds of larger size came flying into the garden, and making straight for the murdered body they bowed their heads over it, crying lamentably and seeking with the warmth of their breasts to restore it to life. Presently, when all their efforts proved vain, they scooped a grave with their claws, and having laid therein the slaughtered bird, they covered it with earth and immediately soared upward and disappeared.

Camaralzaman sat weeping; for the mourning of these birds reninded him in some way of the grief and separation he himself had endured, and as little could he hope for the return of his lost happiness as they for the revival of their dead comrade. As he was thus thinking, once again came the strange cry he had heard before, and looking up he saw the two birds flying back carrying the murderer in their claws. No sooner had they alighted above the grave than falling upon their captive they tore out his heart and entrails, and having drained out his blood as an offering to the slain, they left the body lying, and flew away.

All this while Camaralzaman had looked on in wonder; and surely it seemed to him that if, in the lower order of creation such miracles of devotion and service were wrought, humanity had no cause for despair. And even as he so thought, he saw in the torn body of the bird something that shone brightly, and coming nearer he recognized it as the talisman which he had taken from his wife's girdle.

Instantly all life became changed to him; seizing the stone he wiped it of blood and pressed it a thousand times to his lips. "Now at last," he cried, "I believe and know that my beloved is to be restored to me!"

So sure was he his good fortune had now returned to him that, unable to remain idle and inactive, he seized a hoe, and started to break up the ground at the foot of the tree under which he had been standing. At the third stroke the earth gave back a hollow and metallic sound. Quickly removing the soil he discovered a trap-door, which, when it was opened, disclosed an aperture and a narrow flight of steps. Descending these he found himself in a deep cellar lined with jars, twenty in all, filled with red gold.

Contentment now took hold of his spirit, and having returned to the garden he replaced the trap and continued at his work until in the evening the old gardener returned from the festivities.

On seeing him the old man said, " Rejoice, my son, I bring you good tidings. The ship which you have so long waited for is now in the harbour, and in three days will be ready once more to set sail."

This news so delighted Camaralzaman that taking the old man's hand he kissed it saying, " I too have tidings for you of a happy kind." And leading the gardener to the tree he lifted the trap, and disclosed to his astonished eyes the gold that lay stored below.

" Well," said the gardener, " I am glad that my poor plot of ground should have yielded thee such rich fruit. Take it, my son, and Heaven prosper thee by its aid till thou come once more to thine own land and the heart of thy beloved."

" Not so," replied Camaralzaman, " I will take nothing if I may not share it equally with thee."

So it was agreed. Then said the gardener, " My son, hast thou thought how to convey safely so much gold on a voyage where thou wilt be alone in the hands of strangers ? Surely if they find thee possessed of such

wealth they will kill thee for the sake of it. Hearken,
therefore, to what I shall advise. From this country
we send olives into all parts of the world, and many ships
go laden with them. Fill for thyself, therefore, fifty
jars from the olive-trees which are in this garden, and
at the bottom of each jar lay a portion of the gold:
so shall it be safe, and no man will know of it."

So the Prince did as the gardener advised; and
fearing lest, while on the voyage, he himself might be
robbed, he put the talisman along with the gold in one
of the olive jars, marking it with a number so that
he might know it again. Then he made a bargain with
the owner of the vessel, and on the third day the seamen
came and carried away the jars and stowed them on
board. And the captain said to Camaralzaman, who
had accompanied them, "Do not be long in returning,
for the wind is fair and I only wait for you to set sail."

So Camaralzaman hastened back to say farewell to
the old gardener and to thank him for all that he had
done; but when he arrived at the house he found the
old man so stricken with grief at his departure that
he was already at the point of death. Camaralzaman
therefore sat down by his bed and tended him, holding
him by the hand and speaking many comfortable words;
and toward evening, having made his profession of faith,
as all good Mussulmans do, the old man let fall his head and
expired.

Camaralzaman closed his eyes, wrapped his body for
burial, and having dug a grave in the garden, interred it.
Then he went down in haste to the shore and found
that the vessel had gone.

Once again, therefore, despair returned to him, for
now a second time the talisman was lost, and he had
no hope of recovering it. Also he must needs wait another

year before the ship could return and take him upon
his way. So going to the landlord of the garden he
became a tenant in the place of his dead friend, and
hiding what remained of the gold in fifty other olive
jars, he set to work once more as a gardener until the
time should once more come round for him to embark.

Meantime, under a favourable wind, the ship arrived
at the island of Ebony; and it so happened that as it
came into the harbour the Princess Badoura was looking
out of one of the palace windows toward the sea. No
sooner did her eyes rest upon the sails of that ship than her
heart became uplifted with joy. " Surely," she said to
herself, " either my beloved is there on board or it brings
news of him."

So going down to the shore, accompanied by her
emirs and attendants, she caused the master of the vessel
to be summoned before her and inquired of him what
merchandise he had brought. " O King," replied the
captain, " I have spices, drugs, aromatic scents, and
sweet ointments ; I have also rich fabrics and metal-
work ; and in addition to all these things I have olives
such as are not to be found in any other country, and
these, since I came by them fortunately, I can let you
have cheap."

On hearing this a desire for the olives took hold of
the Princess and she said, " What quantity have you
brought ? " " Fifty jars," answered the master ; "that
is all I have." "Well," said the Princess, "I will take
fifty." And she paid him for them the price that he
asked—a thousand pieces of silver.

Now presently, when the olives had been conveyed
to the palace, there came upon the Princess a strange
desire to taste that which she had just purchased so she

BADOURA WATCHING THE SHIP

(*Page* 184)

24

gave orders for one of the jars to be opened and the contents to be poured into a dish; and as the attendant poured, first came olives and then a heap of red gold.

Then said Badoura to the Princess Hayatelnefoos, who alone was with her, "That is gold!" So she examined further and in every jar found gold in equal quantity. Presently as she emptied one of the jars, along with the gold came the talisman which Camaralzaman had concealed there; and no sooner did the Princess Badoura see it than she knew it again; and she showed it to Hayatelnefoos, saying, "Lo, this is the stone whose loss hath caused our separation; now, finding it again, I know that my beloved will be restored to me."

Then she sent in haste and caused the master of the vessel to be brought before her, and she said to him, "Whence had you these olives? Tell me the truth, or you shall die!"

Thereupon the master being smitten in his conscience dropped to earth and lay there, crying, "Alas, I had them of a poor man who brought them himself to the vessel but did not return at the appointed time; therefore I sailed without him. Be assured, O King, that all the money I got for them shall be honestly paid to him."

Then said Badoura, "As to that I care not. But go back straightway to that country from which you came and find the man and bring him to me, for he is a malefactor against the laws of this kingdom, for he hath stolen from me a precious thing dearer than life itself; therefore is his life forfeit. And if you fail to bring him, then all the merchandise which you have now brought I will hold, and no ship or merchandise of yours shall ever enter this port again. But if you bring him safely, I will reward you abundantly."

The master therefore, being so compelled, left his

188888888888888888888888888888 THE ARABIAN NIGHTS

merchandise in bond and returned with all haste to the
port from which he had set out, and there coming with
his men to the house of Camaralzaman, he knocked ; and
no sooner had the Prince opened than, seizing him, they
carried him off, and bestowed him on board the vessel
as a prisoner.

Camaralzaman said to them, " Masters, why are
you treating me thus ? " They answered, " Thou art
an offender and malefactor against the King of the Ebony
Isles, son to the King Amanos, and hast stolen his wealth ;
yea, a precious thing hast thou stolen from him, and
now he requires it of thee ! "

" Well," said Camaralzaman, " this is the first that I
have heard of it."

So they bore him away, and after they had sailed for
some while they came again to the city of Ebony, and
word was sent to the palace that the master of the vessel
had returned bringing the King his prisoner.

Then Badoura gave orders, and Camaralzaman, still
in his workman's dress, his body wasted with grief,
and his face and hands soiled with the defilements of
his long voyage, came and stood before her. As soon
as she saw him her heart leapt with joy, but she
feared to reveal herself, for how would it appear to her
emirs and chamberlains were she before all eyes
to throw herself into the arms of a common gardener.
Therefore, retaining her disguise, she spoke to him as a
King should do to a peasant, and in a man's voice. And
Camaralzaman, fearful of the unknown charge which
was to be brought against him, stood before her with
bowed head and did not look up.

The Princess asked him but a few questions, of
the country from which he had come, of the time that
he had lived there, and what calling he had followed.

Then she said to him, " Be assured that if thou art innocent of that which is charged against thee, thine honour and integrity shall be made known to all. Even now if thou wilt confess to have taken a thing which is not thine and wilt restore it to me, I am willing to pardon thee, seeing that it was done without thought of evil." But Camaralzaman hearing these words knew not what they meant, for his thoughts were all astray and he did not dream that it was of himself and of the talisman that she spoke.

Then Badoura ordered an officer of her household to take charge of the prisoner and treat him with all care; and having recompensed the master of the vessel and set free his merchandise, she went in to Hayatelnefoos, and told her of all that had come about. And she said to her, " O bosom-friend and comforter of my heart, be sure that what brings happiness to me shall bring it to thee also; for no fortune shall Heaven send me, nor any bliss, however great, that I am not ready to share equally with thee." Then speaking of Camaralzaman she said, " So great a distance divides in men's eyes what seems his present lot from ours, that it were peril to be sudden in this matter lest the truth of our story should not be believed. Therefore we must wait till of his own natural nobleness he shall have raised himself in the eyes of all." And to this plan Queen Hayatelnefoos agreed.

So the next day Badoura gave orders to conduct Camaralzaman to the bath; then she caused him to be clad in an emir's robes and brought forth where all might see; and lo! as a willow branch after rain or the planet of love shining at dusk, so seemed he then to the eyes of all.

Then again she caused him to be brought before her in the Hall of Judgment and pronounced him clear of all that had been charged against him. " For that which was precious to me," she said, " has been restored ; and other hands held it from me, not thine. Therefore as thou hast been proved true I will appoint thee to high honour." Then addressing the emirs and councillors who were gathered about her she said, " My lords, this Camaralzaman whom to-day I admit to my Councils is not unworthy of the high post which I confer on him ; for not only have I tested him as ye have seen on an accusation whereof he is innocent, but he is a man of approved valour, of grace, and learning, being also a descendant of kings."

Great was Camaralzaman's astonishment at finding his name and lineage known to the King of the Ebony Isles ; but not daring to question how his good fortune had come about he prostrated himself before the throne, saying, " O King, only by thy favour have I been raised to this honour, and by that alone can I either deserve or maintain it." So the Council ended, and Camaralzaman was conducted to a large and sumptuous abode with slaves and attendants to wait upon him, and everything that his heart could desire save only his beloved Princess.

After a few days Badoura, wishing to find occasion for Camaralzaman's more frequent presence, appointed him to the office of Grand Treasurer, and thereafter scarcely a day passed that she did not bestow on him fresh honours ; while Camaralzaman, for his part, wondering why such high favours were shown him, served the King diligently, and was greatly respected not only by all the emirs and officials of the Court, but by the common people, who swore by his life, and would have asked no better than for such an one as he to be their ruler.

So time went on, and ever did the wonder of Camaralzaman increase why he alone had been chosen for such

THE FINAL MARRIAGE PROCESSION
(*Page* 190)

great honours. And because this thing seemed to him
without reason, he came at last to fear it. Furthermore,
for loss of his beloved, restlessness and the desire for
travel filled his heart, and in no one place could he find
happiness. So one day coming to the King—that is to
say to Badoura—he spoke as follows : " O King of the
Age, so great is the favour that thou hast shown me, that
I know well it cannot last.   Suffer me therefore to depart
before I have outstayed my welcome ; so shall my gratitude
be undiminished and the nature of thy regard for me
unchanged."

When Badoura heard these words she smiled on him
and said : " If indeed it is thy will to depart, then must
thou take and cast away once more—yea, lose utterly—this
stone whose virtue brought thee back to me, and by
which, while it is in my possession, our lives are bound."
So saying she reached out and put the talisman in his
hand.

When Camaralzaman beheld the stone once more
his wonder was beyond words. " O King," he cried,
" whence came this to thee ?   For herein lies the cause of
all my afflictions and separation from one whom I loved
as my own soul."

" Surely," answered Badoura, " none can part from
that talisman without estrangement and separation.
And since now I have parted from it to thee, our separation
must infallibly begin from this hour. Therefore the
King of the Ebony Isles thou shalt see no more."

So saying she passed out of the chamber, and Camaralzaman stood and wondered, not knowing what to think.

Then Badoura went in haste to a closet, and there
she put on the dress and the girdle which she had worn
on the day of separation ; and taking from her head
the man's turban, she spread her hair and put on a head-

25

dress of fine gold delicately wrought. So she returned to him, and when Camaralzaman saw her he uttered a cry and ran into her arms and held her with kisses as if he could never let her go. And when at last he spoke of things other than his joy—" How," he inquired, " has the King accomplished this miracle ? Surely when he spoke I understood nothing of what he said."

Badoura smiled as she answered : " When the King put the talisman into thy hand, then did his kingship cease, and he returned once more to his true form. O my lord, look upon thy king, who is now become thy slave. Surely hadst thou loved me a little more thou wouldst have known me."

Then she told Camaralzaman of all that had happened to her from first to last ; and on the morrow she went to King Amanos, and to him also made her story plain. Nor would she allow that any deception had been used, " For truly," she said, " I and my beloved are one ; and I did but come before and prepare for him the place which he was destined to fill. Therefore when I married thy daughter, it was Camaralzaman who married her ; and when I accepted of thee the crown, it was Camaralzaman who accepted it. Give me leave, therefore, O King, who hast been to me as a father, to show my beloved to the Queen whom I have won for him, and to the people over whom, in his name, I have ruled."

Greatly was King Amanos astonished to hear a woman utter such words ; and the wonder of Camaralzaman was scarcely less. Yet, as she had brought fortune and happiness to both alike, they consented to do her will ; and so it was agreed.

Therefore from that day on did Camaralzaman take up the power and authority which Badoura had attained for him, rejoicing also in the domestic felicity of two wives, the one as beautiful as the other, each without jealousy, and having no wish or thought out of which estrangement could arise.

Doubtless it was the perfect happiness in which he thus dwelt which caused Camaralzaman to forget altogether the object for which his journey had been begun. No second dream of his father, the King Shahzaman, ever came to remind him of his neglected purpose, while to the dominions of King Gaiour of China he had no wish to return.

EPILOGUE

" This, O King, is the story of Prince Camaralzaman and of the Princess Badoura from the time of their falling in love until the day when all their wanderings of separation were ended. A year later the two Queens each presented him with a son almost upon the same day. And the birth of these Princes was celebrated with every kind of festivity and rejoicing."

As Scheherazade concluded her story the light of dawn grew full. For a thousand and one nights she had given entertainment to her lord, saving at the same time the lives of her fellow-women. During this period she had borne the King three children, all with so strong a resemblance to their father that even he could find no cause in them for casting suspicion upon his wife's virtue.

So the tale being ended Scheherazade rose, and having kissed the ground at the King's feet, said, " O King of the Age, perfect and incomparable, lo in dust and ashes I thy slave come to present to thee a petition." And the King said, " Ask, and it shall be granted thee."

Then Scheherazade called to her attendants and said, " Bring in the children ! " So they brought the children quickly ; one of them walked, one crawled, and one lay at the breast.

So she set them before the King, and said, " These children are thine and mine. In pain I bore them, having little hope of any joy that they might bring me ; for under sentence of death I brought them into the world, and though thrice I have been a mother thou hast not yet pardoned me. Say, therefore, O King, when is my death to be ; or, if it is not to be, then let my suspense be ended."

At these words the King wept ; and embracing his children tenderly, cried : " O Scheherazade, by Allah I swear to thee that before the coming of these children thou wast pardoned already. Nor shall the death of such an one as thou be laid to my charge when Kings come before God to be judged."

Then Scheherazade fell down and kissed his feet and his hands, crying, " God give thee a long life, and power and strength, and dominion and majesty to the world's end."

Joy of that news spread through the palace, and thence to the city and all the people ; and the night of rejoicing that followed was a night not to be reckoned among lives, for its colour was as the rainbow in its promise over young fields of corn, and its light whiter than the face of day.

SINDBAD THE SAILOR ENTERTAINS SINDBAD THE LANDSMAN
(*Page* 199)

SINDBAD THE SAILOR

In the time of Harun-Er-Rashid there was, in Baghdad, a rich merchant named Sindbad the Sailor, the source of whose wealth was a mystery. It seemed to be inexhaustible. For long seasons he kept open house, and his entertainments were the most magnificent of all save only those of Er-Rashid himself. All that riches could buy seemed at his disposal, and he lavished the good things of this life upon his guests. Pages, slaves and attendants there were in great number; his garden was spacious and beautiful, and his house was filled with every costly luxury.

This Sindbad the Sailor has a story to tell—the story of his life—but he never told it to any until, one day, there came to him one Sindbad the Landsman, a man of poor and humble birth. This man pleased him greatly and he was struck with the happy conceit that, now Sindbad the Sailor was at last confronted with Sindbad the Landsman, it would be no bad thing were he to narrate the story of his life.

Accordingly Sindbad the Sailor held seven receptions on severn different days, and, although on each occasion a multitude of guests was assembled to listen, he failed not to address his words from first to last to his simple listener, Sindbad the Landsman.

THE FIRST VOYAGE OF SINDBAD THE SAILOR

My father was a merchant of high rank and rich possessions. He died when I was but a child, leaving me all his wealth. When I reached manhood's estate I used my inheritance with no thought for the morrow, living in a sumptuous manner and consorting with the richest young men of Baghdad. I continued this life for many years until, at last, when reason prevailed with me to mend my plan, I found with dismay that I had sunk to poverty. And then it was that I arose and sold what goods remained to me for three thousand pieces of silver, and girded myself, resolving to travel to other lands and rebuild my fortune by the wit of my mind and the labour of my hands.

With a part of my hoard I bought merchandise for exchange in far lands, and also such things as I should require in my travels. Thus prepared I set sail with a company of merchants in a ship bound for the city of El-Basrah. For many days and nights we sailed upon the sea, visiting islands; and everywhere we bartered, and bought and sold. At length we came to an island unlike the others. It seemed like a garden that had floated from off the sides of Paradise and established itself in the sea. And here our ship cast anchor and we landed.

When all had eaten of the food prepared the shore became a gay scene of sport and play, in which I engaged to the full. But, suddenly, a cry from the master of the

ship put an end to our gaiety. Standing at the side
of the vessel he called loudly, " Hear me, and may God
preserve you ! Hasten back and leave everything ; save
yourselves from sudden death, for this that ye think is
an island is not such. It is a mighty fish lying entranced
in sleep on the surface of the sea since times of old, and
trees have grown upon it ; but your fires and your frolick-
ing have awakened it, and lo ! it moves ; and, if it sink
into the sea, ye will assuredly be drowned. Hasten
then, and save yourselves ! "

At this we all, with one accord, left everything and
fled for the ship, hoping to escape with our lives. While
we were making for safety the island moved with a great
turmoil and sank behind us in the sea, and the waves
leapt against each other above it. For a time I gave
myself up as lost, for I was drawn down fathoms deep ;
but, by God's grace, I rose again to the surface, and
to my hand was one of the large wooden bowls which
some of the passengers had taken on shore for the purpose
of washing. This I seized, and established myself in
it, and thus combated the leaping waves, steadying
myself with my hands and feet. In vain I called
on the master of the ship. He heard me not. He had
spread his sails and pursued his way, thinking that
none beside those who had been taken up were left
alive.

Astride my wooden bowl I gazed longingly at the ship
until it was out of sight. Then I prepared for death as the
night was closing around me. Perchance I swooned, for I
remembered naught else until I found myself stranded
upon a mountainous island. There were trees over-
hanging, and I grasped a drooping bough and drew
myself up from the fretting wave. My limbs were be-
numbed, and, on looking at my legs, I saw the marks

made by the nibbling teeth of fish, and marvelled at my salvation from death.

Staggering forward, I flung myself high on the beach like one dead, and so I remained until the dawn of the next day.

And it chanced, as I took my way to and fro in the island, revelling in the sight of things that God had set there, that on a day when the sea was sounding loudly on the shore I beheld something in the distance which excited my curiosity. It seemed like a wild animal of gigantic size, and, as I approached, I feared it was some fabulous beast of the sea. But, as I drew still nearer, I was overcome with amazement to see a beautiful mare standing high, with mane and tail floating on the breeze. She was tethered to a stake on the shore, and, at sight of me, she screamed loudly and stamped her forefeet on the sand; but, ere I turned to flee, I beheld a man come forth from a cave near by, and he ran after me, calling on me to give an account of myself and my presence in that place. Thereupon I laid my story before him, sparing no detail, even to the wooden bowl by means of which and the grace of God I had come thither.

Gladness seized him at my recital, and he took my hand. Saying, " Come with me ! " he led me into his cave and set food before me. I ate until I was satisfied; and, being at my ease, I repeated my story more minutely, and he wondered thereat. Then I said, " Thou hast the truth of my adventures upon the sea ; now I pray thee, O my master, tell me who *thou* art, that thou dwellest hidden in a cave while thy mare is tethered on the shore." He was in no way displeased at my curiosity, but answered me in plain words. " I am one of the grooms of the King El-Mihraj," he said, " and the others are scattered about the island. For, look you, friend, it is the time of the new moon, when the sea-horse cometh up out of the sea ; and it is our plan to bring our best mares hither and tether them by the shore so that they may lure the sea-horses into our hands."

While I was wondering at the manner of this cunning device a magnificent sea-horse rose from the waves, shaking the foam from its crest and neighing loudly. As it approached, my companion drew me into the cave and placed himself at the opening with a long coil of thick cord in his hand. Presently by means of this he leashed the sea-horse with great dexterity, and fettered him, and subdued him. Then, with the mare and the sea-horse, he led me to his companions, who, when they had heard my story, were all of one mind that I should accompany them to the city of the King. So they mounted me on one of the mares and I rode with them to the King's palace.

As soon as we had arrived at the palace gates they went in to the King and informed him of my strange adventures ; whereupon he sent for me, and they led me before him. He greeted me very courteously and bade me tell him my story, which, when he had heard it, filled him with amazement, so that he cried, " By Allah ! my son, of a truth thou art favoured by fate ; for how else couldst thou escape so great a peril ? Praise God for thy deliverance ! " And he made much of me and caused me to be treated with honour ; and he appointed me master of the harbour and comptroller of the shipping.

My condition then was no longer that of a wayfarer. I rose day by day to a higher and a higher place in the King's favour, and he took me into his council in all affairs of State. Yet my thoughts turned ever to Baghdad, the Abode of Peace. At last, weary of the wonders of that island, I stood one day on the seashore when a great ship drew near and a number of merchants landed from it.

The sailors brought forth their merchandise, and, when I had made an account of it, I inquired of the master of the ship if that were the whole of his cargo. "All, O my master," he replied; "all save some bales whose owner was drowned on our voyage hither; but even these, being in my charge, I desire to sell on behalf of his family in Baghdad." "Sayest thou so?" I cried. "Tell me, I pray thee, the name of the owner of these goods." And he replied, "His name was Sindbad the Sailor, and he was drowned on our way hither."

When I heard this I regarded him more closely and recognized him. Then I cried out, "O my master, I am he; and they are my goods that are in thy hold." And then it was that he and many of the merchants regarded me with fixed looks and recognized me.

Mindful of the King I served, I at once opened my bales, and, selecting the most costly articles, went in to him and laid them at his feet, telling him how I had regained the goods of which they were a part. And the King wondered greatly at my good fortune and graciously accepted my gifts. He also showed me great favour and honour in that he bestowed upon me gifts in return for mine.

Then, having sold my remaining goods at a profit, I bought largely of the merchandise of the city. And soon thereafter I set sail with the others for Baghdad.

Our voyage was fortunate, and, with the aid of favourable winds, we reached the city of El-Basrah in safety. Thence I repaired to Baghdad, and my family and my friends gave me a joyous welcome. And when I had sold my merchandise I set up a large establishment, sparing no cost. And I bought land and houses, and gathered round me wealthy companions, in whose society I soon forgot the dangers and terrors I had suffered in other lands.

THE SECOND VOYAGE OF SINDBAD
THE SAILOR

As I related yesterday, I was living here in Baghdad in the midst of every delight, surrounded by companions after my own heart. But a time came when the wandering spirit seized me again and I longed for the sight, even for the perils, of other and unknown lands.

The step was quickly taken. Having collected suitable merchandise I repaired to the river, and, without a word to anyone, embarked on a new ship finely rigged and manned by a large crew. Together with a goodly party of merchants I sailed away, and we passed over the deep from island to island and from sea to sea, with fair winds filling the sails. And at every place at which we cast anchor we bought and sold and bartered. So we continued until we came to an uninhabited island of great beauty. Selecting a rare spot on the bank of a stream, I sat apart, meditating upon the wonderful works of the Omnipotent One. There the soft zephyrs singing in the trees, and the stream murmuring at my feet, lulled me to slumber; and, when I awoke later, I looked forth upon the sea and lo, the ship was far out on the wall of the ocean sloping to the sky. They had forgotten me and I was left alone upon the island.

Despair fell upon me as I gazed around and realized that I was desolate.

At last I climbed to the top of a high tree, and,

looking forth in every direction, saw only sky and sea
and trees and watercourses. As I gazed, however, my
eye reverted again and again to an object in a distant
part of the island. It was round and white, and of
enormous size. This aroused my curiosity and I resolved
to find out what it was. Having marked its position I
descended from the tree and made my way towards it.
When I reached it I found to my astonishment that it
was a gigantic dome, white and shining. My first
thought was to walk round it to ascertain if there were
some door or opening, but none could I find in its whole
circumference, which was about fifty paces.

While I was meditating on some means to gain an
entrance to this strange structure, behold, the sky darkened; and on looking towards the sinking sun, I saw it
was hidden by a great black cloud—an unwonted thing,
as it was the summer season. While I continued to gaze
the object drew rapidly nearer, and now I could discern
in it the shape of a monstrous bird approaching swiftly
through the air; and this it was that blotted out the
sun.

Marvelling greatly I recalled a story told by travellers
about certain islands where was found a bird of immense
size called the rokh, which fed its young on elephants.
It was then I knew the great white dome I had discovered
was one of this bird's eggs—at which, not the least of the
Creator's works, I wondered greatly. Then, while I so
wondered, the giant bird alighted over the egg, and,
crouching down, spread its wings and brooded over it,
and composed itself to sleep.

Here, thought I, was a chance of escaping from the
island. Unfolding my turban I twisted it into a rope,
and bound one end of it tightly about my waist; then I
approached the great bird cautiously, and fastened the

THE ROKH

Page 206)

other end securely to one of its feet; but it was not until
morning that the bird awoke, and, with a loud cry, rose
from the egg, bearing me aloft. Higher and higher it
soared, until I thought it must reach the stars; then,
gradually, in vast circles, it descended, and finally came
to earth on a high table-land. In great fear lest the
bird should discover my presence I made haste to loose
the turban from its foot, and, having done so, I crept
away, trembling in every limb. Then, as I watched the
bird from a distance, I observed it pick something from the
ground and soar away with it clutched in its talons; and
I looked again and saw that it was an enormous serpent
twisting and writhing in the grasp of the bird as it flew
swiftly towards the sea. And at this strange thing I
wondered greatly as I folded my turban.

But what desert place had I come to by this daring
misadventure? On the one side of the table-land was a
deep valley, and, on the other, a steep mountain which no
foot of man could climb. Had I only remained in the
island I should at least have had fruit to eat and water
to drink, but here was nothing but desolation, from which
I had no hope of escape. There was no course but to
descend into the valley; and this I did, little caring whither
I went.

Now, I had not walked therein but a few furlongs when
I observed that the ground I trod was strewn with diamonds
of large size, but—and this gave me cause for wild alarm—
coiled here and there amongst the stones were gigantic
serpents such as the one I had seen the bird bear away
in its talons. As soon as I was aware of these sleeping
serpents, which were of the same hue as the ground whereon
they lay, I stepped warily lest I should awaken them and
be devoured.

In this way was I proceeding down that valley, my

flesh quaking and my knees a-tremble, when suddenly the
flayed carcass of a slaughtered beast fell with a great noise
before me. This aroused great wonder in my mind and also
called to my recollection a story I had heard in my youth
from a merchant traveller who had visited lands whence
none else had ever come to deny the truth of it—a story
confirmed by others who claimed a reputation for wide
knowledge, and feared to lose it. It was this—that
in a far land, where diamonds are as thickly strewn
as the venomous serpents and other deadly perils which
render it difficult to come at them, the daring merchants
who seek these precious stones employ a cunning stratagem.
They take a beast and slaughter it on the heights above
the valley, and, having skinned it and lacerated the
flesh, they throw it down. And, when it reaches the
bottom of the valley whereon the diamonds lie, the
stones adhere to the moist flesh. From the depths of the
sky descends the watching vulture of the giant kind, and
this bird, seizing the carcass in its talons, soars with it
to the mountain tops ; whereupon the merchants spring
out and frighten the bird away with loud cries, and
then take the stones adhering to the meat and bear them
to their own country. I had my whole life long regarded
this story with a half-shut eye, but now, beholding the
slaughtered beast before me, and guessing full well the
meaning of its presence there, I said within myself,
" By Allah ! no marvel is past belief, for here is the
verification." I surveyed the carcass and, having measured
in a glance the distance to the mountains whence it had
descended, I gazed into the blue sky in whose depths
lurked the watching vulture. A plan of escape then
came to me and I hastened to put it into operation.
First I gathered as many diamonds as I could well
dispose within my garments. Then, unfolding my turban,

I approached the slaughtered beast, and, lying on my back, drew it over me and bound myself firmly to it.

I had not lain long in that position, with the heavy weight of the beast upon me, when a monstrous vulture came out of the sky, and, seizing upon the carcass with a loud scream, gripped it in its powerful talons and rose up and away with it and me. And it rose higher and higher with a mighty flapping of its wings, until at last it alighted on a broad ledge near the summit of the mountain—a place which, judging by the bleached bones lying on every hand, was the favourite feeding-place of these birds. This was clearly known to the merchant who had cast the carcass down, for, no sooner had the vulture deposited his burden and started to tear at the flesh, than he sprang out with loud cries and scared it away.

Half smothered by the weight of the slaughtered beast I lost no time in freeing myself, and soon I struggled to my feet and stood there with my clothes stained and polluted with its blood. When the merchant saw me his fear was great; but his disappointment was even greater when, his fear mastered by the lust of gain, he turned the carcass over and found no diamonds sticking to the flesh. Pitying him in his sad case—for he was smiting hand on hand and calling out against fate—I advanced and said, " Curse not fate, nor fear me, for I am of thy kind, and I bear with me an abundance of these stones the loss of which thou lamentest; and they are of the largest that a man can carry upborne by a vulture's wings. Of these will I give unto thee; therefore forget thy fear and bury thy disappointment."

On hearing this the merchant thanked me and prayed fervently for me and my family; and he ceased not to pray for the prolongation of my life until I had bestowed upon him the largest diamonds I could find within my garments. While he was thanking me for this there came his companions, each of whom had cast down a carcass; and, when they had heard the story of my escape, they congratulated me and bade me come with them, for they said, "By Allah! thou art greatly favoured by fate, since none but thee hath been in that valley and escaped to tell the tale."

I continued with my companions for some space, journeying from island to island and exchanging the diamonds we had acquired for rich merchandise. And, in passing through many countries unheard of in this city, I separated from them and went my way, coming at length to El-Basrah with a princely cargo of goods. Thence I journeyed to Baghdad, the Abode of Peace, and rejoined my family. Wealth I had in abundance, and I resorted to my former life of luxury, bestowing gifts and alms, wearing rich apparel, and eating and drinking with my companions.

THE THIRD VOYAGE OF SINDBAD THE SAILOR

HAVING rested for a space in Baghdad, where I lived surrounded by every happiness and delight, I began again to experience that restless desire for travel and commerce which had drawn me forth on my former voyages. When the desire grew so great that I could no longer withstand it, I set out with a large stock of merchandise and arrived at the city of El-Basrah, where I took ship, together with a goodly company of merchants, and others of high standing and repute.

For many days we sailed outwards, buying and selling among the islands; until, one day, while we were in the midst of the ocean, a storm descended upon us and blew the ship out of its course. The wind continued from one quarter with great violence, and for a day and night we were hurled before it. When morning came it abated and the master of the ship looked forth on every hand to ascertain where we were. Suddenly he uttered a loud cry and plucked his beard. "God preserve us!" he said. "The gale hath driven us to an evil fate. See! yonder is the Mountain of Apes! None hath ever come near it and escaped."

We looked and beheld a high mountain on an island, and, while we were gazing at it, and wondering where lay the danger at so great a distance, behold, the sea around us was swarming with apes which had swum out from the island. They were hideous black beasts, not of large size, but of malignant aspect; and so great was their number that we were powerless to stand against them. They climbed up the sides of the ship and seized upon the ropes, which they severed with their sharp teeth so the sails were powerless and the vessel drifted with tide and wind to the shore. There we were seized by the apes and set on the land, after which they returned to the ship and bent fresh ropes and set the sails and departed over the sea we knew not whither. But we ceased to wonder at the manner of their going, for we were in a desperate plight, since all sailors feared the Mountain of Apes and no ship would ever approach the island to rescue us.

In our wanderings through the island, eating of its fruits and drinking of its streams, we came at length to an open space in which stood a house of gigantic size. The walls and the folding doors of ebony were very lofty, and, when we walked into an immense apartment—for the doors were open—we found everything within it of a corresponding size. The cooking utensils were large enough to cook an ox whole, and, on the couch at the upper end, a hundred men might sit with comfort. But no occupant could we find, so we seated ourselves and rested for a while, and then we slept.

It was about sunset when we were awakened suddenly by a loud noise and a trembling of the earth; and lo, we beheld coming from the farther end of the apartment a gigantic being in the shape of a man. His skin was black, and his eyes blazed like fire; two gleaming tusks protruded from his great mouth, his enormous ears drooped to his shoulders, and his nails were like the sharp claws of a beast of prey. We were stricken with great fear at the approach of this frightful being so that we could neither move nor cry out while he advanced to the couch

A MIGHTY FISH

(*Page* 201)

and disposed his huge limbs thereon. Then, on turning
his head, he caught sight of us and arose and came
towards us. As I was nearest to his hand he seized
me, and, taking me from the ground, turned me over and
over in his palm, feeling my limbs to see if they were fat.
But, by the grace of God (whose name be exalted!) I
was lean and wasted with fatigue and affliction; so he
set me down and seized another, whom he turned over
and felt in the same manner. He, too, was lean, and
he let him go; but he took one after another until he
came to the master of the ship—a big man and fat. With
him he was satisfied. Then, seeing what he was about to
do, we hid our eyes, and did not look again until the
ogre, having cooked and eaten our master, threw his bones
upon a heap of others on one side of the apartment.
Afterwards he arose and laid himself down upon the
couch and slept, and his snoring was like the roll of
thunder.

One said, " By Allah! by Allah! let us kill him!"
and he proposed a plan. "Listen, O my brothers!" I
said on hearing this; " if we seek to kill him let us first
prepare some rafts on which to escape, for we may fail of
our purpose; and on these rafts we can at worst be
drowned, which is better than being roasted." They
answered me, " Thou art right!" So we set to work and
gathered stout pieces of wood and carried them to the
seashore, where we constructed rafts and stowed food
upon them in readiness for a hasty departure. Then
we returned to the giant's house to carry out our plan.

The sound of his snoring told us he still slept, so we
took two sharp-pointed iron spits and heated the points
red-hot in the fire. Then we approached him cautiously,
and, at a given signal, thrust the red-hot points one into
each of his eyes, and bore upon the spits with our combined

weight. He arose with a mighty roar, and we fled right and left; for, his sight being destroyed, we feared his blind rage. He searched for us, but, not finding us, he groped for the door, and went forth uttering loud cries which shook the earth.

In great haste, and lashed by mortal fear, we gained the seashore and launched the rafts; but, scarcely had we gained the water, when we saw the ogre approaching, led by a female more gigantic and more hideous than himself. We swam out, pushing the rafts before us; but they hurled great rocks after us, and many of our number were killed. Three alone, including myself, escaped, and, after much stress and peril, reached another island, and there, when night came on, we slept, but only to awaken to fresh terrors. Lo! in the act of coiling round us was a serpent of enormous size, its folds contracting and its head raised to strike. At sight of this, another and myself were more nimble than our companion, for we sprang clear of the serpent's embrace while he was seized in the huge jaws and slowly swallowed with a horrible crackling of bones. And we mourned our companion and went thenceforth in fear for ourselves. Dreading to sleep again on the ground we climbed a high tree, and, binding ourselves each in a safe position with our turbans, we slept fitfully. But alas! God hath given to all serpents the wisdom of the Evil One. That night the serpent mounted the tree, and, seizing my companion, proceeded to swallow him, while I looked on in helpless fear. Then, in descending the tree, it coiled its vast bulk round the trunk and I heard my companion's bones crack within its paunch.

When morning had come I descended from the tree feeling that my safest course was to drown myself in the waves, for where else could I hide that the serpent could not find me ? But life is sweet, and I pondered long upon a cunning plan to protect myself. Then, repairing to the seashore, I selected some pieces of wood from the raft, and took them to a dry place. Towards evening, when I had eaten of the fruits of the island and drunk of its streams, I bound a long piece of wood crosswise upon the soles of my feet and another crosswise upon my head ; I secured a wide flat piece to my right side, another to my left side, and another to the front of my body ; and there, having thrust my arms under the side pieces, I lay encased. And, as the evening wore on, the serpent saw me, and drew near ; but it could not swallow me because of the pieces of wood. All through the night it tried to come at me, attempting in all ways to effect its purpose ; but in every way it failed, while I lay like a dead man, gazing in speechless horror at the terrible creature. And it ceased not in its efforts to engulf me till morning broke, when it went its way consumed with rage and vexation. Then I freed myself from the pieces of wood and arose, trembling in every limb, but thanking God for my deliverance ; for, look you, I was sorely tried by what I had endured from that serpent.

Not many hours later I had the good fortune to espy a ship far out upon the sea, and, as it was making as if to pass a headland of the island somewhat closely, I ran with all speed and established myself on the farthest point. There I waved my unfolded turban to attract the notice of those on the vessel. At last they saw me, and came and took me on board.

The master of the ship, seeing me without merchandise, came to me, and, taking compassion upon my poor condition, told me of some goods in the hold which belonged to a man whom they had lost during the voyage. He offered me these goods to sell so that, when an account had been rendered to the owner's family in Baghdad, there would be a recompense for my trouble and service. I thanked him gladly for this, and he ordered the goods to be brought up. And lo! when I saw the bales, I knew them, and showed how they were marked with the name of Sindbad the Sailor. Then, seeing that they were perplexed, I shouted in my excitement, " Do you not hear me? *I* am Sindbad the Sailor, and these are my goods!"

The remainder of this, my third voyage, was occupied in buying and selling among the islands on the way to El-Basrah, whence, in good time, laden with wealth and rich merchandise, I proceeded to Baghdad to dwell in peace again, surrounded by my family and friends. Here, for a season, charmed with every delight, I forgot the perils and horrors I had endured. But the longing for travel and adventure found me out again, impelling me to undertake a fourth voyage; and the events of this— more marvellous than those of the preceding voyages, O Sindbad the Landsman—I will narrate to you to-morrow.

THE FOURTH VOYAGE OF SINDBAD THE SAILOR

Led by the desire to associate with other races, and to buy and sell for gain—for the soul is prone to evil— I departed from Baghdad with many precious bales, and set sail from El-Basrah in a large ship on which a company of other merchants embarked in like fashion.

For many days we had a pleasant journey among the islands, and all went well with us until, on reaching the wider sea beyond, a mighty wind came up against us. The sails were rent, the masts were blown away, we sprang a leak, and slowly the vessel began to sink. We gave ourselves up for lost, and, indeed, when the waves passed over us and we sank, many perished. But, in the seething turmoil, it was my good fortune to be cast against a broad plank, which I seized and held. Others were struggling for life near by and I was able to draw some of them to me. Sore buffeted as we were by wind and wave we mounted that plank and sat astride of it. At dawn on the following day the sea cast us like dead men upon an island, where, for many hours, we lay exhausted.

That night we slept upon the shore, and in the morning we arose strengthened and invigorated. When we had broken our fast we set ourselves to explore the island, and had not gone far in this before we came to a great building. As we stood at the door of this, wondering who dwelt within, a party of naked men came out, and without a word, seized us and led us into a spacious

apartment, where we found ourselves standing before their
King. He commanded us to be seated, and they brought
us food of a strange kind, such as we had never seen.
My companions ate largely of this, but my stomach revolted
at it and I ate but little—a thing which preserved me from
a terrible fate. For, as my companions ate, they became
mad with a ravenous hunger, and ate more and more.
Presently they were given coco-nut oil to drink, and,
when they had swallowed it, their eyes rolled in their
heads, and they continued to eat it a frenzy horrible to
behold.

I was consumed with fear at these things and said
within myself, "This is a tribe of the Magi and their King
is a ghoul!" As I observed them attentively I remembered a story of these people : how they seize on travellers
and set this loathsome food before them to eat, and give
them the oil to drink, so that they swell out and eat more
and more until they are fattened to an enormous degree
and their minds are rendered like those of idiots ; whereupon, in due time, they kill and roast them and serve
them up as food to their King.

As for myself, as soon as I observed that I was a
failure in that I would not fatten, and that none took
heed of me nor marked my coming or my going, I arose
in the night and crept away among the trees surrounding
the King's dwelling. Then, when morning came, I went
forth with a heart of fear, knowing not what fresh terror
I should encounter. In my wanderings back and forth
I came about midday to a stretch of green pasture, where
I beheld with sorrow my late companions grazing on all
fours, and fattening like beasts for the slaughter, while
the beastherd sat upon a rock and piped on an oaten
reed. I breathed a silent farewell to them as to those I
should never see again, and turned sadly away.

Journeying in this way I came at length to a grove of pepper trees, and there were men at work in it, gathering the berries. Their aspect seemed to me to be peaceable, so I exposed myself, and they approached me and pressed upon me, asking my name and whence I had come, for my aspect excited their curiosity.

When they had finished their work at the setting of the sun they took me with them to the seashore, and I accompanied them in their vessel to an island, not far distant, where they brought me to their King. And, there, before them and his court, at his command I narrated my adventures since leaving Baghdad, at which his interest was kindled, and he bade me sit with him and eat. And I did so gladly, for my body was thin and meagre, and my vigour was sorely wanting. After that, having shown my gratitude to the King and offered praise to God for His saving grace, I rose, and, with the King's permission, went forth into his city. It was a well-conditioned, flourishing place, thronged with buyers and sellers; and there was an abundance of food and rich merchandise.

As day followed day and time drew on I had cause to rejoice at my arrival in that city, for I found favour with the King, and he magnified me over his people and his great men.

I was yet to learn that he had a further favour in store. One day, while I was sitting at his right hand discussing affairs of state, he looked at me intently and said, " I would marry thee to a woman of high rank among us—one possessed of great beauty and wealth—so that thou mayest continue to dwell with us in pleasure and comfort and with a good heart. Thus shalt thou advantage greatly and receive every good thing at my hands; wherefore, refuse me not, nor oppose my wish."

I remained silent, for I was overwhelmed by his proposal and the stress of bashfulness it brought to my face. Seeing this, he rallied me and said, "Art thou dumb? Is not thy heart with us?" Then of a sudden I replied, "O King! Thy words took away my breath. As thou commandest, so I obey."

Pleased at my compliance the King immediately ordered his officials to bring the lady and the witnesses, and forthwith I was married to her with the King's blessing and the acclamation of all his Court. She was of surpassing loveliness, and she brought me a dowry of abundant wealth and possessions. But there is no strength nor power but in God, and He orders the fates of men as He will. On an evil day a great fear suddenly came to me by reason of a thing which I will make known to you.

A companion of mine suffered a bereavement in that his wife died; whereupon I went to him, and mourned with him, saying, "Take heart, O brother; God will fill her place to thee with one far better." But he continued to weep, saying, "Alas! How can I marry another when this very day I depart this life?" "Nay," said I, "that is not within reason, for thou art in good health and not like to die." He then raised his head and dried his tears, and said to me very slowly, "Hear me, O my brother! Knowest thou not that, to-day, they will bury my wife, and that they will bury me also in the same tomb with her? For such is our custom. When husband or wife is buried the other must be buried also, so that neither may continue to enjoy life alone."

"By Allah!" said I, smiting palm on palm, "this custom is wholly vile, and it toucheth me closely."

And on my return I went in to the King with grief and fear gnawing at my heart. "O King!" I said, "Tell

me why is this : that ye bury the living with the dead ? "
Said he, " O my son, it is the custom of our country and
has descended to us from our ancestors : husband and
wife are one, in death as in life." And I answered him
with a question that concerned me nearly. " O my lord,"
I said, " and the stranger that sojourneth with thee : if
his wife die, do ye treat him in like manner ? " " Yea,"
he replied, " in like manner." Then I departed from him
in grief and mourning lest I should perchance be bereft of
my wife. In vain did I say to myself, " Be comforted !
Maybe thou wilt die before her—none knoweth." In
vain did I give myself up to my manifold occupations.
The fear was not to be dispelled.

And, within a short time, what I had feared came to
pass. My wife was stricken with a fever, and, when I
had reason to hope she would recover, she suddenly
relapsed and died. My grief at this was overwhelming,
but, as if to add to it, there came many to condole with
me on her death and to mingle their tears with mine for
that I should soon be departing this life. The King himself came and commiserated with me on my most unhappy
fate. And he said, " There is no strength nor power in
any but God. Farewell, O my son ! "

And they prepared my wife for burial, arraying her
in her richest garments and her finest jewels. But, when
they carried her to the burial place and cast her down
into the pit, and all my companions pressed upon me to
bid me farewell, my gorge rose and I cried out upon them
that their custom was vile. Loudly I spoke my bitter
mind on the abominable nature of this thing ; they would
not listen, but took me by force and lowered me into the
pit, together with seven cakes and a pitcher of water.
And when I had reached the floor of a vast cavern they
called down to me : " Untie the ropes that we may draw

29

them up!" I answered, "Draw me up with them!"
" Nay, nay," they replied, " we do but follow our custom."
" To the ravens with you and your custom!" I retorted,
for I had no stomach for this proceeding. Then, as I
steadily refused to loose the ropes, they at last threw
them down upon me, and, having closed the mouth of
the pit, went their way.

Now was I in worse plight than I had ever been. On
that cavern floor there were the bodies and bleached bones
of those that had died a natural death cheek by jowl with
those who had perished in the fulfilment of this abominable
custom. And I said to myself, " Better to remain single
and live, than to marry and be buried alive."

Nevertheless, knowing not night from day, I kept
myself from death by eating sparingly of the cakes and
drinking some of the water, for I was in no mood to die
in so vile a manner after having come through great perils
by mountain and sea. At length, when I had eaten all
the cakes and drunk all the water, and hunger and thirst
began to cry out within me, I arose and wandered to and
fro in the cavern, stumbling and falling over dead bodies
and biting the dust of bones that had crumbled long since.
By dint of much groping in the dark I at length found
the wall of the cavern, and, selecting therein a cavity
free from bones and corpses, I stretched myself and
slept.

I was awakened later as if by hunger and thirst knocking
at the door; and, while I sat in gloom thinking of the
plenty in Baghdad—fool that I was to leave it!—I heard
a sudden noise. Looking forth from my cavity, I saw
that the stone had been removed from the opening of
the cavern and a dead body was being lowered. It was
the body of a man and after him was let down the living
body of his wife. She was weeping and wailing for him

and for herself. Then the mouth of the cavern was closed again and all was dark and silent save for the wailing of the woman echoing through the cavern. " Alas ! " she cried, " that I should die this lingering death ! Had I the means to end my life, then would I do it. Would that there were one here to slay me ! "

When I heard this I remembered that I had never been able to resist the pleadings of a woman. So I arose, and, taking a stout leg-bone in my hand, I slew her according to her desire. And I took her seven cakes and the pitcher of water, which she would no longer need, and, retiring to my cavity, I ate and drank. This thing occurred many times during my sojourn in that cavern, for a number of married men and women chanced to die. And, though they did not always cry out for me to slay them, I knew their prayer beforehand and answered it speedily. Thus the cakes and the water bequeathed to me stayed my spirit and I continued to live.

Time passed slowly, but yet it passed. I had no other means of measuring it except to call an hour a day and a day a year. And I was weary to death of it all when an unwonted thing occurred. I was awakened suddenly from sleep by a noise at the far end of the cavern. Then I heard footsteps as of some beast. I arose, and, arming myself with a stout bone, advanced upon the intruder ; but it heard me and fled from me, and I could not come at it. Yet, as I followed its footsteps, I saw its form darken a pin-spot of daylight at the end of a crevice of the cavern. This gave me a glimmer of hope, for, where that beast had passed, I myself might pass, and so gain the outer air. Over jagged points of rock I clambered towards that opening, now losing sight of it, and now gaining view of it again, until at last I reached it and found that it was indeed a communication with the outer country.

With some difficulty I forced my way through it and climbed down by a perilous pathway to the seashore.

I had escaped from the sepulchre of the living and the dead, and I praised God for the sight of the sky and the sea; but, when I had looked into my position and found behind me an impassable precipice, before me the wide stretching sea, and above me the dome of heaven, I sat down on the shore with my head on my knees and said within myself, " There is no way out ! I cannot scale the sheer cliff, neither can I tread the fishes' pathways in the sea, nor walk in the tracks made by birds in the air. There is no way out ! "

But God, in His infinite mercy, willed it otherwise, for one day, sitting sadly on the shore as was my wont, I espied a vessel on the sea. Hope surged high within my breast and I arose and stripped myself of a white garment and mounted it on a staff and ran wildly to and fro, waving it above me. And, when my signal was observed, the vessel stayed its course and sent a boat ashore.

Our journey from that place, where I had suffered so much, took us from island unto island towards the city of El-Basrah. As we proceeded, the places where we cast anchor grew more and more familiar to me, and, as of old, I bought and sold as merchants do. At length we arrived at the city of El-Basrah. There, in the bosom of my family, and surrounded by my companions, I returned to my former habit of life.

THE EPISODE OF THE OLD MAN OF THE SEA

(Page 233)

THE FIFTH VOYAGE OF SINDBAD THE SAILOR

LOOKING back from the position of safety and comfort to which I had returned I came in time to make light of the perils I had encountered and the sufferings I had endured. And, moreover I had conceived the wish to become the owner of a ship, for thus the gain accruing from a voyage to other lands would be so much greater.

Having considered the matter deeply, I arose from my life of luxury and ease and departed with many bales of merchandise for the city of El-Basrah. There in the river I found at length a splendid vessel, which I purchased. I found a master and a crew, over whom I set my own trusty servants; and, having secured a goodly company of merchants as passengers, I embarked their bales and mine, and we set sail. We worked our way outwards, calling at island after island, and doing the usual business that merchants find in those places, until one day we came to a large uninhabited island.

Here, while I was engaged in matters concerning the vessel, the merchants landed and, as I afterwards learned, they found there the great egg of a rokh, such as I had met with on a former voyage. Mistaking it for a deserted structure, and, failing to find an entrance, they had amused themselves by casting stones at it, so that it broke; whereupon a young rokh came forth from the shell. And they set upon this monstrous chicken in its helpless condition, and slew it, and brought great slabs of its flesh back to the ship.

The vengeance of the rokh was sudden and dire. When it saw that its egg had been broken and its young one destroyed it flew above us, looking down at the ship and shrieking in a voice that filled the sky. On this it was joined by its mate, and the two circled round us, their hoarse cries of rage falling like thunder on the sea. In great fear I bade the master and the sailors hoist the sails and seek safety in flight.

Then, as soon as we began to draw off from the island, the rokhs left us and flew inland, so that we thought we had made good our escape. But soon they reappeared and came after us, each bearing in its talons a huge mass of rock. One of them flew above us and dropped the rock, so that we saw death descending upon us. But the great mass missed the ship by a narrow space. Then the other rokh dropped the rock from its talons, and fate ordained that it struck the ship astern with a mighty crash. Amid cries of fear and despair we sank into the sea, and all seemed lost.

When my mind returned to me, I found myself on the shore of an island sitting upon a plank, which, it seemed, had borne me hither. That I had fought against wind and wave I knew, for I was wellnigh exhausted. I could do nothing more than drag myself painfully to a sheltered spot, where I rested and slept.

When I arose later in the day, I was refreshed ; and, having found both fruit and water, I ate and drank and my strength returned to me. I went forth upon the island, and to and fro in it, but I found no other's footprint on the shore, nor any sign of human habitation from coast to coast. But that there *was* a dweller there I was soon to learn, and to my cost.

It was on the following day towards evening, when I was walking among the trees, that I came upon an old man sitting on the bank of a stream. He was a comely old man, with flowing silver locks and an ample white beard. He was clothed, from the waist downward, with the leaves of trees threaded together. As I regarded him for some moments I felt that his whole aspect betokened a disposition of simplicity and mild benevolence. Advancing upon the bank I spoke to him, but he shook his head sadly and sighed ; and I saw that his speech was gone. Then he made signs with his hands as if to say, " Mount me upon thy neck and carry me across the stream."

I felt kindly disposed towards this mild and gentle old man, and wished to do him a service ; so I mounted him upon my neck and took him across the stream. " Now," I said, " thou canst dismount when it pleaseth thee ! " But, instead of dismounting, he wound his legs still more closely round my neck, and pressed his feet into my chest, so that I cried out with pain and rage and attempted to throw him from my shoulders. But my frantic efforts were in vain ; he stuck like a leech, and I could not dislodge him. Indeed, he clung so tight that he nearly throttled me, and I fell to the ground exhausted. Then he belaboured me sorely with his feet until I arose with him again, and, in this way, he compelled me to obey him.

For many days I was ridden hither and thither at the will of this obstinate old fellow, who, though he could not torment me with speech, was truculent enough in his manner. And I reproached myself for having desired to do him a service, saying constantly in my mind, " By Allah ! never again while living will I do a service to any ! "

30

At length one day the old man guided and belaboured me into a space on the island where pumpkins grew in abundance. While he was eating some of these I took others that were ripe, and, having cleaned out the seeds and coarse matter through a small aperture, filled them with the juice of grapes; then I filled up the apertures and laid the pumpkins in the sun. Thus in a few days I procured pure wine, and, every day thereafter, while the old man on my neck ate of the pumpkins, I drank of the wine until I became intoxicated, and laughed and sang and danced about with him among the trees. And when, with fist and heel, he desired to know the cause of this, I showed him the wine that I had made. Seeing that its effect upon me was so agreeable he sought to achieve the same happy result by drinking largely of it himself, so that he grew hilarious and broke a pumpkin over my head, rocking and rolling in his seat with laughter. Then, as he continued to drink, he gradually lost control of his limbs and lolled from side to side; whereupon I grasped his feet and unwound them from my neck and threw him on the ground. And so at last, to rid the earth of such a monster, I slew him, and left him there for the vultures.

After this, happiness returned to me and I went about the island like one relieved of a heavy burden, as indeed I had been. And day by day I sat by the sea watching for a vessel. But I lived upon the island many days before at last I saw a ship approach and cast anchor off the shore. When the passengers had landed I ran towards them and welcomed them, answering their many questions respecting my condition. They listened to my story with great amazement. Then some one said, " This old man of whom thou speakest is surely he whom they call the Old Man of the Sea. He hath ridden many to death, and none hath escaped but thee. Therefore, praise God for thy deliverance."

They took me to the ship and set food before me, and, after I had eaten, they brought me some clean clothes and I clad myself decently. As the ship set sail for El-Basrah my thoughts went before it to Baghdad, The Abode of Peace.

Once more in the lap of luxury, and reposing in the bosom of my family, I returned to my former life of revelry and ease, and soon forgot the hardships I had endured.

THE SIXTH VOYAGE OF SINDBAD THE SAILOR

On a day when I was living happily in Baghdad, having forgotten the perils and dangers of my former voyages, I was sitting at ease in my garden when a party of merchants came to me, and their tales of travel aroused within my bosom a great longing to engage again in the hazardous delights of those things. I pondered long upon the matter, and, though I had said within myself, "Never will I set forth again," I found that my mind was made up in spite of me. Therefore I set about collecting merchandise, and, having packed a goodly number of bales, I departed for El-Basrah, where I took ship with a company of merchants and others of high repute.

The outward voyage was pleasant and fortunate, and we did as others do, buying and selling and amusing ourselves in different cities. But there came a day of disaster, when the master of the ship suddenly discovered that we had wandered from our course, and had lost our reckoning. He plucked his beard and smote his breast, and cried out in despair that we had sailed into an unknown sea, where dire perils awaited us. And so it proved, for not long afterwards, while we were sailing in a calm sea, a sudden wind burst upon us and, before the sails could be loosed, the rudder was broken and the ship drifted and was driven at last upon the sides of a high mountain rising up to heaven. She was dashed to pieces by the violence of the waves, and, from that terrible wreck, few

survived. There were some others besides myself who
clung to the sides of the mountain, and, by tooth and
nail, climbed to a place of safety.

Little by little, when the tide receded, we made our
way down among the crags until we came to a strip of seashore, and from this point we could see that the island was
of large size, its interior being sheltered from storms by
the front of the mountain. But what took our wonder was
this : on the seashore was amassed the wealth of a thousand
wrecks. And this was not all, for, when we proceeded
through the island, we found a spring of pure ambergris
overflowing into the sea ; and by this the whales are
attracted, but when they have swallowed it and dived to
the depths of the sea it turns in their stomachs and they
eject it, so that it rises to the surface in solid lumps such
as are found by sailors. But the ambergris that is cast
about the opening of the spring melts in the heat of the
sun, and its perfume is blown about the island, wafted
sweet upon the breeze like fragrant musk.

When we had explored the island and wondered at the
many strange things it contained, we searched among the
wreckage on the shore and found some few barrels of
preserved meats, and on these we stayed our hunger.
With the provisions on the shore and the fruit we secured
on the island we were in no danger of starvation, but a
kind of fever seized upon our company and one after
another sickened and died. This was a time of stress
and despair. Day after day the living buried the dead
until there was only one left, and that one was I.

But God in His mercy led my footsteps forth and I
roamed in the island, restless for the end. In my wanderings I came to a river gushing forth out of the side of a
mountain, and, after flowing for a space between banks of
verdure in a valley, entering again another mountain.

—" The King of Sarandib sends greeting. Peace be on thee, O Brother, from the King of Sarandib, who commands a thousand elephants, and in whose palace are ten thousand jewels. By the bearer of this we send thee a gift, for we have a deep affection for thee. The gift is all too trifling, but we beseech thee to accept it graciously and reply to us. Peace be upon thee! " The present with which I was entrusted was a goblet of ruby, the inside of which was set with sparkling diamonds and priceless pearls—truly a kingly gift.

Having bade farewell to the King and such of his people that I had associated with I embarked in a large ship which was bound for El-Basrah. In good time we reached that port and I journeyed up the river to Baghdad.

My first thought was to deliver the letter and the gift into the hands of the Khalifeh. So I lost no time in approaching him and fulfilling my pledge to the King of Sarandib. He was greatly pleased with the letter, and, when he saw the sparkling goblet of ruby and precious stones, he was filled with delight.

He then thanked me for my faithful service and bestowed rich gifts upon me, and bade me seek my own house in peace and content. There in the bosom of my family I lived at ease, having put behind me the perils of travel and set fixedly before me the determination never to seek them again.

THE SEVENTH VOYAGE OF SINDBAD THE SAILOR

WHILE I was sitting one day thinking on this and saying within myself, " I am here in the Abode of Peace and Allah be praised ! I shall never quit it for the haunts of trouble " ; lo ! there came a messenger summoning me to the Khalifeh. I arose and followed him, and presently I was before his majesty, saluting him and kissing the ground. " Welcome, O Sindbad ! " he said. " Know that I have a matter of importance for thee to execute." " Sire," I answered, " I am thy slave."

Then the Khalifeh unfolded to me his wish : which was that I should go to the King of Sarandib bearing a letter and a gift.

It was not for me to disobey the command of the Prince of the Faithful, and I bowed my head in submission. I took from his hands the account of the items composing the gift, together with a letter and a sum of money for my expenses ; and, bidding him farewell, went forth, saying to myself that fate was against me.

The Khalifeh's gift to the King of Sarandib was one of great magnificence. First there was a splendid white horse, the equal of which was not to be found in the length and breadth of Arabia. Its saddle and trappings were adorned with gold and set with brilliant jewels. Then, in addition to this, there were a priceless robe, fit for the king of all the earth ; a great quantity of rich stuffs from Egypt and Greece, and a wonderful crystal goblet of such a kind

31

not in their career until they came to a valley in which were a great number of elephants' bones and teeth and tusks. On a heap of these the king-elephant set me down very gently; and, after that, he and the others turned and walked away, leaving me there.

I looked about in the valley and saw a wealth of gleaming white tusks on every hand, and I said within myself, " The elephants liked not the death of one of their number every day, and they have done this to show how I may come by an abundance of tusks without further slaughter."

Then I found my way back over a great distance to the abode of my master. He welcomed me as one returned from the dead, for, when he had found the tree torn up by the roots, he had concluded that the elephants had made an end of me. I told him what had befallen me and described the position of the valley where the tusks lay. When he heard this he was greatly excited and lost no time in mounting me behind him on an elephant and setting forth to find the spot where so much wealth was stored. We reached the valley without mishap and I showed my master the ivory, at sight of which his joy knew no bounds. We then laded the elephant with as much as he could carry and returned with it to the house.

This adventure of mine placed me in a most favourable light in my master's eyes; and, because I had been the means of revealing to him a source of enormous wealth, he set me free and gave me permission to return to my own country. He was even better than his word, for, not many days later, he set me on board a vessel bound for El-Basrah and presented me with a large sum of money for my passage and expenses, together with many bales of merchandise. And my return journey was very fortunate. The traffic I did at the different cities on the way brought me great profit, and I bought many rare things suitable for gifts.

On my arrival at Baghdad I went in to the Khalifeh and told him all that had befallen me; and he was so astonished thereat, and so delighted at my return, that he commanded his scribes to write my story in letters of gold. And he said to me " O Sindbad, my son; thou hast done well, and now thou shalt have the wish of thine heart and keep thy vow; for, unless thou so desirest, thou shalt go forth no more upon the sea."

*   *   *   *   *

This, O Sindbad the Landsman, is the end of the story of my voyages; and now, as I have conceived an affection for thee, thou shalt dwell with me and be my boon companion; and we shall pass our lives together in a state of the utmost joy and happiness, strengthened by God (whose name be exalted!) the Great! the Omnipotent Creator of sea and land!

ALADDIN AND THE WONDERFUL LAMP

ONCE upon a time, in a far city of Cathay, there dwelt a poor tailor who had an only son named Aladdin. This boy was a born ne'er-do-well, and persistently resisted all his father's efforts to teach him a trade by means of which he would be able in future to earn a livelihood. Aladdin would sooner play at knuckle-bones in the gutter with others as careless as himself than he would set his mind to honest business; and, as to obeying his parents in the smallest matter, it was not in his nature. Such was this boy Aladdin, and yet—so remarkable is the favour of fate—he was strangely predestined for great things.

Stricken with grief because of the waywardness and idle conduct of his son the father fell ill and died, and the mother found great difficulty in supporting herself, to say nothing of the worthless Aladdin as well. While she wore the flesh off her bones in the endeavour to obtain a meagre subsistence Aladdin would amuse himself with his fellow urchins of the street, only returning home to his meals. In this way he continued until he was fourteen years of age, when his extraordinary destiny took him by the hand, and led him, step by step, through adventures so wonderful that words can scarce describe them.

One day he was playing in the gutter with his ragged companions, as was his wont, when a Moorish Dervish came by, and, catching sight of Aladdin's face, suddenly stopped and approached him. This Dervish was a sorcerer who had discovered many hidden secrets by his black art; in fact, he was on the track of one now; and, by the look on his face as he scrutinized Aladdin's features, it seemed that the boy was closely connected with his quest.

The Dervish beckoned to one of the urchins and asked him who Aladdin was, who his father was, and indeed all about him. Having thus learned the whole history of the boy and his family the Dervish gave his informer some coins and sent him away to spend them. Then he approached Aladdin and said to him, " Boy, I seem to recognize in thee a family likeness. Art thou not the tailor's son ? " Aladdin answered him that he was, and added that his father was dead.

On hearing this the Dervish cried out with grief and embraced Aladdin, weeping bitterly. The boy was surprised at this and inquired the cause of such sorrow. " Alas ! " replied the Dervish with tears running down his cheeks, " my fate is an unhappy one Boy, I have come from a distant country to find my brother, to look upon his face again, and to cheer and comfort him ; and now thou tellest me he is dead." He took Aladdin's face in his hands and gazed searchingly upon it as he continued : " Boy, I recognize my brother's features in thine ; and, now that he is dead, I will find comfort in thee."

Aladdin looked up at him in wonder, for he had never been told that he had an uncle ; indeed, he was inclined to doubt the truth of the matter ; but, when the Dervish took ten pieces of gold from his purse and placed them in his hand, all doubt was out of the question, and he rejoiced at having found so rich an uncle. The Dervish then asked him concerning his mother and begged him to show him the way to her house. And, when Aladdin had showed him, he gave the boy more gold and said, " Give this to thy mother with my blessing, and say that her brother-in-law, who has been absent forty years, has returned and will visit her to-morrow to weep with her over the place where his brother is buried." With this he departed, and Aladdin ran to his mother to tell her the news.

On the morrow the Dervish sought Aladdin in the street where he had seen him the day before, and found him there among his disreputable friends. Taking him aside he kissed him and embraced him ; then, placing ten gold pieces in his hand, he said, " Hasten now to thy mother and give her these gold pieces and say that her brother-in-law would come to sup at her house this night."

So Aladdin left him and ran home to his mother with the gold pieces and the message. Then the widow busied herself and prepared for the coming of this new-found relative. She bought rich food, and borrowed from the neighbours such dishes, utensils and napery as she required. When the supper was ready, and the widow was about to send Aladdin to hasten the guest, the Dervish entered, followed by a slave bearing fruit and wine, which he set down, and then went his way. The Dervish, weeping bitterly, saluted the widow and immediately fell to asking questions about the departed.

Then, when he was comforted and they all sat at supper together, the Dervish turned to Aladdin and asked him if he knew any art or trade. At this Aladdin hung his head, and, as he was too ashamed to answer, his mother dried her tears and answered for him. " Alack ! " she said, " he is nothing but an idler. He spends his time as thou didst find him, playing with ragamuffins in the street, and is never at home except at meal times. And I—I

am an old woman and ugly through toil and hardship, and
grief at his behaviour. O my brother-in-law! It is
he who should provide for me, not I for him."

" I am grieved to hear this of thee," said the Dervish,
turning to Aladdin; " for thou art no longer a child.
Wouldst thou like to be a merchant?" he asked. " If
so I will give thee a shop with all kinds of merchandise,
and thou shalt buy and sell and get gain, and rise to a
position of importance."

At this Aladdin clapped his hands with glee, and his
mother was rejoiced. And she chid her boy for his own
good, and counselled him straitly to obey his uncle in
all things. The Dervish also gave Aladdin much sound
advice on the conduct of trade, so that the boy's head
was bursting with buying and selling, and he could not
sleep that night for dreams of rich stuffs, and bales of
merchandise. At last, when the Dervish arose and took
his departure, promising to return for Aladdin on the
morrow and take him to buy his merchant's dress, the
wizard felt that he had proved himself undoubtedly
the best of brothers-in-law, and the best of uncles.

True to his word the Dervish came on the morrow,
and Aladdin, holding him affectionately by the hand, went
with him forth to the market. There they entered a
shop full of the finest materials, and the Dervish asked
to be shown some dresses such as a wealthy merchant
might wear. The owner of the shop laid a great variety
before him and the Dervish said, " Now, my son, choose
what dress you like." This delicate favour of choice
pleased Aladdin greatly, for it seemed that he had now at
last reached the age of discretion. He picked out one that
he liked, and the Dervish paid the price without any
attempt at bargaining. Then they went together to the
Hammam, and, when they had bathed and rested, Aladdin

clothed himself in his new dress and came forth in great delight, kissing his uncle's hand and thanking him again and again.

After they had rested the Dervish suggested a walk, and he led Aladdin through garden after garden until they came to the confines of the city, beyond which stood a high hill. " Shall we return, O my uncle ? " said Aladdin, who was in no mood for climbing the hill. " There are no more gardens outside the city." " Nay," replied the Dervish, " on the hill-side is the loveliest garden of all. Bear up, my son, and be a man ; we shall soon be there." And, as they went, he beguiled the boy with anecdotes, so that Aladdin forgot both the length of the way and his weariness.

At last they came to a place on the hill-side where the Dervish paused and looked about him, saying to himself, " This is the spot I have journeyed so far to find." But to Aladdin he said, " Rest here awhile, O my son, and, when thou art refreshed, gather some wood and we will make a fire ; then, if thou wish to see a most wonderful thing, I will show thee that which will take thy breath away."

At this Aladdin's curiosity was excited, and, with no thought of resting, he began at once to gather wood. When he had collected a sufficient quantity the Dervish lighted the fire, and, taking from his wallet a little box, drew some fine powder from it and scattered it over the fire, uttering an incantation. Immediately, amid rumblings of thunder, the earth reeled and opened. At this Aladdin fled in terror, but the Dervish, powerless to effect his purpose without the boy's aid, flew after him in a rage, and smote him over the head, so that he fell to the ground stunned.

When, presently, he regained his senses, he sat up and

wits together then, my son," said the Dervish, well pleased; "and descend, for verily thou art a man of mettle, and not a child. Yea, thou, and thou only, art the rightful owner of all this great treasure. Come now!"

Filled with courage from the wizard's words, and enticed by the dazzle of untold riches, Aladdin descended the twelve steps and passed through the fourfold chamber with the utmost care lest he should touch any of the golden jars therein with so much as the fringe of his garment. When he came to the door at the far end he paused to repeat the names of his ancestors, and opened it; then, lo, before him lay a beautiful garden where the trees were laden with many coloured fruit, while sweet-voiced birds sang in the branches. He took the pathway that lay before his feet, and, as he followed it, he looked up and noticed that the trees bore, not fruit as he had supposed, but sparkling jewels flashing with many colours.

But Aladdin, though dazzled by the glitter, thought these sparkling things were but coloured glass; and it was for such that he plucked them with boyish delight until his pockets were full. "These are lovely things to play with," he said, and proceeded to fill his girdle also.

As he made his way along the garden path, plucking the bright jewels as he went, he caught sight of the alcove at the far end, and, remembering his uncle's instructions, hastened towards it. There was the stairway of forty-nine steps, and there, hanging from a crystal beam, was the Lamp. He paused, looking up at it. How should he reach it? His uncle had said that the stairway was neither for Aladdin nor for himself, and yet he saw at a glance that the only way of reaching the Lamp was by mounting seven steps of the stairway. He hesitated, then, concluding that the Lamp was the whole object of his quest, and that he must reach it at all costs, he ventured. With some misgivings he mounted the seven steps and, reaching out, took the Lamp from its fastening and descended with it. Then, emptying out the oil, he placed it securely in his bosom, saying, " Now, as my uncle said to me, with this Lamp in my bosom all is mine ! "

As Aladdin was returning along the pathway among the trees, laden with the precious jewels, fear assailed him lest his uncle would be angry at his delay, for it was borne in upon him that no great delight can come to a mortal without his having to suffer for it. Whereupon he hastened his footsteps, and, passing through the fourfold chamber without touching the golden jars—for the fear of that was still upon him—he arrived quickly at the foot of the stairway of twelve steps. Heavily weighted as he was with the jewels and the Lamp he proceeded to mount the stairs at a run. But the jewels grew heavier, and the Lamp weighed upon his bosom, so that he was exhausted by the time he was half-way up. Kneeling on the seventh step he looked up and saw the Dervish urging him on with the greatest impatience.

" Bear with me, O my uncle," he said. " I am heavily weighted and am out of breath. I will soon come to thee." Then he climbed three steps and one step more, and sank exhausted before the last, which was far higher than the others. The jewels and the Lamp oppressed him with heaviness and he could not mount that last step. " O my uncle, give me thy hand and help me up," he cried. But the wizard dare not touch him, for so the spell of fate was worded and he must abide by it. " Nay," he called down, " thou art man enough ! It is the Lamp that hampers thee. Reach up and place it on the ledge here ; then thou canst mount easily thyself."

The Dervish held out his hand expectantly for the

33

Lamp and his eyes glittered. Aladdin saw the evil light in them, and, having some mother wit, replied, " O my uncle, the Lamp is no weight at all ; it is simply that I am exhausted and this step is too high for me. Give me thy hand and help me up." " Give me the Lamp ! " cried the Dervish, holding his hand out for it, and beginning to rage. " Place it on the ledge before thee, and then I will help thee up." " Nay," returned Aladdin, growing obstinate, " if thou wilt not give me thy hand I will not give thee the Lamp, for it is in my thoughts that thou wantest the Lamp more than thou wantest me."

This enraged the Dervish to a point beyond control, and he said within himself, " If I get not the Lamp then may it perish with him ! " And, taking a box from his wallet, he threw some powder on the embers of the fire, muttering curses and incantations as he did so. Immediately a flame shot up, and its many tongues went hither and thither, licking the air. The earth shuddered and groaned with a hollow thunder ; then the marble slab closed of itself over the aperture, the hill-side rushed together above it, and all was as before, save that Aladdin was sealed within that cavern without hope of escape.

Long and loud did Aladdin call to his supposed uncle to save him from a living death ; but there was no answer to his cries, and, at last, when he was almost exhausted, he took counsel of himself and plainly saw the truth of the matter. The Dervish was no uncle of his, but a cunning wizard who had made a catspaw of him to secure treasure which, by the laws of magic and destiny, he was powerless to come at in any other way. The whole thing, from the very beginning, was a trick ; and he saw it clearly now that it was too late. The way out was sealed, and the darkness pressed heavily upon him. Frantic with the desire to escape from this dungeon he thought of the garden and the stairway in the alcove; but, when he had groped his way to the end of the passage, he found the door closed, and all his efforts failed to open it. The names of his ancestors were of no avail against the magic of the Dervish. At this he wept loudly, and continued to weep throughout the night, until his rage and despair were spent. At last he sank down exhausted on the lowest step of the stairway by which he had first descended, and, feeling himself utterly abandoned by man, he raised his hands to God, praying for deliverance from his calamity.

Now, while he was holding his hands in supplication, he felt the ring upon his middle finger—the ring which the Dervish had placed there saying, " In whatever difficulty thou mayst find thyself this ring will be thy protection ; thou hast only to—but of that I will tell thee later." The Dervish had perhaps given him the ring to gain his confidence, and had purposely omitted to reveal its secret. But now, in answer to Aladdin's prayer, the power of the ring was revealed as if by the merest chance ; for, when he felt the ring, he looked at it ; and, seeing a light from the jewel therein, he breathed upon it and rubbed it with his palm to increase its lustre. No sooner had he done this when, lo, the Slave of the Ring appeared, and gathered shape before him, first in a luminous haze, and then, gradually, in clearer and clearer contour.

" Ask what thou wilt, and it shall be done," said the apparition; " for know that I am the Slave of the Ring and the slave of him on whose finger my master placed the ring."

Aladdin, seeing before him an Efrite after the order of those invoked by the Lord Suleiman, was terrified, and his tongue clave to the roof of his mouth, so that he could not speak. But the Efrite reassured him with kindly speech.

" Thou hast only to ask," he said, " and thy wish will be fulfilled ; for, since my master's ring is on thy hand, I am thy servant."

At this Aladdin took heart, and, having considered his wish, resolved to put the matter to the test.   " O Slave of the Ring ! " he said, " my wish is that thou take me from this dungeon and place me in the light of day where the sun shines and the breezes blow—if indeed it *is* day, for here have I been for many, many hours."

Scarcely had he spoken the words when there was a clap of thunder. The cavern opened, and, by some mysterious power, he was conveyed through the opening. Then, when he sat up and looked around him, he was in the light of day upon the hill-side, and everything was as it had been when he and the Dervish had first reached the spot.

Aladdin marvelled greatly at this, and said within himself, " I wonder if it was all a dream ! "   But, when he looked at the ring upon his finger and felt the Lamp and the jewel-fruit he had gathered from the trees in the garden, he knew it was not a dream.   Besides, there was the spot where the fire had been ; and it was now but a heap of grey ashes on the ground.   Turning himself about, he saw the path by which they had ascended, and the gardens stretching below. Nothing had changed. The side of the hill which the Dervish by his magic had opened for his entrance, and the Slave of the Ring had now closed up behind him, was as it had been when he first saw it.

Seeing that he was safe and sound in the outer world, Aladdin fell on his knees and gave thanks to the most High for his deliverance from a terrible death.   Then straightway he arose and took the path that led down the hillside and through the gardens of the city in the direction of his home. At length, with wearied body, but elated mind, he reached the doorway of his dwelling, and, entering, found his mother weeping.

"Where hast thou been, my son?" she cried. "All night long I lay awake, anxious for thee; and now it is again near nightfall, and thou comest like one about to die. Where hast thou been, and where is thine uncle?"

But Aladdin could not answer her. What with utter weariness, and the joy of gaining his home once more, he fell in a swoon at her feet. Quickly she dashed water on his face and restored him. Then, when she had made him eat, she inquired gently what had befallen him.

"O my mother," said Aladdin, "how much thou art to blame! Thou gavest me over to a devil of a sorcerer who tried, by his evil arts, to compass my ruin." And thus, having vented his anger at the false conduct of the Dervish, he proceeded to tell his mother, first about the lamp and the jewel-fruit, then about all that had happened on the hill-side, from the opening of the earth by a magic spell, to the closing of it again, and his subsequent escape through the Slave of the Ring.

Then Aladdin took the Lamp and the precious stones from his bosom and placed them before his mother, albeit neither knew why the Lamp had been so coveted by the Dervish, or that the stones were more valuable than any possessed by kings.

Now, neither Aladdin nor his mother had rested for two days and two nights, so that, exhausted at length with weeping and with heaping maledictions on the Dervish, they slept; and, when they awoke, it was about noon of the following day. Aladdin's first words on pulling his wits together were to the effect that he was hungry. "Nay, O my son," replied his mother, "there is nothing to eat in the house, for thou didst eat yesterday all that there was. But stay, I have some spinning that is ready for the market. I will take and sell it and buy some food."

She was busying herself about this when Aladdin suddenly called out to her, " Mother ! bring me the Lamp, and I will take and sell that ; it will fetch more than the spinning." Now, although Aladdin and his mother knew that the Dervish had greatly coveted the Lamp, they both imagined that he had some strange reason of his own for this ; and, as the Lamp was an article that would command a ready sale, the mother quickly agreed to Aladdin's proposal and brought the Lamp to him in answer to his call. On regarding it closely, however, she observed that it was very dirty. Well knowing that it would fetch a better price if it were clean and bright, she set to work to polish it with some fine sand ; when lo, as soon as she started to rub the Lamp, the air before her danced and quivered and a chill gasp of wind smote her in the face. Then, looking up, she saw, towering above her, a being monstrous and terrible, with a fierce face in which gleamed fiery eyes beneath frowning brows. She gazed at this apparition in fear and astonishment, for she knew it was surely a powerful Efrite such as were under the power of the Lord Suleiman. Then the being spoke : " Thou hast invoked me ; what is thy wish ? " But she only gazed at him, dumb with terror. Again the awful being spoke : " Thou hast summoned me, for I am the Slave of the Lamp which is in thy hand. What is thy desire ? " At this the poor woman could no longer endure her fear, and, with a cry, she fell in a swoon.

Aladdin had heard the Efrite's words and had hastened to his mother's side. He had already seen the power of the Slave of the Ring, and he guessed that now the Slave of the Lamp had appeared, and was ready to do the bidding of the one who held the Lamp. So he quickly took it from his mother's hand, and, standing before the Efrite, plucked up courage and said, " I desire food, O Slave of the Lamp ! the finest food that ever was set before a king."

No sooner had he spoken than the Efrite vanished, but only to reappear immediately, bearing a rich tray of solid silver, on which were twelve golden dishes with fruits and meats of various kinds. There were also flagons of wine and silver goblets. As Aladdin stared in amazement at this magnificent repast the Efrite set the tray down before him and vanished in a flash. Then Aladdin turned to his mother and dashed cold water on her face, and held perfumes to her nostrils until she regained consciousness and sat up. And when she beheld the sumptuous repast set out upon the golden dishes she was greatly astonished, and imagined that the Sultan had sent it from his palace. But Aladdin, who was very hungry, fell to eating heartily ; and, while persuading his mother to eat, he would tell her nothing.

It was not until they had satisfied their hunger, and placed the remainder aside for the morrow, that Aladdin informed her what had happened. Then she questioned him, saying, " O my son, was not this the same Efrite that appeared to thee when thou wast in the cavern ? " " Nay," he answered. " That was the Slave of the Ring ; this was the Slave of the Lamp." " At all events," said she, " it was a terrible monster that nearly caused my death through fear. Promise me, O my son, that thou wilt have naught further to do with the Ring and the Lamp. Cast them from thee, for the Holy Prophet hath told us to have no traffic with devils."

" Nay, nay, O my mother," protested Aladdin ; " it

were wiser to keep them, for did not the Slave of the Ring deliver me from death ? and has not the Slave of the Lamp brought us delicious food when we were hungry ?" "That may be so," replied his mother, "but hear my words, my son ; no good thing can come of these dealings with accursed spirits, and it were better for thee to have died in the cavern than to invoke their aid." And thus she pleaded with him to cast away the Ring and the Lamp, for she was sore afraid of the power of the Evil One. But Aladdin would not undertake to do this, although, in respect for her wishes, he agreed to conceal the objects so that she might never need to look upon them. He also agreed to invoke neither of the Efrites again, unless it were a case of dire necessity. And with this his mother had to rest content.

Mother and son continued to live on the food that remained, until, in a few days, it was all gone. Then Aladdin took up one of the dishes from the tray, and, not knowing that it was of pure gold, went out to sell it and buy food with the proceeds. In the market he came to the shop of a Jew—a man of exceeding vile methods of buying and selling ; and he showed the dish to him. This Jew, as soon as he saw the dish, knew it for pure gold and glanced sharply at Aladdin to find whether he knew its value. Then, preferring that others might call him a rogue rather than that the event might prove him a fool in his own eyes, he took a single gold piece from his pocket and handed it to Aladdin.

As for Aladdin, he hastened home and gave the gold piece to his mother, begging her to buy food with it. She did so, and they ate, and were comforted. And so, from day to day, they lived on the proceeds of one dish after another, which the unregenerate Hebrew bought at cheaper and cheaper prices, saying always that the metal was

THE SULTAN AND THE VIZIER LOOKING FOR THE MAGIC PALACE
(Page 310)

inferior and that the demand for such goods was not what it used to be. And, when at last the dishes were all sold, Aladdin, who, in deference to his mother's wishes, had concealed the Lamp and the Ring against a necessitous occasion, brought forth the former and rubbed it, for so, he concluded, was the Slave invoked. His conclusion was right, for no sooner had he rubbed the Lamp than the Efrite suddenly appeared before him, immense and of terrible aspect.

" What is thy wish, O my master ? " said the Efrite ; " for I am the Slave of the Lamp and of him who holds it." " My wish," answered Aladdin, " is that you bring me another tray of food similar to the one you brought before." Immediately the Efrite vanished, and, in a moment, appeared again, bearing a tray of food exactly similar to the one he had brought before. He set this down before Aladdin and then disappeared.

And they ate and drank and were merry, the food lasting them some days. Then, when the food was all gone, Aladdin proceeded to dispose of the dishes as before. Taking one of them he went forth to find the Jew, but it chanced that on his way he passed the shop of a fair-dealing man—that is to say, not a Jew—who had no vile methods of buying and selling, but was just, and feared God. When this man saw Aladdin passing he called to him, and told him that he had frequently seen him selling things to the Jew, and warned him about it.

Then Aladdin showed him the dish of gold and he took it, and weighed it on the scales. " My son," he said, " here is the price if thou wouldst sell."

He counted out seventy gold pieces and handed them to Aladdin, who took them and thanked the merchant heartily for his honest exposure of the Jew's wickedness. And thereafter he brought the remaining dishes, and at last the tray, to that merchant, and received from him their full value; so that Aladdin and his mother were placed above want and in a comfortable position for people of their station in life.

During this time Aladdin had changed his ways greatly. He no longer consorted with the ragamuffins of the street but selected for his friends men of standing and integrity. Often he would watch the jewellers at their work, and the goods they handled; and, through knowledge thus acquired, he began to suspect that the jewel-fruit he had gathered in the garden of the cavern was not glass, as he had imagined, but real gems. By this and that, and by comparing and asking questions, he came at length to the certainty that he actually possessed the richest jewels in all the earth. The smallest among them was bigger and more sparkling by far than the largest and finest he could see in any jeweller's shop.

One day he was in the jewellers' market, taking note of things, when a herald came by, crying to all people: " Take heed! By command of the Sultan, King of the Age and Lord of the Earth, let all doors be closed, and let none come forth from shop or dwelling on pain of instant death, for the Sultan's daughter, Bedr-el-Budur cometh to the bath! Take heed! "

Now, on hearing this, a great longing arose in Aladdin's breast to look upon the face of Bedr-el-Budur, the Sultan's daughter. " All people extol her loveliness," he said to himself; " and I—even if I die for it—I will look upon her face; for something—I know not what—impels me to gaze on Bedr-el-Budur the beautiful."

Hastening to the Hammam he secreted himself behind the door so that, unobserved himself, he might see her when she came in. And presently the Sultan's daughter arrived; and, as she entered, she lifted the veil from her face, so that Aladdin saw her features clearly.

What a wondrous beauty was there! The witchery of her eyes! The ivory of her skin! The jet of her glossy tresses! These, and the swaying of her graceful body as she walked, caused Aladdin's heart to turn to water and then to spring wildly into flame.

Like one walking in a dream Aladdin went home and sat him down in dejection of spirit. For a long time he answered not his mother's questions as to what ailed him, but continued like one who had beheld a vision so lovely that it had deprived him of his senses. At last, however, he looked up, and said, " O my mother, know that until to-day I had believed that all women were of thy fashion of face, but now I find they are not; for to-day I saw the Sultan's daughter, and she is more beautiful than all others on earth." And Aladdin told her how he had hidden behind the door of the Hammam, so that, when Bedr-el-Budur had entered and lifted her veil, he had seen her clearly; and how, on that, a great love had leapt up in his heart and filled him to the exclusion of all else. "And there is no rest for me," he concluded, "until I win the Lady Bedr-el-Budur, and make her my wife."

At these daring words Aladdin's mother regarded him sharply, with fear on her face. "Art thou mad, my son?" she cried. "Nay, O my mother," he answered, "I am not mad. But, as I risked my life to see her, so will I risk it again to win her; for, without her, life is of no account to me. I will go to the Sultan and ask him to give me the lovely Bedr-el-Budur for my lawful wife."

Seeing his determination his mother was sore afraid, and knew not what to do. For a long time she reasoned with him anxiously, pointing out what a scandal it would be for the son of a poor tailor to aspire to the Sultan's daughter.

These arguments, and more, his mother put before him ; but Aladdin shook his head at all of them, and remained firm in his determination. "And further, O my mother," he said, " I wish now that thou go thyself to the Sultan and put my request to him, for am I not thy child ? And is it not thy duty to perform this office for me ? "

" O my son," she cried in despair, " wilt thou bring me into thy madness ? I, a poor woman, of humble birth, to go in to the Sultan and demand the princess for my son ! Besides, O my son, how shall I even gain access to the Sultan's presence for this purpose without bearing a rich gift to offer him ? "

" Mother," answered Aladdin, " thy words have served me well, for they have called to my recollection a thing which, through excess of love for the Lady Bedr-el-Budur, I had forgotten. Thou sayest that thou canst not approach the Sultan without a rich gift. Then, O my mother, if I place in thy hands an offering richer than any King in the world can make to any other, wilt thou carry out my desire ? "

Thinking his words were wild as the wind, and that he could produce no such offering, his mother agreed ; but, remembering the Slave of the Lamp, and what had already been done in that way, she stipulated with Aladdin that she would carry out his wish only on condition that it required no further invoking of the Efrite. Aladdin assured her on this and asked her to fetch him a china bowl. Wondering greatly she arose, and brought the bowl to him. Then Aladdin emptied into it all the sparkling jewels which he carried within his garments, and, when they were heaped together in the bowl they shone with a dazzling splendour. But, since he realized that it was not impossible that the project might fail, and that he

THE NUPTIAL DANCE
(*Page* 296)

might have to seek to the Slave of the Lamp for advice
and help in difficulty, he spoke to his mother on the
matter. "O my mother," he said, "it was the condition
of thy promise that I should not invoke the Slave of the
Lamp in the furtherance of this my desire; yet it must
be understood between us that if thou make a blunder—
which thou needst not do—then, to extricate us from a
dire calamity, I am free to rub the Lamp and see what
its Slave can do for our salvation."

His mother assented to this, for she knew, if she failed
with the Sultan, all was lost; and, in such case, even
the aid of a demon would be acceptable.

When morning dawned Aladdin's mother arose and
prepared herself for the visit to the palace, and, wrapping
the bowl of jewels in a cloth, went forth early. When the
audience was full the Sultan came in and seated himself
on the royal divan. All bowed down before him, and
then stood waiting with folded arms for his permission
to be seated. And, when he gave permission, all sat
down in their due order of precedence. Then he listened
to their petitions in the same order, and gave his decisions,
until the hour grew late, and the audience was declared
closed. The Sultan arose and went into the palace, and
the princes, with the nobles and the people, went their
ways. Among them went Aladdin's mother, thinking
to herself that this would be a matter of many days.
And every day thereafter she stood in the audience
with the bowl of jewels under her arm and heard the
petitions, but dared not for very timidity address the
Sultan. And in this way she continued for a whole
month, while Aladdin was nursing his impatient soul and
waiting on the issue.

Now the Sultan, being observant, had noticed the
woman present herself constantly at the levee. So he

the Sultan required to know nothing further than what was before him in the bowl.

" O Vizier," said the Sultan. " What sayest thou ? The man who sends me this kingly gift is worthy of my daughter. I, the Sultan, King of the Age, having power over all men, do withdraw my former promise to thee to bestow her on thy son. Bedr-el-Budur, the one beautiful jewel in the treasury of my heart, is my gift in return to the man who has sent me these priceless jewels."

The Grand Vizier bit his lips and pondered awhile. Then he spoke. " Peace be on thee, O King of all the Earth. But is not thy promise worth most of all ? Thou didst pledge me thy daughter for my son, and with that pledge I went, thinking that the whole earth and all therein were not its value. Wherefore, O King, I pray that thou wilt allow this matter time. If thou wilt pledge this foster-mother of a prince that thou wilt comply with her request in three months' time, then it seems to me that, by so doing, thou wilt cement the good feeling and loosen the griefs of all parties concerned. And in the meantime—yea, I have good reason for saying it— there will come before thee, O King of the Age, a gift compared to which this thou hast seen is but dross."

The Sultan weighed the Grand Vizier's words in his mind, and accordingly, he said to the woman, " Tell thy son that he hath my royal assent, and that I will give him my daughter in marriage ; but, as every woman knows, these things cannot be hastened, for there are garments and necessaries to be prepared ; wherefore thy son (on whom be peace) must abide in patience, for, let us say, three months. At the end of that time he may approach me for the fulfilment of my promise."

Satisfied with this, Aladdin's mother thanked and blessed the Sultan, and, buoyed up with a burden of

delight, almost flew back to her house. There Aladdin
was awaiting for her, and, when he saw her hastening,
and noticed that she had returned without the bowl of
jewels, his heart rose high to meet her.

Then she related to him the details of the interview,
laying stress upon the fact that, although the Sultan
had been moved at the sight of the jewels to make immediate arrangements for the marriage, a private word from
the Grand Vizier had led him to delay the ceremony for
three months. "Take heed, my son!" she concluded.
"The Grand Vizier hath a motive for this counsel of
delay. He is thine enemy. I saw it in his face. Beware
of him!"

Aladdin was greatly relieved by her news. He felt
like one jerked out of the grave; and, where the Sultan
was favourable to his suit, he was in no mood to fear a
Grand Vizier. "Nay, nay," he said, "the jewels have
the eye of the Sultan more than the Grand Vizier hath his
ear. Fear nothing, O my mother! The Sultan's word is
good, and I rest content to wait; though I know not how
such a long time as three months can be got into the
calendar."

Two of these long, weary months went by, and Aladdin
nursed his soul in patience. Then a thing happened
which gave him seriously to think. On a day in the
first week of the third month his mother went forth into
the market place about sunset to buy oil, and she saw
that all the shops were closed, and the people were adorning
their windows with bright garlands as if for some festivity.
She wondered greatly at this, thinking the Sultan had
either changed his birthday or that another child had
been born to him. Yet she had gleaned nothing of any
great event from the gossip of her neighbours. Having,
after much difficulty, found an oil shop open, she bought

"Take that scurvy thief," said Aladdin to the Efrite, pointing to the Vizier's son, "and bind him and lodge him in the wood-closet for the night." And the Efrite did so. He took up the Vizier's son in one hand, and, reaching with the other for cords, drew them from the invisible and bound the miscreant securely. Then he placed him in the wood-closet and blew an icy blast upon him to comfort him. Returning to Aladdin he said, "It is done, O Master of the Lamp! Is there aught else thou dost desire?" "Naught but this," replied Aladdin. "In the morning, when the Sultan is proceeding towards their chamber to wish them long life and happiness, convey them back thither in a state of sleep so that the Sultan's knock at their door may wake them." "I will obey," said the Efrite, and, in a moment, the air closed over him and he was gone.

And Aladdin smiled to himself to think that this thing had been done. Then he turned to the Lady Bedr-el-Budur, who was sitting weeping on the couch. "O lovely one," said he, "weep not; for I would not hurt one hair of thy head, nor sully thine honour in any way. Know that I love thee too much to harm thee; but, since thy father the Sultan promised me thee, and has violated his word, I am determined that none other shall call thee his. Rest in peace, lovely lady; for neither am I thy husband nor the thief of thy husband's honour. Wherefore, weep not, but rest in peace."

So saying he took a sword that hung on the wall of his chamber, and, having placed it by her side in token of security, he stretched himself upon the couch so that they lay with the sword between them. Thus they passed the night. The Sultan's daughter wept the long night through, and Aladdin could not close his eyes for thinking of his unfortunate rival's condition in the wood-closet. Towards morning Bedr-el-Budur, utterly exhausted with weeping, fell asleep; and, as Aladdin gazed upon her, he saw that indeed her loveliness was rare; and, the more he gazed, the more he thought of the unhappy fate of the Vizier's son. Never was a man so badly treated as to be bound fast on his wedding night and laid in a wood-closet in deadly fear of the dreadful apparition that had placed him there.

In the morning, while Bedr-el-Budur still slept, the Slave of the Lamp appeared according to Aladdin's command. " O my master," he said, " the Sultan hath left his couch and is about to knock at the door of the bridal chamber. I am here to perform thy bidding on the instant." " So be it," answered Aladdin. " Convey them together on the couch back to their place." And scarcely had he spoken when the Efrite vanished and reappeared with the Vizier's son, whom he quickly unbound and laid upon the couch beside the sleeping Bedr-el-Budur. Then, lifting the couch with the two upon it, he vanished, and Aladdin knew that, before the Sultan had knocked at the door of the bridal chamber, everything would be as it had been. Everything? No, not everything; for the Lady Bedr-el-Budur must awake as from a terrible nightmare; and, as for the Vizier's son, would he sing a song to the Sultan about spending the night in the wood-closet? Aladdin pondered over this and decided that nothing less than a repetition of the affair would wring the truth from either of them.

At this moment the Sultan knocked at the door of the bridal chamber in the palace, and the Vizier's son, still cold from the wood-closet, arose and opened to him. The Sultan advanced to the couch, and kissed his daughter, and asked her if she was happy and content. By way of answer she glared at him in sullen silence, for she had not forgotten, in dreams or in waking, what had happened to her. The Sultan, not understanding what had befallen, and feeling annoyed, turned and left the chamber to lay the matter before the Queen, to whose ear their daughter's tongue might the more easily be loosed. So he came to the Queen and told her how Bedr-el-Budur had received him, concluding his recital with the remark, " Thus it is ; there is trouble behind the door of that bridal chamber."

But the Queen smiled at his serious fears and answered him : " O my lord the King, thou knowest little of the heart of a woman. When it is happiest, a trifle makes it sad ; and, when it would send tears of laughter and joy to the eyes, it sometimes turns perverse against itself for very gladness, and sends tears of pain instead. Wherefore, be not angry with her, but let me go and see her. She will surely confide in me."

So saying, she arose and robed herself, and went to the bridal chamber. At first sight of her daughter's dejected attitude and pained expression she imagined that some lovers' quarrel over a mere trifle had occurred ; but when she kissed her, wishing her good morning, and Bedr-el-Budur answered no word to her salutation, she began to think that some grave trouble rested on her daughter's mind. And it was not until she had coaxed her, and used every argument known to a mother, that she received an answer to her questions. " Be not angry with me, O my mother," said Bedr-el-Budur at last, raising her sad beautiful eyes, " but know that a terrible thing has happened—a thing which I hardly dare tell thee lest thou think I have lost my reason. Scarcely had we retired, O my mother, when there suddenly appeared a huge black shape—terrible, horrific in aspect ; and this—I know not what nor who—lifted the couch whereon we lay and conveyed us in a flash to some dark and vile abode of the common people." And then to her mother's astonished ears she unfolded the tale of all that had happened during the night till, suddenly, in the morning, she awoke to find the monstrous shape replacing them in the bridal chamber at the moment her father the Sultan had knocked at the door. "And that, O my mother," she concluded, "is why I could not answer my father, for I was so bewildered and stricken with unhappiness that I thought that I was mad; though, now I have thought about the affair from beginning to end, I know that I have my wits like any other."

"Truly, O my daughter," said the Queen with great concern, "if thou were to tell this story to thy father he would say thou wert mad. Wherefore, I counsel thee, child, tell it to him not; neither to him nor to any other one." "Nay, O my mother," answered Bedr-el-Budur, "dost thou doubt me? I have told thee the plain truth, and, if thou doubt it, ask my husband if my tale be true or not." But the Queen replied, "Sweep these fancies from thy mind, O my daughter; and arise and robe thyself to attend the rejoicings which this day have been prepared in the city in thine honour. For the whole people is in glad array, and the drums will beat and music will delight the ears of all; and the musicians will sing thy praises and all will wish thee long life and happiness."

Leaving Bedr-el-Budur, then, with her tirewomen, the Queen sought the Sultan, and begged him not to be angry with their daughter, for she had been distressed with unhappy dreams. Then she sent for the Vizier's son to come to her secretly, and, when he stood before her, she related to him what Bedr-el-Budur had told her, and asked him if it were true or if he knew aught of it. "Nay," he answered, for he had thought the matter over and feared that the truth might rob him of his bride; besides, his acquaintance with the wood-closet seemed to him discreditable, and he felt little inclined to boast of it. "Nay, O my lady the Queen," said he; "I know naught of these things beyond what thou hast told me."

From this there was no doubt left in the Queen's mind that her daughter had suffered from a nightmare so vivid that she had been unable easily to cast it from her. Nevertheless, she felt assured that, as the day wore on, with its gaieties and rejoicings, Bedr-el-Budur would be enabled to rid herself of these troublous imaginings of the night, and resume her former self.

At eventime, when the wild rejoicing of the city had fatigued itself against replenishment by wine, Aladdin retired to his chamber and rubbed the Lamp. Immediately the Slave appeared and desired to know his wish. "O Slave of the Lamp," said Aladdin, "do as thou didst last night. See to it that thou convey the bridal pair hither again as man and maid at the eleventh hour of their innocence." The Slave of the Lamp vanished in a moment, and Aladdin sat for a long time; yet he was content, for he knew that the wily Efrite was but waiting his opportunity. At length the monster reappeared before him, bearing in his arms the bridal couch with the pair upon it, weeping and wringing their hands in excess of grief and terror. And, at Aladdin's word the Slave took the Vizier's son as before and put him to bed in the wood-closet, where he remained, bound fast in an icy chill. And when it was morning, and the Sultan was about to knock at the door of the bridal chamber in the palace, the Slave of the Lamp appeared and conveyed the bride and the bridegroom swiftly back to their place.

The Sultan had come to wish his daughter good morning, and to see also if she would behave towards him as on the former occasion.

ALADDIN FINDS THE PRINCESS IN AFRICA

(Page 313)

At this the Grand Vizier bowed his head and went forth exceeding wroth, and proclaimed the annulment of the marriage to all the people.

Whether the Sultan had swiftly forgotten, or tardily remembered, his pledge, Aladdin troubled not to inquire. He waited patiently until the three months had expired, and then sent his mother to demand of the Sultan the fulfilment of his promise.

The Sultan, who had not now the bowl of jewels before him to blind his vision, regarded her intently, and saw that she was of humble state. "What is thy thought on this, O Vizier?" he said. "My word is my word, and I regret that thou shouldst have explained it away; yet it seems to me that this woman is not of the kind that could mother-in-law my daughter. Hast thou a plan which is not a trick? If thou hast, whisper it in mine ear."

The Grand Vizier was pleased to hear the Sultan appealing to his ready wit in this way. "O King of the Age," he said, "thy pledge holds good, as ever it did; yea, as good as marriage vows. But verily, if this common woman's son desireth thy daughter for his wife, there should be a settlement befitting such a suit. Wherefore ask of him forty bowls of gold filled with jewels of the same blood and tincture as the woman brought at first, with forty female slaves to carry them, and a fitting retinue of forty. This thing, which is a Sultan's right to ask, it seemeth to me he cannot contrive to execute, and thus thou shalt be free of him."

"By Allah!" said the Sultan, "thou art of ready wit, O Vizier! Truly a marriage settlement is needed." Then, turning to Aladdin's mother, he said: "O woman! know that when one asketh the daughter of the Sultan one must have standing, for so it is in royal circles; and, to prove that standing, the suitor must show that he is able to provide for the Sultan's daughter and keep her in that state to which she has been accustomed. Wherefore he must bring to me forty golden bowls filled with jewels such as thou didst bring, with forty beautiful female slaves to carry them and forty black slaves as a retinue. Coming like this, thy son may claim my daughter, for the Sultan's word is the Sultan's word."

A sad woman then was Aladdin's mother. She returned to her son sick at heart. " O my son," she exclaimed, weeping, " said I not to thee that the Grand Vizier was thine enemy? The Sultan remembered his pledge, but the Vizier—may his bones rot!—spake in his ear, and the outcome is this : forty golden bowls of jewels, forty female slaves to carry them, and forty slaves as an escort. With this dowry, O my son, thou mayest approach the Sultan and claim his daughter as thy bride."

Loudly Aladdin laughed to scorn. And when his mother had brought him food, and he had eaten, he arose and went into his chamber. There he brought out the Lamp, and, sitting down, he rubbed it. Immediately the Slave appeared.

In less than an hour he returned and led before Aladdin forty beautiful maidens, each carrying a golden bowl of jewels on her head, and each accompanied by a magnificent black slave. And when Aladdin's mother saw this array she knew that it was done by the Lamp, and she blessed it for her son's sake. Then said Aladdin, " O my mother, behold, the dowry is ready according to the Sultan's requirement. It is for thee to take it to him, to show him what is in my power, and also that no time hath been lost in complying with his request."

Then the maids, with the golden bowls of precious

stones, arrayed themselves in the street outside the house,
and by each maid stood a slave. Thus, led by Aladdin's
mother, they proceeded to the Sultan's palace; and the
people crowded in the streets to see this unwonted sight,
for the maids were richly dressed, and all, with the sun
shining on their raiment and flashing in the jewels they
bore, made a magnificent spectacle. Never had the people
seen such jewels, never such beauteous damsels, never
such magnificent slaves.

Thus, in due course, came Aladdin's mother before the
Sultan, leading the cortège into the Audience Hall.
The maidens took the bowls of jewels from their head and
set them on the ground. Then they made obeisance,
they and the slaves prostrating themselves before the
Sultan; and, having done this, they all arose and stood
before him in humble reverence. And, when the Sultan's
gaze at last left the beauteous damsels and fell upon the
bowls of jewels at their feet, he was beside himself with
wonder and admiration. When he found words, he commanded that the whole cortège should present itself,
with the jewels, to the Lady Bedr-el-Budur in her palace.
Then he added to Aladdin's mother: "Tell thy son he
need fear not but that I shall keep my promise; but bid
him come hither to me with all haste, so that I may
look upon his face and accept him as my son-in-law;
for the marriage shall be this very night."

The Grand Vizier turned white with rage—whiter than
his false heart had ever been, even when a boy. After
a dagger-thrust of glances between them, Aladdin's
mother made obeisance to the Sultan and thanked him.
Then, with contempt for the Grand Vizier written plainly
on her face, she withdrew, and returned home, walking on
the air.

Now Aladdin, when he saw his mother returning swift-

THE LADY BEDR-EL-BUDUR

(Page 290)

footed and on wings of joy, knew that good tidings came with her. But, before he could speak, his mother burst in upon him and embraced him, crying, " O my son ! thy heart's wish is fulfilled. This very night thou art to wed the Sultan's daughter, and so it is proclaimed before all the world." Then did Aladdin rejoice that his expectations were fulfilled, and was continuing to rejoice when his mother addressed him suddenly. " Nay," she said, " I have not told thee all. The Sultan bids thee go to him immediately, for he desires to see his son-in-law. But how shalt thou approach the Sultan in thy merchant's garments ? However, I have done all I can for thee, and it is now thine own affair."

So saying, she withdrew to rest a little, and Aladdin, having blessed her, retired to his chamber and brought forth the Lamp. With a set purpose in his mind, he rubbed it, and at once the Slave appeared. " Thou knowest me : what is thy desire ? " " I wish," answered Aladdin, " that thou take me to a bath which hath no equal in all the kingdoms, and provide me there with a change of raiment of resplendent glory, richer than any the Sultan has ever worn."

No sooner had he spoken than the Efrite bore him away in his arms, and deposited him in a bath the like of which no King could compass nor any man describe. Then he sought the jewelled hall and found there, in place of his merchant's garb, a set of robes that exceeded all imagination. At the door of the bath, he was met by the Efrite in waiting, who took up and bore him in a flash to his home.

" Hast thou still some further need ? " asked the Slave of the Lamp, about to vanish. " Yea," replied Aladdin. " Bring me here a Chief of Memluks with forty-eight in his train—twenty-four to precede me and twenty-four to

follow after ; and see that they have splendid horses and
equipments, so that not even the greatest in the world can
say, ' This is inferior to mine.' For myself I want a
stallion such as cannot be equalled among the Arabs,
and his housings must be for value such as one could
purchase only in dreams. And to each memluk give a
thousand gold pieces, and to the Chief Memluk ten thousand ; for we go to the Sultan's palace and would scatter
largesse on the way. Wait ! Also twelve maidens of
unequalled grace and loveliness in person to attire and
accompany my mother to the Sultan's presence. And
look you ! whatever of grace and beauty is lacking in
my person supply it to me on my natural plan of being.
See to it, O Slave of the Lamp ! "

" It is already done," said the Slave of the Lamp ;
and, vanishing on the instant, he reappeared at once
at the doorway of the house, leading a noble white
stallion gorgeously equipped, while behind came the
twelve damsels and forty-nine memluks on magnificent
chargers.

Now, when the Sultan had received word that Aladdin
was coming, he informed his nobles and grandees of the
meaning of this thing ; so that, when Aladdin arrived,
there was a vast concourse of people, and all the stateliest
of the land were there awaiting his entry. As the sun
rises in glory upon a waiting world, so came Aladdin
to the palace. At the door of the Hall of Audience he
dismounted, while hands held his stirrup that had never
performed such an office before.

The Sultan was seated on his throne, and, immediately
he saw Aladdin, he arose and descended and took him to
his breast, forbidding all ceremony on so great an occasion.
Then he led him up affectionately, and placed him on his
right hand. In all this Aladdin forgot not the respect due

to kings. Forbidden to be too humble, he was not too lofty in his bearing. He spoke :

" O my lord the Sultan ! King of the Earth and Heaven's Dispenser of all Good ! Truly thou hast treated me graciously in bestowing upon me thy daughter the Lady Bedr-el-Budur. Hear me yet further, for I have a request to make. Grant me a site whereon to build a palace, unworthy as it may prove, for the comfort and happiness of thy daughter, the Lady Bedr-el-Budur ? "

Then the Sultan conversed with Aladdin and was greatly charmed with his courtliness and eloquence. Anon he ordered the musicians to play, and together they listened to the music in the utmost content. Finally he arose, and, taking Aladdin by the hand, led him forth into the palace banqueting hall, where a splendid supper was awaiting them with the lords of the land standing ready in their proper order of degree. Yet above them all sat Aladdin, for he was at the Sultan's right hand. And, while they ate, the music played and a merry wit prevailed ; and the Sultan drew nearer to Aladdin in their talk, and saw, from his grace, his manner of speech, and his complaisance, that indeed he must have been brought up and nurtured among kings. Then, while they con- versed, the Sultan's heart went out with joy and satis- faction to Aladdin, and the whole assemblage saw that it was not as it had been with the Vizier's son.

The Grand Vizier himself would have retired early had it not been that his presence was required for the marriage ceremony. As soon as the banquet was over and the tables cleared away, the Sultan commanded the Vizier to summon the Kadis and the witnesses, and thus the contract be- tween Aladdin and the Lady Bedr-el-Budur was duly executed. Then, without a warning word, Aladdin arose to depart. " Wherefore, O my son ? " said the Sultan.

" Thy wedding is duly contracted and the festivities are about to begin."

" Yea, O my lord the King," replied Aladdin ; " and none rejoiceth at that more than I ; but, if it please thee, it is my thought to build a palace for the Lady Bedr-el-Budur ; and if my love and longing for her be anything, thou mayest rest assured that it will be completed so quickly as to amaze thee." At this the Grand Vizier tugged the Sultan's sleeve, but received no attention. " It is well," said the Sultan to Aladdin ; " choose what site seemeth best to thee and follow thine own heart in the matter. See ! this open space by my palace ! What thinkest thou, my son ? " " O King," replied Aladdin, " I cannot thank thee enough, for it is the summit of my felicity to be near thee."

Then Aladdin left the palace in the same royal manner as he had approached it, with his memluks preceding and following ; and again the people praised and blessed him as he passed. When he reached his house he left all other affairs in the hands of his Chief Memluk with certain instructions, and went into his chamber. There he took the Lamp and rubbed it. The Slave appeared on the instant and desired to know his pleasure. " O Slave," answered Aladdin, " I have a great task for thee. I desire thee to build for me in all haste a palace on the open space near the Sultan's Serai—a palace of magnificent design and construction, and filled with rare and costly things. And let it be incomplete in one small respect, so that, when the Sultan offers to complete it to match the whole, all the wealth and artifice at his command will not suffice for the task." " O my master," replied the Efrite, " it shall be done with all speed. I will return when the work is finished." With this he vanished.

It was an hour before dawn when the Slave of the

Lamp returned to Aladdin, and, awakening him from sleep, stood before him. " O Master of the Lamp," he said, " the palace is built as thou didst command." " It is well, O Slave of the Lamp," answered Aladdin; " and I would inspect thy work." No sooner had he spoken than he found himself being borne swiftly through the air in the arms of the Efrite, who set him down almost immediately within the palace.

Most excellently had the Slave done his work. Porphyry, jasper, alabaster and other rare stones had been used in the construction of the building. The floors were of mosaics the which to match would cost much wealth and time in the fashioning, while the walls and ceilings, the doors and the smallest pieces of detail were all such that even the imagination of them could come only to one dissatisfied with the palaces of kings. When Aladdin had wondered at all this, the Slave led him into the Treasury, and showed him countless bars of gold and silver and gems of dazzling brilliance. Thence to the banqueting hall, where the tables were arrayed in a manner to take one's breath away; for every dish and every flagon was of gold or silver, and all the goblets were crusted with jewels. But, when the Slave led him farther and showed him a pavilion with twenty-four niches thickly set with diamonds and emeralds and rubies, he fairly lost his wits. And the Slave took him to one niche and showed him how his command had been carried out in that this was the one small part of the palace that was left incomplete in order to tempt and tax the Sultan to finish it.

When Aladdin had viewed the whole palace, and seen the numerous slaves and beautiful maidens therein, he asked yet one thing more of the Efrite. " O Slave of the Lamp," he said, " the work is wonderful, yet it still

38

memluks to his palace to make ready for the reception of his bride, Bedr-el-Budur. And, as he went, all the people thronged him, shouting, " God give thee happiness ! God bless thy days ! " And he scattered gold amongst them.

Bedr-el-Budur, watching him from a window in her father's palace, felt her heart turn over and over in her bosom, and then, saying within herself, " He is my husband and none other," she renounced herself to the exquisite joy of sudden love.

At eventime the Sultan commanded an escort to conduct the Lady Bedr-el-Budur to her husband's abode. On this the Captains of guards, the officers of state and nobles, well equipped, were mounted in readiness and waiting at the door of Bedr-el-Budur's apartments. Presently, preceded by female slaves and eunuchs bearing lighted tapers set in jewelled candlesticks, came forth a vision of loveliness. Bedr-el-Budur, aflame with love for Aladdin, appeared on the threshold like a pure white bird about to fly into space. All too slow was the procession that escorted her to Aladdin's palace. The stately pomp and splendour accorded not with the beating of her heart. She saw not Aladdin's mother nor the beauteous damsels, nor the mounted guards, nor the emirs, nor the nobles—her only thought was Aladdin, for her heart was consumed with love.

Thus from the Seraglio to Aladdin's palace, where Bedr-el-Budur, as one floating in a dream, was taken to her apartments and arrayed for presentation to the Court assembled. And of all that Court and multitude of people the only one who had no voice was Aladdin, for, when he looked upon his bride in her surpassing loveliness, he was reft of speech or thought, and stood silent before a joy too great for tongue to tell.

At last, when the presentation was over, Aladdin sought the bridal chamber where he found his mother with Bedr-el-Budur. And there, in the apartment all sparkling with gold and precious stones, his mother unveiled her and Aladdin gazed into her eyes and took no thought for the lustre of jewels. And while his mother went into raptures over the splendour of the palace, Aladdin and Bedr-el-Budur exchanged one look of love —a thing which none could purchase with all the treasures of the earth. And so it was with Aladdin and his bride.

Great was the Sultan's wonder and admiration when he saw the architecture and masonry of the structure, for, even without, it was all of the rarest and most costly stone inwrought with gold and silver and fashioned with consummate skill; but when he entered and viewed the entrance hall his breath was snatched away from him, for he had never seen anything so magnificent in his life. At length, finding speech, he turned to the Grand Vizier and said, " Verily, this is the greatest wonder of all. Hast thou ever, from first to last, beheld a palace like this ? " " O King of the Age," replied the Vizier gravely, " there hath never been the like of this among the sons of men. It would take ten thousand workmen ten thousand days to construct it ; wherefore, as I told thy Felicity, its completion in a single night is the work of sorcery." At this the Sultan was not pleased. " Verily, O Vizier," he replied, " thou hast an envious heart, and thou speakest foolishly with thy mouth."

At this moment Aladdin approached the Sultan to conduct him through the rooms of the palace. And, as they went from one to another, the Sultan was simply astounded at the wealth of metal and precious stones on every hand, and at the workmanship thereof. As for the Vizier, he had said all he had to say, and followed sullenly, appearing on the instant. "I desire thee to complete the niche which was left incomplete," answered Aladdin. "I hear and obey," said the Slave, and vanished. In a very short space of time he returned, saying, "O my master, the work is complete." Then Aladdin arose and went to the kiosk, and found that the Slave had spoken truly; the niche was finished. As he was examining it, a memluk came to him and informed him that the Sultan was at the gates. At this Aladdin hastened to meet him. "O my son," cried the Sultan as Aladdin greeted him, "why didst thou not let my jewellers complete the niche in the kiosk? Wilt thou not have the palace whole?" And Aladdin answered him, "O my lord, I left it unfinished in order to raise a doubt in thy mind and then dispel it; for, if thy Felicity doubted my ability to finish it, a glance at the kiosk as it now stands will make the matter plain." And he led the Sultan to the kiosk and showed him the completed niche.

The Sultan's astonishment was now greater than ever, that Aladdin had accomplished in so short a space that which he himself could command neither workmen nor jewels sufficient to accomplish in many months. It filled him with wonder. He embraced Aladdin and kissed him, saying there was none like him in all the world. Then, when he had rested awhile with his daughter Bedr-el-Budur, who was full of joy and happiness, the Sultan returned to his own palace.

As the days passed by Aladdin's fame went forth through all the land.

Now it chanced that the Sultan's enemies from distant parts invaded his territory and rode down against him. The Sultan assembled his armies for war and gave the chief command to Aladdin, whose skill and prowess had found great favour in his eyes. And Bedr-el-Budur wept when

Aladdin went forth to the wars, but great was her delight when he returned victorious, having routed the enemy in a great battle with terrible slaughter.

Now the fame of Aladdin penetrated even to distant parts, so that his name was heard even in the land of the Moors, where the accursed Dervish dwelt. This sorcerer had not yet made an end of lamenting the loss of the Lamp just as it seemed about to pass into his hands. And, while he lamented, he cursed Aladdin in his bitter rage, saying within himself. " 'Tis well that ill-omened miscreant is dead and buried, for, if I have not the Lamp, it is at least safe, and one day I may come by it." But when he heard the name " Aladdin," and the fame attached to it, he muttered to himself, " Can this be he ? And hath he risen to a high position through the Lamp and the Slave of the Lamp ? " Then he rose and drew a table of magic signs in the sand in order to find if the Aladdin of Destiny were indeed alive upon the earth. And the figures gave him what he feared. Aladdin was alive and the Lamp was not in the cavern where by his magic he had first discovered it. At this a great fear struck him to the heart, and he wondered that he had lived to experience it, for he knew that at any moment Aladdin, by means of the Slave of the Lamp, might slay him for revenge. Wondering that this had not occurred to Aladdin's mind he hastened to draw another table ; by which he saw that Aladdin had acquired great possessions and had married the Sultan's daughter. At this his rage mastered his fear and he cursed Aladdin with fury and envy. But, though his magic was great, it could not cope with that which slumbered in the Lamp, and his curses missed their mark, only to abide the time when they might circle back upon him. Meanwhile, in great haste, he arose and journeyed to the far land of

39

Cathay, fearing every moment that Aladdin would bethink him of revenge by means of the Slave of the Lamp. Yet he arrived safely at the City of the Sultan and rested at an inn where he heard naught but praises of Aladdin's generosity, his bravery in battle, his beautiful bride Bedr-el-Budur and his magnificent palace.

Taking his instruments of divination, he soon learned that the Lamp was not on Aladdin's person, but in the palace. At this he was overjoyed, for he had a plan to get possession of it. Then he went out into the market and bought a great number of new lamps, which he put in a basket and took back to the inn. When evening was drawing nigh, he took the basket and went forth in the city—for such was his plan—crying, " New lamps for old ! Who will exchange old lamps for new ? " And the people hearing this, laughed among themselves, saying he was mad ; and none brought an old lamp to him in exchange for a new one, for they all thought there was nothing to be gained out of a madman. But when the Dervish reached Aladdin's palace he began to cry more lustily, " New lamps for old ! Who will exchange old lamps for new ? " And he took no heed of the boys who mocked him and the people who thronged him.

Now Fate so willed it that, as he came by, Bedr-el-Budur was sitting at a window of the kiosk ; and, when she heard the tumult and saw the pedlar about whom it turned, she bade her maid go and see what was the matter. The girl went, and soon returned, saying, " O my lady, it is a poor pedlar who is asking old lamps for new ones ; and the people are mocking him, for without a doubt he is mad." " It seems proof enough," answered Lady Bedr-el-Budur, laughing. " ' Old wine for new ' I could understand, but ' old lamps for new ' is strange. Hast thou not

THE LADY BEDR-EL-BUDUR AND THE WICKED MAGICIAN
(*Page* 318)

an old lamp so that we might test him and see whether his cry be true or false ? "

Now the damsel had seen an old lamp in Aladdin's apartment, and hastened to acquaint her mistress with this. " Go and bring it ! " said the Lady Bedr-el-Budur, who had no knowledge whatever of the Lamp and its wonderful virtues. So the maid went and brought the Lamp, little knowing what woe she was working Aladdin. Then the Lady Bedr-el-Budur called one of the memluks and handed him the Lamp, bidding him go down to the pedlar and exchange it for a new one. Presently he returned, bearing a new lamp, and, when the Princess took it and saw that it was a far better one than the old one, she laughed and said, " Verily this man is mad ! A strange trade, and one that can bring him small profit. But his cry is true, therefore take him this gold to cover his losses." And she gave the memluk ten gold pieces, and bade him hasten. But the memluk returned anon with the ten pieces, saying that the pedlar had disappeared, having left all his new lamps with the people. The Lady Bedr-el-Budur wondered at this, but knew not, nor guessed the terrible consequences of her act.

As for the Dervish, as soon as he had got the Lamp, he recognized it. Placing it in his bosom, he left all else and ran, which to the people was only a further proof of his madness. On and on he ran, through the city and its outskirts, until he came to the desert, where at last he was alone. Then, and not till then, he took the Lamp from his bosom and rubbed it. In a flash appeared the Slave of the Lamp. "What is thy wish? I am the Slave of the Lamp which is in thy hands." And the Dervish replied, " I desire thee to take the palace of Aladdin, with all it contains, and convey it to the land of the Moors in Africa, and set it down upon the open space within the who obtained it by a stratagem told me of its virtues, and how he had achieved this thing by its aid." And immediately Aladdin heard this he knew that it was indeed the Dervish who had worked this woe upon him.

" Tell me, how doth this accursed man treat thee ? " he asked. " He cometh once a day," she replied, " and he would fain win my love and console me for thy loss, for he saith the Sultan, my father, hath struck off thy head, and at the best thou wert of poor family and stole thy wealth from him. But he gets no word from me, only tears and lamentations." And Aladdin embraced her again and comforted her for what she had suffered. " Tell me," he asked again presently, " where doth this accursed keep the Lamp ? " " Always in his bosom," she replied, " where he guards it with the greatest care and none knows of it but me." Aladdin was overjoyed when he heard this, for he thought he saw a way to obtain the Lamp. " Listen, my beloved," he said, " I will leave thee now and return shortly in disguise. Bid thy maid stand by the side door to let me in. Then I will tell thee my plan to slay this accursed one and take the Lamp."

Then Aladdin went forth upon the road that led to the city, and he had not journeyed far before he met a poor peasant proceeding to his daily toil. Stopping him he offered to exchange his own costly garments for those the peasant was wearing. But the man demurred, whereat Aladdin set upon him and effected the exchange by force. Then, leaving the peasant battered and bruised but dressed like a prince, he went on into the city, and, coming to the market, purchased some powder of benj, which is called " the son of an instant," for it stupefies in a moment. With this he returned to the palace, and, when he came to the side door where the maid was waiting, she recognized

him and opened immediately.   Very soon he was exposing
his plan to Bedr-el-Budur.

"O my beloved," he said, "I wish thee to attire
thyself gaily, and adorn thyself with jewels in the sparkle
of which no grief can live ; and, when the accursed cometh,
greet him with a smile and a look from thy lovely eyes.
Then invite him to sup with thee, and, when thou hast
aroused a blinding passion in his bosom, he will forget
the Lamp which lieth there. See," he drew forth the
powder, " this is benj, the ' son of an instant.' It cannot
be detected in red wine. Thou knowest the rest : pledge
him in a cup and see to it that the benj is in his and not in
thine. Thou canst do this ? "

" Yea," replied Bedr-el-Budur. " It is difficult, but
I will dare all for thee ; and well I know that this accursed
wretch deserves not to live." And on this assurance
Aladdin withdrew to a private chamber and sat him
down to wait. He realized his extreme danger, for he
knew that if the Dervish so much as suspected his existence
in the flesh a rub of the Lamp and a word to the Slave
would bring him instant death ; but he did not know that
Bedr-el-Budur, having learnt the virtues of the Lamp,
had exacted a pledge from the Dervish that he would
make no further use of it until she had given him her final
decision as to whether she would come to him of her own
free will and accord, which she maintained was a better
thing than subsequently to be compelled by the abominable
power of sorcery.

When the Dervish appeared, she sat weeping as usual,
and it was not until, in his protestations of love, he said
words that were suitable to her purpose that she paused
and half dried her tears as if it needed little more to make
her weigh his petition with care. Observing this he drew
near and sat by her side, and now, though no longer

loving cup, for it is the fashion in my country for the lover to take the loved one's cup and drink it." " O lovely one of my eye," he replied, " I will honour thy custom, since thou hast so greatly honoured *me*."

At this Bedr-el-Budur took his cup and filled it for herself, while a slave girl, who knew what to do as well as she hated the Dervish, handed him the cup which, though it contained the benj, she had just filled as if for her mistress. She even had to be told twice that it was not for her mistress but for the guest. So the Dervish took it, and looked into the eyes of Bedr-el-Budur brimming with love. They drank, and immediately the Dervish fell senseless at her feet, while the cup, flung from his nerveless hand, clattered across the floor.

In the space of moments Aladdin was on the spot. Bedr-el-Budur's arms were round his neck, and she was sobbing on his breast, while the Dervish lay stretched helpless before them. And when he had comforted her she went, and the slave girls with her. Then Aladdin locked the door, and, approaching the Dervish, drew the Lamp from his bosom. This done, he stood over him and swore a fearful oath, then, without further shrift, he drew his sword and hewed off his head, after which he drove the point of the sword through his heart, for only in this way can a wizard be warned off the realm of mortals.

Once in possession of the Lamp Aladdin lost no time. He rubbed it and immediately the Slave appeared. " I am here, O my master; what is thy wish ? " " Thou knowest," replied Aladdin. " Bear this palace and all that is in it to the Land of Cathay and set it down on the spot from which thou didst take it at the command of that." He pointed to the dismembered wizard. " It is well," said the Slave, who served the living and not the

dead; "I hear and obey, on the head and the eye."
Then Aladdin returned to Bedr-el-Budur, and, in the
space of one kiss of love, the palace with all therein was
carried swiftly back to the original site from which it had
been taken.

Now the Sultan was in grievous mood ever since the
loss of his daughter—the apple of his eye. All night long
he would weep, and, arising at dawn, would look forth on
the empty space where once had stood Aladdin's palace.
Then his tears would flow as from a woman's eyes, for
Bedr-el-Budur was very dear to him. But, when he looked
forth one morning and saw the palace standing as it had
stood, he was rapt with joy. Instantly he ordered his
horse, and, mounting, rode to the gates. Aladdin came
out to greet him, and, taking him by the hand with never
a word, led him towards the apartments of Bedr-el-Budur.
She too, radiant with joy, was running to meet him. Like
a bird of the air she flew to his arms, and for some moments
neither of them could say a word for very happiness.
Then in a torrent of words, she told him all about the
accursed Dervish; how by his sorcery he had conveyed
the palace to Africa, and how Aladdin had slain him, thus
releasing the spell and restoring everything to its place.
But not a word did she say about the Lamp and its virtues.
Then they arose and went to the chamber which contained
the trunk and severed head of the Dervish. And, by
the Sultan's orders, these remains of the Sorcerer were
burnt to ashes and scattered to the four winds of heaven.

And so Aladdin was restored to the Sultan's favour,
and he and the Lady Bedr-el-Budur dwelt together in the
utmost joy and happiness.

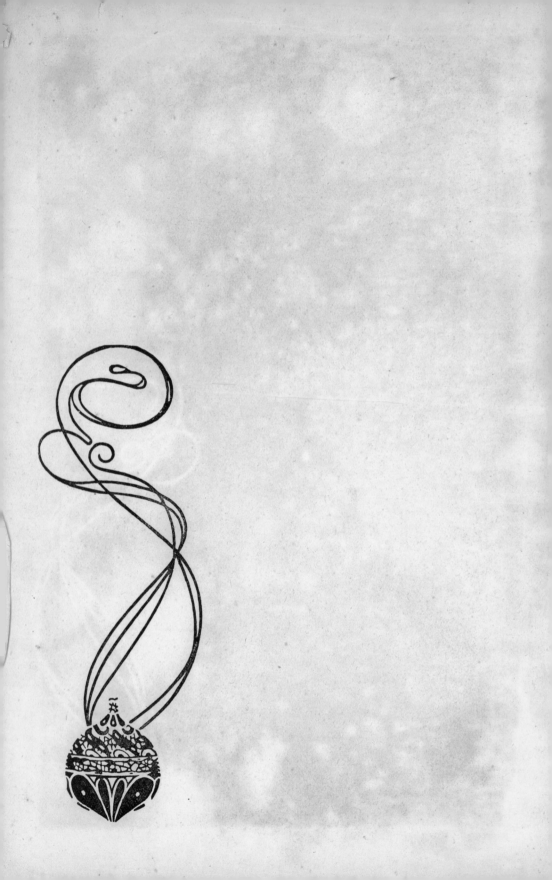